Whatever It Takes

by

Joy Wood

Published by FeedARead.com

First printed July 2024

For my courageous friend Tess Doyle who fought so hard to stay with us.
1955 ~ 2023

Between hello and goodbye, there was love . . . so much love.

Chapter 1

Dan made his way into the kitchen as Lorna placed a bowl of muesli on the breakfast bar for him and poured some milk on it from the carton. "Is this enough or do you want some toast as well?"

"This is fine. Aren't you having any?" he asked taking his seat and picking up the spoon.

"Not today, it's Amy's last day at work before the wedding. She's bringing pastries and cakes in for breakfast."

"Oh yeah, that's right, I forgot," he said, "and you're out after work, aren't you?"

"Yeah, we're at the Strugglers so I won't be back until late-ish. Sarah's picking me up for work this morning and bringing me home so I can have a drink tonight."

"Have a nice time then," he said taking another spoonful of cereal and picking up the newspaper, "any male stripper-grams or surprises for the bride?"

"God no, nothing like that. Not when Elspeth's going to be there. I wish she wasn't coming actually. She'll only spoil it. You think she'd have the sense not to come. Who wants the boss at their party?"

"Well Amy must have invited her?"

"Only out of politeness, she never expected her to say yes."

He carried on eating and flicking through the sport at

the back of the newspaper as Lorna made her way to the kitchen window and reached to separate the venetian blind and peer out.

"That's why we won't be too late," she said, almost as if she was talking to the blind, "the party will be over and done with after we've eaten. We see enough of Elspeth at work."

"Maybe she won't come, or just pop in for a drink to be polite," he stared at her, "what are you looking at anyway?"

"To see if anyone's arrived next door yet," she moved her head to get a better look. "I'm curious to know what the new neighbours will be like."

He folded the paper, preferring to read the rest in the evening when he had more time, "Long as they haven't got a wretched barking dog, I'm not bothered," he tossed his spoon into the empty bowl.

"They've taken the lease for six months, Hilary mentioned before she left. That isn't long, is it?" She eased the blind into place running her finger over some dust, "I wonder why only six months?"

"Could be anything. They might be working here temporarily, or having a house built. Who knows? I'm sure you'll be the first to find out."

"Mmmm, could be," she said, moving to the kitchen island to retrieve her orange juice. She took a sip. "I'm just hoping they're our age, I couldn't face two old dears either side of us. We don't want anyone in their seventies; we've got enough with nosy Phyllis next door."

"You are awful about her, if you spent a bit of time with her and got to know her properly, you'd see what a nice old lady she is."

"No, thank you. You spend enough time with her for both of us. She's always got you on some job or other. I think half of it's pretend to get your attention." She injected a whiney tone to her voice, *Could you help me get my suitcase out of the loft, Dan. Can you check the TV Ariel, Dan."* She glared, "It's no good looking at me like that, you know I'm right."

"If you say so."

"You want to try saying no sometime, she might stop asking then."

"She's no bother, she's a nice old lady, and I'd like to think someone would be kind to you if you were ever widowed suddenly."

"Well, I wouldn't be calling on a neighbour, that's for sure, and taking advantage of their nice nature. I'd get someone in and pay for jobs."

"She might not have the money to do that, for all we know."

"Course she's got money. I hardly think she's poor affording to live in a house in Campden Place. Anyway, enough about her, I might take a card round to the new residents next door tomorrow and some cakes or something. You know, play the good neighbour."

He raised an eyebrow. "They'll know you're just being nosy."

"Who cares? I want to know who's going to be living alongside us for the next six months."

He stood up. "Well, I'm sure you'll see them soon enough. Right, I'd better dash, I've got an early meeting, and one at six tonight, so I'll be late home myself." He made his way towards the dishwasher with his empty bowl and coffee mug.

"Okay," she answered passing him her empty glass, "does your meeting include food and drink?"

"No, just a client coming to the office, he can't make it during the day. I'll see to myself so don't worry, you enjoy your night."

"How was Ruth yesterday?" she asked stopping him from leaving the kitchen.

"Pretty much as you'd expect," he sighed, still feeling desperately sorry for his sister-in-law and wondering where the hell his errant brother was. It had been almost three weeks now since he'd gone missing and there hadn't been any urgency from the police. Their response had been, *People go missing all the time and eventually turn up. You just have to be patient and hope he returns home.*

He carried on, "She said she wants to start back at work to take her mind off things. I think it's a mistake but it must be hard sat at home each day, waiting around to hear something."

"That brother of yours is despicable," Lorna sneered, "he must have known how frantic you'd all be about him. Surely, when he was planning his disappearing act, he thought about the implications for the people that love him. It's not on to just up sticks and vanish, cutting all contact."

"I agree. Lord knows what he's thinking," he

shrugged, "I wish we knew."

She raised her eyebrows, "Do you seriously think he's out there somewhere still?"

"I'm sure of it. He'll turn up soon you see with his tail between his legs, begging for forgiveness."

"Maybe Ruth won't forgive him," she raised her eyebrows, "I know I wouldn't. If he wants to leave her, why doesn't he do that? Not just disappear into the night so nobody knows where he's got to. He does have responsibilities to his family and work."

"I know. We've been over this. You know Connor, he's impetuous."

"That's still no excuse though, is it? He needs to grow up. Half the trouble is you've mollycoddled him over the years. That's why he behaves like he does. He knows he can get away with it as you bail him out every time."

He shook his head, fed up with the conversation. He'd heard it all before.

"I haven't got time for this right now. I'm well aware of my faults and don't need them pointing out. Right now my brother's missing, so I'd rather save the post mortem until after we've found him, if you don't mind. I've got enough on trying to support Ruth and the kids and keeping the business afloat."

"Yeah, well when he does crawl out of that hole he's hiding in, you need to sack him."

"You can't just sack people," he sighed, "especially when they're on their uppers. And he is good at his job, managing everything at the office."

"Yes, but anyone can do that, so you don't need him

specifically."

"I can't just get rid because he's gone AWOL with some woman or other. And he is my brother don't forget."

"Oh how could we ever forget that?" she said flippantly. "You definitely think he's run off with a woman, then?"

"I have no idea. But he has form. The only thing I would say is, he loves the twins so the biggest concern is that he's not been in touch with them."

"Yeah, so that just shows his character. If he doesn't want to be with Ruth, just tell her, for God's sake, not leave everyone out of their minds with worry. I feel for the girls, they're only young."

"I know. But they have Ruth and I'm trying my best to support them." He checked his watch, "I really must be off." He went to kiss her and she gave him her cheek and pulled away almost immediately his lips touched her, "See you tonight after the party," she said, turning towards the sink.

"Okay. Say hello to Sarah for me."

He took his car keys out of the drawer in the hall and let the front door close behind him. Although he was twitchy about Lorna's scorn, she was absolutely right about his brother. Much as it narked him, he couldn't deny he had indulged him over the years, certainly into adulthood. But there was no point in analysing that now.

Dan clicked his car fob as he made his way towards his car. His mind was still on his brother. Unlike everyone else when Connor had initially disappeared, he'd always felt he was alive. He couldn't verbalise why, it was an innate feeling. What he couldn't fathom was why he had gone into hiding and cut off all contact.

Phyllis Dixon, their elderly neighbour called out, which prevented him from any further analysis of his brother.

"Good morning, Dan."

He turned towards her, coming down her drive adjacent to theirs separated by low brick wall. She was a good egg and had coped brilliantly since her husband had died earlier that year.

"Morning, Phyllis. Is the smoke detector behaving itself?" He'd replaced the batteries for her a couple of days earlier. Lorna might get irritated that she was always asking him to do small jobs, but he didn't mind. Her husband had been a paratrooper in the Falkland's war and he felt it was the least he could do for the widow of a well-regarded man.

"Oh yes. Funny how I didn't realise they had batteries as well as being powered by the mains. That's why I was so puzzled at it going off all the time."

"You'll know now if any of the others start alarming. Ours do it sometimes, it's just a safety thing, batteries as well as mains. Anyway, I'd better get off and try and beat the traffic. I try every day but invariably it beats me no matter what time I set off. You have a nice day."

"You too, dear. And drive carefully. Better to get there in one piece."

He saw her out of his rear-view mirror stood at her gate waving him off. It was nice. It reminded him of his mother waving his father off to work each day. Only a small gesture, but it was sweet. Lorna would never do that. She wasn't the 'waving her husband off' sort at all, much as he'd like her to be.

Exactly as he'd predicted, the drive into the city was slow. Stop start, stop start. Despite the slowness each day, the drive to and from work was his favourite time. He used it as his thinking time. As he pulled at some traffic lights, he put the car in neutral and applied the handbrake. He watched through the windscreen as a man with his two sons, held each of their hands as they crossed the road. The boys looked a similar age, one slightly taller than the other. It reminded him of himself and Connor walking to and from school. They'd always been close as brothers but completely different in temperament. Connor was the one with everything, a cheeky chappie who everyone fell in love with, while he was seen as steady Dan, three years older than Connor and always thought of as much smarter. He wasn't though. Connor was equally as smart but had a laid-back approach and a much shorter fuse.

Sadly, over the years, he'd indulged his wayward brother. He couldn't help it. He was his only family. When their parents had been killed and they'd been taken into care, Connor was all Dan had. And he loved him unconditionally. All the scrapes Connor got into, Dan was always there to bail him out. Good old dependable Dan.

Thirty minutes later, he arrived outside the Butler and Lloyd Accountants offices; he pulled into his parking space and cut the engine. He took a deep breath. He hoped his sister-in-law Ruth didn't ring and ask him to call round after work. It wasn't that he didn't want to support her, he was trying his best. But today, he couldn't look her in the eye and continue the charade of not knowing anything when he had heard from his brother. Only a text from a number he didn't recognise saying he was okay and would be in touch when he'd cleared his head. Angry as Dan was at the casualness of a text, it was an enormous relief and the message he'd been praying for. At least Connor was alive.

He was furious with his brother for putting him in this position. He'd have to inform the police he'd received the text from him. Not that they were carrying out extensive searches – a missing bloke in his thirties who'd disappeared once before was not something high on their priority list. But he still needed to let them know.

Even from a distance, Connor had the ability to make him feel guilty. That very morning he'd not been entirely truthful with Lorna, and he was going to most probably do that today with Ruth. Initially, she'd been frantic, imagining Connor had thrown himself onto railway lines, or was hanging in the woods somewhere remote, but the longer time went on, and no word or sighting of him materialised, she was coming round to the idea he was in hiding somewhere, hence her trying her best to carry on as normal.

The question that had kept Dan tossing and turning all night was, did he tell Ruth he'd had a text? He hated lying of any description and if he didn't tell her, he felt he'd be lying by omission.

And his sister-in-law and deserved better.

Chapter 2

Perry Hunter took a huge bite out of his burger. He and his wife Ingrid were travelling in their Range Rover to a temporary home in Campden Place, an exclusive development in Nottingham they would be renting for the next six months. Much as he wanted to crack on and get there, his rumbling stomach had forced him to stop and grab a snack, which he'd bought from the drive through and then pulled into a vacant space in the car park.

"Mmm, this is heaven," he said closing his eyes dramatically as he savoured the burger with the bacon and cheese topping, "I've died and gone to heaven."

Ingrid paused from eating her chicken salad and pressed the electric window to let some air into the car and stop the interior from steaming up. "Are you serious? All the gourmet food you get to eat and yet you salivate over that junky crap."

"You can't beat it," he said taking another bite, "everything in moderation, that's what I always say. One burger won't hurt you, you should have one."

"No, thank you. I don't want my arteries furred up by the time I'm forty." She glanced at the clock on the dash, "We've made good time, haven't we?"

"Yeah, not long now."

"Have you been to Nottingham before?"

"Only to view the house with the estate agent."

She took a forkful of food, "Aren't you worried once the neighbours get to know us, they'll try and check us out?"

"No, why would they? I'm not going to tell them loads. It's best to keep lies to a minimum if you can. Blokes aren't usually that bothered about trivia anyway. They take things on face value as to what you tell them. I'll be deliberately vague."

"Yeah, well women are different. The wife might be quizzing me as she gets to know us."

"She won't. But if she does, just stick to the story and if the going gets tough, just change the subject. It'll be fine, I promise you. Don't go imagining trouble when there won't be any."

"I hope you're right. How long realistically do you reckon we're going to be slumming it with the natives for?"

"No longer than three months, I would have thought. I've signed the lease for six months though so as not to draw attention. All being well, we need to have it all sorted by August. We can't delay much longer than that."

"Right. I guess it'll all depend on if they're keen to play ball. They might not be the sociable types for all we know."

"Then it's your job to make them."

Her eyes widened, "My job?"

"You know what I mean," he winked, "you're the one with all the charm. You're more the brawn, while I'm more the brains."

She slapped his arm playfully, "Cheeky bugger, any more talk like that and you're on your own."

"I'm only kidding. We can't do any of this without you. And I'm confident that, as soon as they meet you, they'll not be able to resist you," he leant across and kissed her, "like I can't."

"Flatterer. You've said it now."

He kissed her again, deeply, and she responded like she always did. He pulled away. "Right, considering we're being watched by dozens of people stuffing their faces, we'd better not go there. He wiped the grease off his fingers and put his rubbish in the brown paper bag and waited while she dropped her plastic carton in. "I'll just chuck this and drink my caffeine fix, sugar-laden coffee on the way."

She laughed, sipping from her bottle of water as he got out of the car to walk the short distance to the bin. He screwed the bag up in his hands, making it smaller, while his mind focussed on his future. He was ready . . . ready to begin the next part of his life. For a few months, he just needed to play a part. And he knew he could do it. Hadn't he been playing a part most of his adult life? In a few short months, everything he ever wanted would be his. And he'd have a future to look forward to with the woman he loved.

As he approached the bin and chucked the rubbish in it, two girls walked past and he caught them eyeing him. He was used to it . . . he was a fit bloke and his mixed-race heritage always seemed to be a winner with females.

But the days of casual relationships and sex were a thing of the past for him now. He'd found the woman he was going to spend the rest of his life with.

He got back behind the wheel and fastened his seat belt. "Are you ready for the next part of our lives?" he asked raising an eyebrow.

"Yep. Bring it on," she smiled brightly – too brightly. He spotted the hesitancy in her eyes.

"You don't look very sure." He leaned towards her, "Hey," he said lovingly as he tucked a stray strand of hair behind her ear, "you need to speak up now if you're having second thoughts."

"I'm not. It's just . . ."

"Just?" he tilted his head.

"What if something goes wrong? I'm fine most of the time, but I still get scared. I don't want to spend the rest of my life in jail."

"Nobody's going to jail. I've told you. There are no risks to you at all. It's going to be me taking them all. But I can't do this without you. So you need to say now if you don't want to go ahead. We can easily pull out. All we've done is taken a lease out on a house for six months. We can scrap that and go back now. You just need to say the word."

He stared at her, desperately hoping she wouldn't back out. He stayed silent with his determined eyes fixed on hers, willing her to comply like she always did.

After no more than five seconds, she nodded. "It's okay, I'm fine. I'd do anything for you, you know that. And if this secures our future together, then from now on, there's no turning back. Let's do this."

"You're sure? No more wobbles?"

She shook her head, "No more wobbles. We're in this together."

He raised his hand and she slapped it, giving him a loving grin. She adored him, he knew that.

He started the ignition and put the car into gear. The sat nav indicated forty more miles to the arrival at their home for the next few months. Not long now. Thanks to his tenacity, soon he'd have all he wanted right in the palm of his hand. He winked at his wife, who smiled lovingly back at him. Ingrid was vital to making it all happen.

There was no going back now.

Chapter 3

Lorna leant on the bar and was trying her best to attract the barmaid. They'd arrived after work for Amy's pre-wedding send off and had each put twenty pounds in a kitty for drinks. Both her and Sarah had drawn the short straw of having to go to the bar and get them.

Lorna glanced at the piece of paper Sarah had jotted the drink requirements on. "I see Elspeth's a weakling with a lime and soda. How did I know she wouldn't have anything alcoholic? I'm surprised she even came."

"Yeah, why would you? Who would want their boss, who we have to suffer all day at work, on a night out with them? Surely she could have made up an excuse when Amy asked her to come?"

"You would have thought so. I can't bring myself to be sociable with her," Lorna scowled. "I have to talk to her at work, but I'm not going to on a night out."

"You be careful," Sarah lowered her voice, "for some reason she's got your card marked."

"Who cares? Work was fine until she joined the practice. I really wish Maureen hadn't retired."

"Yeah, me too, but she has, so we'll have to get along with Elspeth or get another job."

"Now there's an idea . . ."

The barmaid interrupted them, "What can I get you?"

Lorna put the tray of drinks down on the table and waited until her work colleagues had each selected theirs before sitting down with her own. Sarah handed out drinks to the adjacent table where the bride-to-be and Elspeth sat and returned to sit down beside her, clutching hers.

She raised her wine glass and caught Amy's eye. "To you, Amy," she called and those seated around her lifted their glasses and shouted cheers in unison. Taking a huge gulp of the refreshing white chardonnay, she was determined to have a few more before the evening was through. Alcohol was exactly what she needed to be in the same room as her boss.

"Thank God we haven't been landed with Dame Elspeth," she whispered to Sarah as the others were engrossed in a conversation about a drama on TV the previous night. It was a relief their boss had chosen to sit at a different table – she really couldn't have coped chatting to her all evening. Covertly watching her, it seemed she was the only one out of them all who'd had time to reapply her make-up. Neither of them had, they'd been far too busy until the surgery doors closed. Lorna had long suspected Elspeth had plastic surgery of some sort as her skin seemed too tight on her forehead and she always wore lashings of foundation, as if she had either a birthmark or a skin condition she needed to cover up.

"She's probably better away from the office," Sarah said, unconvincingly, almost as if trying to persuade herself, "you never know?"

"Oh, I do know. Her type are never any better. They're rigid either at work or socially. That's why she isn't married. Can you see her having sex? She'd be dusting the headboard while some poor bloke was hard at it."

Sarah laughed out loud, "Shush, she'll know we're talking about her."

"Who cares," Lorna dismissed, "I bet I'm not far wrong. Anyway, I'm pleased you're at least having a glass of wine so I'm not drinking on my own."

"Yeah, I'll just make it the one though with having to drive."

"You'll be fine. Get some of the buffet food down you and you might manage another small one."

Sarah shook her head, "I'm not bothered, honestly. I have to take Harry to football first thing and, as if that isn't bad enough, I'll be on the touchline for the duration of the match."

"Where's Neil?"

"Where do you think? Working."

"Good job you love it really," Lorna said, never quite understanding how anyone could get excited about twenty-two males kicking a ball up and down a football pitch.

Sarah gave a wry smile, "Yeah, sure I do. Anyway, how are things, any news on your brother-in-law?"

"Nah, nothing. But don't let's talk about him on a night out, he irritates me to death and I'd rather forget about him."

Sarah ignored her and carried on, "You must have

some idea about what has happened to him? Do you reckon he's done a runner?"

"Initially, I thought there'd been some sort of accident, I think we all did. I was expecting the same as his wife, Ruth that we'd get a call they'd found him dead in the woods or something, but now I'm not so certain."

"What, so you think he's lying low and hiding somewhere?"

"I'm pretty certain that's it, yes. And Dan thinks the same. He doesn't say much about it, but I know he believes he's hiding somewhere."

"But why? Why do such a thing when he has a wife and family?"

"I don't honestly know. Mind you," she took a sip of her wine, "he works with Dan and that's enough to send anyone over the top."

Her friend tapped her arm playfully, "You are terrible. Your Dan's lovely."

Lorna gulped down another mouthful of wine, purposely not responding.

"He must be frantic," Sarah said, resting her drink down. "I know how close he is to his brother."

"Yes he is, but he knows deep down what he's like. He loves him, maybe too much and that's half the problem, but he is worried. Dan lives his life with everything and everyone in its own little box and woe-betide anyone who dares to step out of it. It can get a bit boring at times, or should I say Dan can get a bit boring at times."

"Dan's not boring. He's one of the nicest men I

know."

"Yeah right. I tell you what, we'll do a swap. I'll have your jokey, young at heart husband, and you can have old, dull as dishwater, Dan. How about that?"

Sarah shook her head, "You wouldn't swap him for the world. You're all talk. Come on, they've opened up the buffet by the looks of things. Let's go get some food, shall we?"

The wedding evening wasn't Lorna's idea of a night out and she spent most of the evening talking to Sarah. And drinking, she did plenty of that. The girls from the GP practice she worked at were okay, but she only really liked her friend. Sarah was a good egg and they had become close since she started work at the practice two years earlier. Lorna couldn't help being slightly envious of her friend's perfect life, with her perfect husband and perfect children. Even at the office, Sarah's work was extemporary, and unlike her, she never made mistakes. It was as if she had a photographic memory of some sort as she rarely missed a thing. Diligence was Sarah's middle name. She always gave her best.

Lorna had consumed far more wine than she should have and felt suitably inebriated as she got into Sarah's car and fastened her seatbelt for the twenty-minute journey back to her house. Her head was swimming. It had infuriated her that Elspeth had stuck around all evening, droning on about the impression she'd got when Amy first came to the practice, her efficiency, and then carried on about what a fine wife she was going to make, as if anyone was interested. What the hell did she know about marriage when she was Miss Elspeth Jenkins? That was half her problem, if she had a bloke at home seeing to her, she might well not be so bloody stiff.

"I think it all went well tonight, don't you?" Sarah asked, putting the car into gear and checking over her shoulder as she moved off.

"Yeah, it was nice. We gave her a good send off. She's bloody lucky, having a honeymoon in the Maldives, don't you think?"

"Too right. But her and James aren't paying. It's a honeymoon gift from James's parents by all accounts."

"Whatever. I'd kill for that holiday. I've always wanted to go there."

"Why don't you, then?"

"Cause Mr Bean Counter wouldn't spend that sort of money on a holiday."

"Yeah, well, in fairness to him, it is expensive. We looked when we were getting married and just for a week it was something like seven grand even then, so God knows what it would be now."

"God, Sarah you sound just like him. I showed him one of those bungalows once, you know the ones with stilts on the water. This one had a tiny slide on the side so you just needed to step up from your sun lounger and slide into the water. It was gorgeous. He seemed quite taken himself until he looked at the price. That was the kiss of death."

"Neil would be exactly the same. Maybe you could go for something less pricey, like a hut on the beach? I've looked at those before and they're really nice."

"Why should I, though? If I'm going there, I want to do it in style."

Her eyes felt heavy and she tried desperately to keep them open. It'd be rude to sleep while Sarah was driving her home. It was an effort to force herself to sit upright and carry on a conversation. "I think Amy's pleased to have vouchers from us all instead of those junky presents that only get stuck in cupboards. You don't need all the towels, bedding and crockery. Having the money or vouchers to be able to select your own is so much better."

"Yes, you're right. I got plenty of those, did you?"

"I guess so." Lorna yawned, "Although I can barely remember my wedding to be honest."

"Can't you? I can. I remember mine like it was yesterday."

"Yeah, well yours was probably more joyous than mine."

Sarah turned her head, "Why, what was wrong with yours?"

"Erm . . . I don't know really, it just wasn't what I'd expected."

"What, like too big, or too small?"

"I don't know. Too rushed maybe?"

"You must have wanted to get married though, didn't you?"

"Yeah, course I did. It's just that . . ." Lorna tutted,

"I've never told anyone this, but between you and me, Dan wasn't my first choice."

"Really?" Sarah widened her eyes, "Tell me more."

Lorna shrugged. "Nothing much to tell. It's just that I met Dan after I'd been dumped, by the love of my life, and I was in a pretty bad way. Dan took care of me and it just snowballed from there. And before I knew it, we were getting married."

"But you love Dan, don't you? You haven't any regrets?"

"I do love him, yeah, course I do, but he's a bit . . . I can't think of the word." Lorna squeezed her eyes shut and opened them again trying to clear her foggy brain. "Measured, maybe? And it's so boring. I often find myself wondering what might have been, you know, if I'd married the one I really wanted to."

"What's he doing now . . . this love of your life, do you know?"

"Married and living the dream in New Zealand by all accounts."

"Do you keep in touch?"

"God, no. I just know of him from my old neighbourhood."

"You're happy with Dan though, yeah?"

"Mmmm, I suppose so. I'm happy enough, but I still find myself wanting more. Dan loves me, he'd never let me down. He's honest and trustworthy. But I'd love some excitement. I don't know how to describe it really," she shrugged, "it'd be nice for him to come in from work and grab me for frantic sex on the kitchen table rather than in bed last thing at night, or to have breakfast in bed with the Sunday papers and him not twittering about getting ink on the sheets and crumbs in the bed. You know, stuff normal couples do. Our life is just so exact. As if the bed's for sex and the table is for eating dinner on."

"Well, give me exact any day. With two kids there's no frantic sex in the kitchen for us, and the only breakfast in bed I get is on Mother's Day. That's a typical marriage for you. I reckon you're chasing a dream. It might be like you say when you first get together, but it soon settles down when domesticity creeps in and the bills have to be paid."

"But it should be like that for us. We don't have kids. We should be doing more stuff together, maybe travelling, going away for weekends, but we just plod along. My weekends are spent shopping while Dan's at the gym or playing golf. Some days I just yearn for more in our lives, a bit of excitement rather than our mundane existence. Dan even monitors my spending. I have to hide stuff so he doesn't see it. I mean, how bad is that, hiding stuff you've bought from your husband."

"He's an accountant though. It's his job to manage money."

"Yeah, I know." She sat up again from the slouched position she'd slipped back into as they approached her house. "Take no notice of me, it's the drink talking. I'm fine, honestly. I just get a bit fed up. You know, sort of looking round the corner for some excitement but running into a brick wall every time."

The car came to a halt and Sarah applied the handbrake and turned off the ignition. She turned to Lorna, "Look, we all get like that sometimes. Just keep reminding yourself of what you have got. A husband that loves you and a beautiful home, there's a lot to be said for that. Maybe concentrate on that rather than looking for this elusive excitement, or before you know it, you'll end up having an affair or something."

Sarah astutely picked up on her silence and scrutinised Lorna's face. A scowl furrowed her brow, "Please don't tell me that has already happened?"

"No," Lorna said quickly – possibly a little too quickly, "Don't be daft."

"Lorrrnnnaaa." Sarah dragged out her name out in a disbelieving way.

"No, honestly, nothing like that has happened," Lorna dismissed, determined to get her friend off the subject. "What chance have I got to have an affair? When I'm at home it's with Dan, and then I go to work. And correct me if I'm wrong, but I've never noticed any potential affair material at our place."

Sarah grinned, "That's true. Anyway, I'm glad to hear you haven't done anything like that. Dan would be devastated, you could end up losing it all." She squeezed her hand, "Just be content with what you've got. Stop looking around for anything more."

Lorna nodded. Sarah had no idea how she felt with her perfect life, perfect husband and perfect children, but she meant well. She was a kind person.

"Right, lecture over," her friend smiled kindly.

"Don't be daft. You never lecture. And you're absolutely right, I'm being stupid. Put it down to too many glasses of wine."

Sarah nodded. "Hey, before I go, and you can tell me to mind my own business if you want to. I know you always say not having kids is a choice thing for you and Dan, but do you think you might one day change your mind? That might be something for you to concentrate on. You'd not be yearning for something else then, you'll be too bloody busy." Her voice softened, "And you'd make a lovely mum."

"Nah, that's never going to happen, I've never really wanted kids. I think that's what attracted Dan to me."

Her friend frowned.

"Before I met Dan, he and his first wife Victoria had a little boy that was born with some heart abnormalities. Don't ask me what it's called as I don't honestly know. Dan won't talk about it much. He only lived a year. After he died, Dan and Victoria split up. Dan swears he could never go through that again. He has a fear that the same abnormality could be passed on, even though the doctors said it wasn't hereditary. But Dan has always been adamant that he couldn't face any more children and that sort of heartache, so they've never been on the cards for us."

"That's so sad. But they can do all sorts now, you know, screening and stuff to check. And there's IVF where they can select the embryos to make sure they're perfect."

"Yeah, I know, but Dan's not interested. So, when I

came along, the rigid anti-kids woman, I think it was another box ticked in my favour. And we've got our nieces who Dan adores, so we have the best of both worlds, we can spoil them to bits and then give them back." Lorna grinned, "On that note, I'll love you and leave you," she leant across and hugged her friend, "thanks for a lovely evening, and sorry for going on. Take no notice of me. You won't say anything will you about what I've said about Dan? I feel a bit disloyal now."

"Course I won't. It's forgotten already. Right, make sure you have some water before you go to bed, and they reckon a banana is good so you don't wake up wrecked. It's something to do with the potassium."

"Oh, God, I'd rather have a hangover than eat a bloody banana right now."

Sarah grinned, "Shall we reschedule swimming tomorrow afternoon?"

Lorna frowned.

"Swimming, remember? You said you wanted to go. I can see how keen you are if you've forgotten already."

"I hadn't forgotten," Lorna screwed her face up, "well maybe for a minute. I still want to go though . . . if you can make it. Sounds like you're busy tomorrow with football duties. I can go on my own if you want. It'll be fine."

"Don't be daft. Neil will be home by lunch so it'll give me an excuse to leave him with the kids. I could do with some exercise to help me lose a bit of weight."

"Yeah, you and me both."

Sarah frowned, "I still can't fathom out this sudden urge

of yours of wanting to swim. It's a bit out of character, even for you. When's the last time you went swimming?"

"Ages ago, but I used to love it as a kid. My weight's creeping on so I need to do something about it. And out of every exercise, I'd rather swim than go to a gym or aerobic classes. I couldn't face anything like that."

"No, me neither. Okay then, I'll text you at lunch and fix up a time. See how you're feeling though. If you're a bit rough, we can do it next week."

Lorna leaned towards her friend and gave her another hug. "Thanks again for being my taxi, it's my turn next time."

She opened the car door. "See you tomorrow. All my love."

"You too," Sarah nodded.

Lorna stood at the gate and waved to her friend as she drove away and smiled at Sarah blinking the indicator lights at her. As she turned to open the gate, her eyes were drawn to a Black Range Rover parked in the adjacent drive. The new neighbours were finally in. She couldn't help but admire the sleekness of the car and its personalised number plate. She knew it most likely would have easily cost seventy grand if not more. Lucky buggers, she'd love to drive a car like that, but not a chance, even as their main car. Dan was happy with his conservative Mazda CX5 and he thought he'd given her the earth buying her a Mini Cooper, which he'd had the cheek to give her as a birthday present when in fact she needed a car for work so it was hardly a gift.

She reached in her bag for her door keys as she turned

to walk up the drive and she spotted Phyllis's motley cat, Oscar sat on the wall. Lorna hated that cat and if it could talk, it would say it hated her, too. It wasn't an endearing cute cat, it had a crusty nose that must have been bitten in a fight, and it had short front legs which always looked odd to her. But it was its constant crapping on their back lawn which infuriated her. Why couldn't it crap on its own lawn, for God's sake? Dan dutifully cleared it up, and she was always nagging at him to tell Phyllis, but as he pointed out, what exactly could she do? Cats roamed around at night and that's what they did. Lorna stared Oscar in the eyes and leaned forward, hissing loudly at him. He speedily jumped off the wall and headed to the security of his back garden – it'd had been on the receiving end of her before and wasn't taking any chances.

As if Phyllis sensed her precious Oscar might be in trouble, the curtain moved in her upstairs front bedroom and her wrinkly old face peered out of the window.

Nosy old git. Lorna was tempted to wave at her but thought better of it. Her legs were unsteady and she needed to get to bed, so she continued to walk down the drive. The security light came on, activated by her movement. The hallway was in darkness as she put her key in the lock. Dan wouldn't be waiting up. He was a 'News at Ten' and then bed man. She turned and looked again at the adjacent house that had been empty earlier but now had tenants. The curtains were closed in the upstairs bay window, but there was a light on in the bedroom. As she closed the front door and turned the latch she decided she'd call round to meet the new occupants the following day and introduce herself.

It was the neighbourly thing to do.

Chapter 4

Lorna woke with a thumping head. The digital clock next to her bed showed eight o'clock. She turned to see the bed vacant next to her. She could hear Dan downstairs so he hadn't left for golf. With a bit of luck he'd take pity on her and make her some breakfast.

She reached for her new cerise pink *Desmond and Dempsey* housecoat she'd hung on the bedroom door the previous day, so it appeared she'd had it ages. Dan would have a fit if he knew what it had cost. The labels were hidden in her bedside drawer; she needed to remember to get rid of them later when he'd gone to golf.

She made her way downstairs to the kitchen. Dan was in the place he liked best, at the breakfast bar reading the sports page. "Morning, sleepyhead," he smiled lovingly, "I left you as you were snoring your head off. Good night?"

She ran a hand through her tousled hair, "Too good. I feel crap."

"Come and sit here and I'll get you some coffee." He stood up, "Can you eat anything? I could do you a bacon or egg sandwich. Or we can push the boat out and you can have both."

She climbed on the chair. "An egg sandwich would be marvellous, thank you."

He passed her a mug of freshly made coffee and

reached into the cupboard where they stored tablets and gave her a pack of Nurofen.

"Thanks." She pushed two out of the blister pack and sipped her coffee while Dan cracked a couple of eggs in a pan and buttered two slices of bread. Why she'd criticised him the night before to Sarah, she didn't know. She didn't normally say much about him at all. It was best that way. He was a good man and had always taken care of her, so she was unfair being disloyal.

She put the two tablets in her mouth and groaned as she swallowed them. "God, I feel rough," she grasped her thick wavy hair away from her face in a pretend ponytail her fingers, "I dread to think what I must look like."

He grinned lovingly at her as he continued frying the eggs. "You look beautiful to me. You always do. Is your housecoat new?"

"No, I've had it a while."

"Have you? I don't think I've seen it before," he frowned, "I'd have remembered if I had, that colour suits you." He put the plate with the sandwich in front of her on the breakfast bar, "There you go, that should sort you out."

"Thank you, this is just what I need."

"Yep, Doctor Lloyd's remedy, that'll cure you in no time." He took a seat on the stool opposite, "I take it the bride got a good send off?"

"Yeah, she seemed to enjoy it," she replied taking a bite out of the sandwich.

"Good," he took a sip of his coffee. "Before I forget,

I've had a text from Victoria and I'm meeting her for lunch on Friday, if that's okay?"

"Why wouldn't it be okay, you do it every year?"

"I know I do. I'm just telling you that's all."

"I'm fine about it."

"I know you are. I just like you to know."

"Why would you suddenly think I'd be worried about Victoria? You split up with her long before you met me, and you're both married to other people now." She wiped the yolk that had run on the plate with the crust. "Is she any happier with her husband? I know you said last time you met, you weren't entirely sure."

"No, I'm still not, I just had a feeling last year when we met that things weren't right. But we haven't spoken since, only the usual text before we meet each year to check we're still on. And when we do meet up, we don't really talk much about personal stuff, it's more about Tommy."

"That's good then. The day is about remembering your son. You both clearly feel the need to meet every year, so must get a lot from it."

He frowned, "Is that a subtle attempt at sarcasm, because if it is, it doesn't suit you."

"No. It's just I would have thought as time went on, you'd have not felt the need to meet up every year on his birthday."

"Well, that's where you're wrong. We both feel the need to meet. We loved our son. And it is only one day out of the year." He reached for the kitchen roll, tore a piece off and passed it to her.

"I know it is. And if you get a lot out of it, who am I to criticise," she wiped her mouth and fingers.

"Exactly." He looked at his watch, it was a distraction, she could tell he wasn't happy with her. But her head ached too much to care. He'd given up asking if she wanted to join them both for a drink. Typical Dan. He'd been worried she might think he'd been having an affair. As if. And why would she even want to meet with them both? As far as she was concerned, they should knock the yearly meeting on the head. It wouldn't bring their child back. It had been nine years since he'd died, after all.

"Right," he said, getting off his stool, "I told Steve I'd meet him. We're going to grab a coffee before we tee off. You'll be alright?"

"Yeah, sure. I might go back to bed for an hour or so though."

"I would. There's nothing spoiling." He leant forward and kissed her head, "Hope you feel better after a sleep. I'll see you later on today."

"Okay."

She finished her coffee and felt less queasy having something inside her stomach. Dan was good doing that for her. He was a kind man, anyone who knew him would vouch for that. She should be happy, but she wasn't. She regretted the conversation she'd had with Sarah on the way home the previous evening. Thankfully, she'd only told her friend half of what she was feeling and she'd successfully deflected away from the affair question. Nobody knew about that. And she wanted it to stay that way. Alcohol had loosened her tongue and she needed to be more careful. But Sarah wouldn't say anything, she was sure of it. She was a loyal friend and would keep her confidence.

Late morning, Lorna made her way down the new neighbour's drive and tapped the chrome door knocker on the gleaming black front door. She was clutching a Roses tin filled with fairy cakes she'd bought from Sainsbury's and taken out of the packets so it looked like she'd made them. Dan had been absolutely right, she was being nosy. But it was important to her to greet the new neighbours and make them feel welcome.

It was a few seconds before she heard footsteps coming towards the door and it was opened by a petite, pretty girl about five years younger than she was and with the most beautiful, thick and long blonde, almost white hair. By contrast, her skin colour was a light brown – she could almost be a walking advert for living in a warm climate, like Australia or something. She looked cute in tight white shorts and a halter neck top.

"Hi," Lorna gave one of her friendliest smiles, "I'm Lorna Lloyd from next door," she nodded to her house, "I've brought you some cakes and a card by way of a little introduction and to welcome you to the neighbourhood."

"Oh, how kind," the blonde smiled, displaying a perfect white set of teeth as she took the tin from her, "I'm Ingrid Hunter, pleased to meet you. Have you got time to come in and meet my husband?" She pulled a playful scowl, "Although I'm not sure how sociable he'll be, you know what it's like, the DIY tools are out, so a divorce could well be the likely outcome."

Lorna laughed knowingly, "It's okay, you carry on, I can meet your husband another time. I just wanted to say a quick hello and welcome you."

"Who is it, love?" a voice called from further inside the house.

"You've been caught," Ingrid grinned, opening the door wider, "you'll have to say hello now. Please, come through."

Lorna followed Ingrid through the hallway, happy she'd got the chance to go in. They made their way down the dark hallway to the back of the house, which was similar to theirs with a kitchen living area. Ingrid's husband turned from the job in hand, which looked as if he was putting up shelves as he was standing back with a screwdriver in his hand. Unlike blonde Ingrid, he was a complete contrast. He was of mixed race, with a beautiful olive colour complexion and deep, brown eyes. His head was completely shaved and his firm jaw was dark with stubble.

"This is Lorna from next door," Ingrid said, "this is Perry, my husband."

Lorna reached out a hand, "Pleased to meet you."

"Nice to meet you, Lorna," he grasped her hand tightly.

She tilted her head, enjoying the warmth of his touch. "That's an unusual name, I don't think I've ever met a Perry before. Is it short for anything?"

"Nope, just Perry. I think my mother liked some sixties singer by all accounts. So the story goes, anyway."

"Well, don't let me stop you working, I just called by to introduce myself really."

Ingrid held up the tin. "And you'll be glad she did as she's brought cakes."

"Ah well," he grinned, "if you've come armed with cakes, you're definitely welcome in this house."

"Have you got time for a coffee?" Ingrid asked, "I was just about to put the kettle on."

"Erm," Lorna glanced at her watch as if she had something on, "thank you, that'd be lovely, if you're sure I'm not disturbing you? I can't stop long," she pretended, "but I can manage a quick one."

"Good. Do you want to follow me or keep Mr Handyman company?"

"I'll join you I think," she grinned and followed Ingrid into the kitchen and stood watching while she filled the kettle and switched it on.

"How long have you lived here?" Ingrid asked and nodded to the small round table with four chairs, "please have a seat." Ingrid waited until she settled herself down. "You'll have to tell me all about the neighbours."

"We've been here four years roughly, and there really isn't much to tell. It's a cul-de-sac where everyone says hello, but keep themselves to themselves."

"What about the lady who owns this house. Did you know her at all?"

"Oh yes, Hilary and Ron, they were lovely. They've moved to Cornwall to be nearer to their grandchildren, hence trying the rental market. I'm sure they'll sell it eventually."

"Not while we have the lease I hope."

"How long have you signed it for?" Lorna asked, knowing full well it was six months as Hilary had told her. "Sorry, that's a bit intrusive of me."

"Not at all. It's for six months, and then we'll be off. Coffee or tea?"

"Coffee please. Just milk, no sugar."

She watched Ingrid making their drinks. She was really attractive in a completely natural way. Lorna could see she didn't have any make-up on, and her blonde, lustrous hair was fastened in a ponytail. But even that pulled-back look suited her as her face was pretty. And glancing at her figure, it was perfect with a pinched in waist and a flat tummy to die for. But unlike her, she was lacking in the breast department, and the absence of a bra only emphasised her flat chest. Lorna always felt blokes must feel cheated having a partner with barely any breasts. Didn't all men lust after women with a small waists and pert breasts? The flat chest spoilt Ingrid as far as she was concerned. Normally, Lorna didn't like attractive women, certainly any she thought rivalled her in the looks department, but this Ingrid was no competitor, although her husband was seriously hot, anyone could see that.

Ingrid handed her a coffee and was about to pick up the two others when Perry walked into the kitchen.

"Did someone mention cake a few minutes ago?"

"I swear he can smell food from ten miles away,"

Ingrid said taking the lid off the tin. "Are you okay to sit in here, Lorna, I was going to go through to the conservatory."

"Here's fine. As I said, I can't stay long."

Ingrid took a seat at the table and Perry remained standing and reached for a cake.

"That's a sure way to my husband's heart," Ingrid smiled adoringly at Perry as he took a huge bite.

"A bit like mine then, he loves the sweet stuff, although he can eat as much as he wants because he spends endless hours at the gym and playing golf."

"Golf?" Perry playfully widened his eyes and turned his head towards his wife, "Can you make a note that the G word has already been mentioned and it wasn't by me."

Ingrid rolled her eyes, "Please God, don't tell me I'm going to become a golf widow this quickly."

"I need to find out more," Perry wiped a finger along his lips and licked it, "what's your husband's name?"

"Dan."

"Then I need to meet Dan ASAP. How about you both come round for drinks one evening? It'd be nice to get to know you and I can find out where he plays golf."

"That'd be lovely, but you don't need to have us round, I can tell you. He's a member of the club on Lovett Lane, it's only down the road, about two miles, that's all. Although I think it's fair to warn you, it's rather elite and there's a waiting list to join."

"Bugger, that's a shame. But maybe Dan might take pity on me and let me be his guest and play a few rounds?"

"I'm sure he'd love to do that."

"Then you must come round. What night suits you? Do you have to get a babysitter or anything?"

"No, there's just Dan and I." She looked at Ingrid, "I expect you need a bit of time to settle in, maybe in the next week or two?"

"No, this week's fine," she said, "how about . . . Saturday?"

"If you're absolutely sure," Lorna nodded, "we could make that."

"Course we're sure, we'd love to have you."

"Okay, Saturday it is then."

"Great. How about seven thirty?"

"Perfect." She drained her coffee cup. "I'd better get off and leave you two to it. Do yell out if you need a hand with anything." She stood up. "It's been lovely meeting you, thank you for the coffee and we'll look forward to Saturday." Perry reached in the tin for another cake, and she smiled, typical man that could eat sweet stuff and never gain a pound. "Enjoy."

He took a bite and winked, "You've stolen my heart, Lorna."

Ingrid shook her head, "Take no notice. If you were ninety-two with a hunched back and brought him food, he'd be in love with you."

Lorna grinned as they made their way down the hall. They seemed like fun.

Ingrid opened the front door for her, "Thanks for coming, and for the cakes and card, that is so welcoming of you."

"It's nothing, honestly," Lorna said, "I'll see you on Saturday."

"Will do. Bye for now."

Lorna let herself into the back door of her own house, pleased with herself for going round. They were a really attractive couple. Ingrid seemed nice enough but out of the two of them, it was the husband that oozed charisma.

Chapter 5

Dan approached Carmichael's restaurant on foot having parked his car in a nearby car park. With everything going on with his brother and work being even more hectic than usual of late, he was looking forward to a leisurely lunch with his ex Victoria as he did on the same day every year. It was 23rd May, which had their son lived, would have been his tenth birthday.

Victoria was seated by the window and waved as soon as she saw him. Her face lit up and she looked as beautiful to him as she always did. Everything about her was perfect. His eyes quickly absorbed her light blue jacket with her hair loosely cascading around cheeks, shorter than she usually wore it, resting above her shoulders. As he approached her, a familiar rush surged through him. Time hadn't diminished how much he'd once loved her, even though time had ensured they'd both moved on.

"Hi," he said as he stopped in front of her. She stood up to hug him and slid effortlessly into his arms. For a few seconds, he inhaled her familiarity, the scent of the heart-warming memories he'd craved for so long after they'd split up. After such a length of time, she still wore the same perfume, all sultry, warm and feminine, and in the few short seconds he held her, he was transported back to a completely different life than he had now.

They'd been together since childhood, separated for a couple of years during university but found each other afterwards and had been inseparable. They'd had their son Tommy for one precious year, and after Tommy died, their love had somehow died too. Or it seemed to. They had both moved on, she'd re-married first and he followed with Lorna. But every year they met on Tommy's birthday. He'd never let his son's special day go past without honouring him in a small way.

"You look well," Victoria's eyes flickered with warmth as she took her seat.

"I'm not sure I do, but thank you for saying so," he smiled, "how are you? You never look any different, you always look great." And she did. Her shorter hair in a wavy bob suited her, and always with the minimum of make up as she didn't need it.

"I'm okay . . . you know, still doing what I do best, working hard." She shrugged, "Perhaps a tad too hard."

"Yeah, me too."

The waiter interrupted them with menus. "Can I get you a drink while you're looking through the menu?"

"That'd be nice. What would you like, Vic?"

"I'll have a glass of white wine I think."

"Yeah, me too. Have you got a Pinot Grigio?" he knew it was a favourite of Victoria's.

"We sure do."

"Make that two then please."

"Will do. I'll be back shortly."

He picked up the menu. "Let's have a quick look at what we want then we can chat."

He surreptitiously watched her as she perused the menu. He'd loved her so much and always regretted they hadn't stayed together. He often considered what their life might be like had they worked through their grief and managed to hang on. But that ship had sailed a long time ago.

After the waiter had returned with their drinks and taken their order, he lifted his glass, "To Tommy."

She clinked hers, "To Tommy." No tears were left. The first couple of years were hard, but as time marched on, their annual meeting had become more of a catch up than anything. They talked about their precious little boy, of course, but it had become less and less. Not that he shared that with Lorna who never understood his need for meeting Victoria.

She took a sip of the chilled wine. "That's nice," she said, licking her lips, "Now, tell me about Connor. I've followed it all in the newspapers but I'm guessing there's still no news?"

He needed to tell someone. Bottling it up was doing him no good at all. And Victoria knew Ruth and Connor well anyway. They'd had years together as a foursome, even going on holiday occasionally when they were younger. They had been close as a family.

"There has been some news actually," he cleared his throat, "but nobody knows yet. I've only recently found out he's alive, and I'm hoping to go and get him."

Her eyes widened, "Really? Gosh, what a relief. I must say I feared the worst. What's holding you back? Why haven't you gone for him straight away?"

He sighed, "Because I'm not sure exactly where he is. I've had a text, not from his phone though. He's sent it from someone else's. It says he's okay and trying to sort himself out. I've begged whoever the person is to let me know where he is so I can go to him."

"God, that's awful, Dan." She reached for his hand, "I know how close you both are. Do you know why he's taken off like he has?"

"No. That's what's so baffling. Ruth said things were fine, but you know Connor of old, he has form, especially where women are concerned. But Ruth doesn't think it's anything like that. She's been an absolute brick. I honestly can't get over how she's coping."

"She's always been strong though, hasn't she? He's lucky to have her. I know he's your brother, but he's not reliable like you are. In fact you're total opposites."

"Yeah, I know. But I have to go get him and bring him home, I can't just leave him."

"No, of course you can't."

The waiter arrived and placed their meals in front of them.

"Would you like any sauces?" the waiter asked, "or perhaps more wine?"

"I'm fine with water," Dan raised an eyebrow, "what about you, Vic, are you driving?"

"No, I'm not. So yes," she smiled, "another small one would be nice."

"Coming right up."

As soon as the waiter was out of earshot, Dan's eyes were drawn to Victoria's kind face. It was almost therapeutic having someone to talk to. She had the most mesmerising eyes, as one of them was blue and the other brown and they changed colour depending on her mood. He often used to tease her and sing an old song about brown eyes turning blue.

"Anyway, enough about Connor." He scooped up some pasta, "How are things with you and Mike?" he asked, forking it into his mouth. He stifled the urge to ask if she was happy. If she wasn't, there wasn't anything he could do.

She rested her knife and fork but hesitated before answering, as if she was thinking carefully about her response. "Okay, he's busy at work too. We're a bit like ships that pass in the night if I'm totally honest. But we've got a holiday booked next month so I'm looking forward to that."

"Good, where to?"

"The US. We're going to drive a bit and see a bit. Eight states in three weeks, I think."

"Sounds great. Which states?"

"Florida to begin with and then working our way up the eastern states."

"That's my sort of holiday. I can't think of anything better than a big Yankee truck with a suitcase in the boot, I'd absolutely love it."

"Why don't you go?" she asked, taking a mouthful of chicken.

"It wouldn't be Lorna's idea of a holiday. She'd hate living out of a suitcase. She prefers a luxury hotel with all the facilities."

"Ah, well, there's nothing wrong with that. You both work hard, it's nice to just sit back and let others spoil you for a little while. Gives you chance to recharge your batteries."

"Yeah, you're right. This pasta's lovely, how's your chicken?"

"Perfect, thank you." She took a sip of her wine. "How's everything with you and Lorna? I know the answer because I ask you every year, but are you still adamant about no more children?"

"Yep, absolutely. He tried hard to look upbeat, even though she'd touched a nerve. "I couldn't face it, Vic. The pain of losing Tommy was just too much. I could never go through that again. And the good thing is, I don't get any pressure from Lorna as she's very anti children anyway."

"Is that why you went for her, do you think?" A pained expression passed across her face, "Sorry, I didn't mean to imply that's the only reason you married her."

"Don't be daft, I didn't think that at all. You're right though, that was a consideration. After you and I split up, I thought if I ever did meet anyone, it would have to be someone that didn't want children."

Her eyes shone with unshed tears. "You were a great dad, Dan. You should have more."

"And you should too." He looked at her tenderly, "But it's not meant to be for you either."

"Yeah, but that's no reason to stop you. You can still father a child."

"I know."

"And take that look off your face. I don't blame you, I never have done."

Victoria was such a gracious woman and he was grateful for that. Nevertheless, his stomach tightened. "It was the hardest decision I ever had to make."

"You had no choice. The doctors told you, a hysterectomy was the only way they could save my life. You had to consent. And I'm grateful you did because I'm here now, with a lot of living left to do, I hope."

"It's so bloody unfair though, isn't it? If Tommy had lived, you'd at least have a child."

"Yeah, but whoever said life was fair? It isn't. And I'm happy enough, and you are. That's what matters. We had Tommy for that precious year and you and I had many happy years together before he died. I'm just glad we can still meet like this, even if it is only once a year on Tommy's birthday. "

"Me too. Mike's okay about us still meeting?"

"Sure he is, why wouldn't he be?"

She said it too quickly. He knew things weren't right between Victoria and her husband. He knew her too well. Every movement of her face, every mannerism he could read. But her marriage wasn't his concern. He needed to put any thoughts about that out of his head. He had his own wife to think about, and his errant brother. He couldn't sort everyone out. It was best he stopped analysing her. After today, he wasn't going to see her for another year. A tightness formed in his throat. He reached for the jug of water and poured himself a glass. The hysterectomy always caused him angst, even after all this time. She'd just given birth to their precious son who was fighting for his life. And she was too. Victoria was going to haemorrhage to death if he didn't give consent for them to stem the bleeding by removing her womb. It was the only way the doctors had told him and time had been of the essence. He remembered the day as if it was yesterday, it haunted his dreams still. That and staring at his tiny new-born son fighting for his life in an incubator, not knowing if he was going to live or die, and then signing his wife away to a life without any more children. He had to put the memories away, they were too painful. He swallowed a mouthful of water.

"Hey, can you remember when we took Tommy to Hall Farm, and how much he loved the donkeys?" he smiled, fondly remembering the delight on his son's face as he deftly moved the conversation along.

Victoria's face lit up.

His heart rate settled.

They were back on terra firma, talking about their beloved son.

Chapter 6

"I can't believe you've accepted an invite to go round to their house," Dan scowled as he stood in his boxers with his hand on the wardrobe door, staring inside at his vast array of shirts and trousers.

"It's just drinks, I don't know what you're getting so het up about." Lorna continued layering her lashes with mascara, sitting at the dressing table mirror.

"Because we don't know them, that's why," he said, reaching for a navy polo shirt and some stone-coloured chinos.

"So? We will do once we've had drinks with them. What did you want me to do, tell them no when they invited us? I could hardly have made an excuse up that we were out for the evening when we live next door and it's evident we're not. What's the problem anyway?"

"There isn't a problem," he said, pulling the polo shirt over his head, "but I've told you, I don't want to get too cosy with the neighbours."

"Jesus Christ, it's a few drinks. We won't be there long. Look, instead of moaning to me, do something useful and find a nice bottle of wine to take. I've got Ingrid some flowers."

"Oh right, we're taking gifts now are we," he said sarcastically as he zipped up his trousers and fastened the belt.

He reached in the drawer at the side of her for his socks while she brushed a bronze colour on her face. His disapproval would be evident; she knew he preferred her without lashings of make-up. She didn't need it, she was a beautiful woman. When they'd first met, she didn't wear nearly as much, but lately she seemed to slap it on. And while he acknowledged she was clever with it and always looked lovely, he preferred her with less. He'd lost count of the times he'd told her that, always in a nice way, not critical, but she took no notice. Compliance was not something Lorna had in abundance – rebellion was more her bag.

"I don't want to be there until all hours either," he said sitting on the bed to put his socks on.

"Oh God," she groaned, "we're on a deadline now are we, Cinderella?"

"No. I'm just saying, don't let's be late. I've got to drive to the hotel tomorrow so I don't want loads to drink."

"Well, don't have *loads to drink*, but don't go ruining everyone else's evening. Normal people have Sundays off. Why can't you just drive to Scotland on Monday?"

"Because I don't want to be late. It's a hell of a way, so I'd rather break the journey up."

"That's fine then, but like I said, don't spoil everyone else's fun."

As he made his way downstairs, he continued to silently curse her for arranging the evening with the new neighbours. He really didn't need it tonight of all nights. He still hadn't told Lorna why he was really heading to

Scotland the following day. He'd told her about a conference he wanted to attend about business marketing strategies on Monday. What had really happened was he'd rang the number that he'd received the text from Connor on, but only got an answer machine so he'd been forced to plead with his brother to contact him. He'd eventually received a call back from the number. The owner of the phone had explained he lived in the vicinity of the cottage that Connor was currently staying in. The man really didn't want to be involved initially, but had reluctantly agreed to lend his phone for Connor to send a text. Dan quickly realised that the man, who identified himself as Arthur, thought there might be some sort of criminal activity going on, but once he'd explained everything about who he was and more importantly who Connor was, Arthur had divulged where his brother was staying in the Cairngorms area of Scotland. Only Connor could have gone hundreds of miles away to the far end of Scotland to hide.

Dan was on the phone to Arthur much longer than he'd anticipated. He turned out to be a well-educated and engaging man, explaining that he lived almost a reclusive lifestyle since his wife had died prematurely. He seemed to want to talk. He wasn't after sympathy though, far from it. He'd said that he was happy living in solitude, preferring to spend the remainder of his life that way. Seemingly, he'd undergone major surgery for cancer and although in remission, his exact words were that he 'hadn't got long for this world'.

The task now for Dan having finally located Connor, was to drive to the Cairngorms and somehow persuade him to come home. He'd asked Arthur not to discuss their conversation which had amused him and he'd explained that was most unlikely. Although neighbours, he'd said there was quite a distance between the two cottages. Dan's fear was Connor might get an inkling he was coming and move on before he had chance to see him. That was one of the reasons he hadn't mentioned going to Lorna or Ruth. He wasn't sure if he did locate him, whether or not he'd return home.

With all this playing on his mind, the last thing Dan needed was an evening with the new neighbours. He hated small talk, he had to do it with clients at work for business, but at home he loved solitude. Golf and the gym were his home life pursuits, and getting too close to neighbours was not something he relished. He lived his life as a 'what if' man – what if there was an argument which caused friction, or they were rowdy, partying all night. The last thing he wanted was to be friends. Plus he didn't really want them knowing his and Lorna's business and he knew exactly what his wife could be like after a few drinks, she'd be telling them their life stories. It wasn't that they had anything to hide, but Lorna had form and he'd have to be on his guard so she didn't say anything inappropriate.

Forty minutes later, suitably attired with Lorna clutching white lilies and him with the wine, they knocked on the door to their new neighbours promptly at seven thirty. It was opened by a male who looked to be in his mid-thirties, mixed race and taller than he was, fit looking with a shaved head. He was clean shaven which Dan liked. He wasn't fond of the unshaven stubble, he liked the well-groomed look.

"Welcome." Perry had a huge friendly smile that lit up his whole face, "You must be Dan," he held his hand out and gave a firm handshake before turning his attention to Lorna and embracing her in a bear hug which seemed a bit too familiar for Dan's liking. But Lorna would relish it, she was a woman that loved that sort of thing.

"Fantastic you could both make it, welcome to our humble abode."

"Thank you for inviting us." Dan handed the bottle of wine to him, "Hope you like red," and Lorna thrust the bunch of flowers at him, "these are for Ingrid."

"That's kind, she'll love them. Thank you, and you Dan for the wine, we love red. Please come in."

Dan stood back to let Lorna go in front and they followed Perry down the hallway towards the back of the house. It had a similar layout to theirs using the back as a living area too. Their own lounge with their carefully selected top of the range sofas at the front of the house wasn't used that often although Dan liked to read in the bay window in his favourite armchair when he got chance.

"Please, take a seat," Perry nodded towards a leather Chesterfield sofa and placed the flowers and wine on a console table. He was a charmer, Dan could see that immediately – he'd be a hit with women, no doubt. He waited while Lorna took her seat and sat down beside her. His wife was a beautiful woman and knew it. She'd most probably spend the evening subtly flirting, which had become a habit, and despite her always excusing it as being friendly, he didn't buy it. She knew exactly what she was doing but he tried not to let himself get too riled. With her being ten years younger than him, he'd learned to cope with flirty. As long as that's all it was and fortunately she'd never given him a reason to think it was anything more.

"What can I get you to drink?" Perry asked in an educated southern accent, "Ingrid shouldn't be long."

"Whatever you've got," Lorna smiled, "white wine for me would be nice."

"Beer if you've got one?" Dan asked.

"Yep, I can manage both of those. Give me a minute." As he turned, a petite blonde woman came through the door wearing a pretty cream sun dress with a fitted bodice and a flared skirt displaying beautifully toned legs. She appeared to be late twenties maybe, with an attractive impish face and stunning blonde almost white hair tied on top of her head, showing off her ears with tiny silver studs which twinkled in the late afternoon sun invading the south facing room. She had made less of an effort than Lorna, but she didn't need to. She was a natural beauty.

"Ah, at last," Perry kissed his wife's cheek lovingly, "and how gorgeous you look too." He kept his arm around her waist as he eased her forward, "This is Dan, Lorna's husband, and Dan, this is Ingrid, my wife."

Dan stood up and reached to take her small delicate hand. "Pleased to meet you, thank you for inviting us."

"Thank you for coming," she smiled displaying the most perfect teeth, "please, sit down."

"Lorna's brought you some flowers," Perry nodded towards them.

"That's so kind, thank you." Ingrid smiled gratefully.

"I'll leave you to chat while I get the drinks, love," Perry said as he made his exit, picking up the bottle of wine Dan had brought on his way out.

Ingrid didn't appear to be in a rush to get the flowers into a vase as she sat down on the chair opposite them both. Her sleeveless dress displayed her toned arms and legs, they were a lovely bronze colour, but natural, which he liked; he hated it when Lorna went in for a tan spray. He knew categorically that Lorna would hate Ingrid for her attractiveness, she liked to be top dog. It didn't take much for the green-eyed monster to rear its head with his wife.

"How are you settling in?" Lorna asked, making a sweeping movement with her head around the room, "You look comfortable."

"Ah, don't be fooled," Ingrid smiled, "most of our stuff is still in boxes. We've managed to sort out the lounge and kitchen, but upstairs is still a bit of a muddle. We'll get there though, there's no rush."

While Dan listened, his eyes were drawn to the open-toe sandals Ingrid was wearing, exposing delicate feminine feet with perfectly manicured toe nails. He vaguely recollected a time when Lorna had hers done in a similar way for a holiday. Some sort of French manicure she called it. It was pretty, much nicer than colour, as far as he was concerned. The sparkling gold chain around Ingrid's slim ankle was cute, and for some bizarre reason, his thoughts drifted to her navel and whether she might have a decorative ring adorning it. He straightened up and inwardly chastised himself for the way his mind was wandering – he really needed to get a grip.

Perry's return was a welcome distraction as he came through the door with a tray of the drinks and handed them round before taking his seat in the chair next to his wife.

Dan felt the need to welcome them to the neighbourhood properly and raised his glass, "Let's have a toast shall we. A warm welcome to you both, we hope you'll be very happy while you're here."

"Cheers Dan," Perry said, and Ingrid smiled at him, "I'm sure we will. And it's great to have neighbours a similar age to ourselves."

Ingrid sipped her drink, and Dan took a gulp of his beer. As she put the wine glass on the table, Dan noticed her tiny little bud of a tongue as she wiped it around her moist lips. And that innocent little act caused something to shift within him. He took another gulp of his beer, at a loss as to what was happening. He was aghast. Fidelity was part of his make-up, he'd never cheat. He needed to control himself.

"Dan," Lorna said sharply, "you're not listening, and that's before you've even finished your beer. I was just warning them about nosy Phyllis next door to us and that blinking cat of hers."

"Sorry, I was miles away," he smiled at Perry and Ingrid, "it's hard to switch off sometimes, I don't know if you find that?"

"Sure," Perry nodded, "all the time. What sort of work do you do?"

Dan explained how he'd bought the small accountancy firm from an ageing accountant who'd stayed on initially during the take-over but had remained with him on a part-time basis, and how his brother Connor managed the practice.

"And it's doing well, is it?" Perry asked.

"I think so. I'm pleased with the progress we've made."

Lorna interjected, "Dan's being modest, he's transformed it and built up a huge client base."

"I wouldn't say huge, love," Dan pulled a face, "but it's doing okay, I'm pleased to say. What about you two, what do you do for a living?"

"A bit of this and that," Perry said, "we're into property mainly. We work for a company that buys old, dilapidated properties nobody wants, revamps them and then sells them on."

"Ah, I see. A good business to be in, I would have thought?"

"It is. We are expanding in the Midlands hence being here for a few months to look for potential properties."

"That sounds quite exciting," Lorna said, "do you both work for the same company?"

"Yes, we do," Ingrid said, "but I tend to do more admin than hands on. Perry's the one checking out the properties although I do accompany him to auctions. I quite like those."

"What's the company called?" Dan asked, wondering if he'd heard of it, but Perry interjected, "What do you do, Lorna?"

"Nothing exciting really. I work in a GP practice as an administrator. Luckily only part-time, I'm not sure I could stand working there full-time. It's a relief to finish each day."

"Oh, I bet," Ingrid said, "I'd hate to work with the public. My father used to have a hardware shop and was really charming to the customers to make sales, but his advice when I was looking at career options as a teenager was not to go into any occupation where you have to deal with the public."

"Anyone ready for another?" Perry asked.

Dan passed him his glass, "Why not?"

"Same again for me, please, that's a lovely wine."

"Can you fetch the nibbles, darling?" Ingrid asked Perry, "or shall I come?"

"No, you stay and talk, I'll get them."

As Perry left the room, Ingrid took up the conversation. "Tell me how you two met. Have you always lived in Nottingham?"

Lorna was centre stage where she loved to be, reminiscing about their first encounter. Dan's eyes were drawn to the lilies on the console table. Strange that Ingrid had not taken them to the kitchen. Maybe she wasn't fond of them, like him? He hated their smell, yet despite knowing it, Lorna always bought them.

Listening to Lorna and Ingrid chatting, he started to relax. Perry and Ingrid actually seemed a nice couple. He was warming to them both.

Either that or the gravity of the beer was high.

Chapter 7

Ingrid climbed into their comfy bed next to Perry as he flicked through the TV with the remote. He wasn't looking for anything specific, his mind was on their evening. The initial contact with Lorna and Dan had gone well. They'd achieved exactly what they'd set out to do.

"So . . . what did you think of them?" Ingrid asked.

"Nice enough." He put the TV on mute and flung the remote on the bed, "Pages apart though, didn't you think?"

"In what way?" she asked, biting her thumb nail.

"Well, she's attractive, bright and outgoing, while he's a bit of a steady Eddie boring accountant by the looks of things."

"I wouldn't say boring, he seemed nice enough to me."

"I'm not saying he wasn't nice. But you can tell he's a bit rigid, although he was better after a couple of beers. I bet she's got her work cut out with him."

"Do you reckon? She's much younger than him though, what do you think the age gap is?"

He shrugged, "Maybe eight, ten years between them, or thereabouts. Hard to judge his age."

"You know her age though."

"I know I do. Maybe he's not as old as he came

across?"

"Who knows? We'll find out soon enough. Anyway, did you manage to arrange a game of golf with him?"

"No. He was a bit vague about golf, as if he didn't want to talk about it, so I didn't push. There's a bit of time yet. I don't want them smelling a rat this early on."

"You're not really going to join the golf club, are you?"

"Definitely not. There's a waiting list anyway, but I'm not going to be filling out forms and things with names and addresses. I don't mind a few rounds to reel Dan in, but that's about as far as it goes. We really don't want other people remembering much about us when we've gone."

"Hey, they bought that we're into property development, although it was a bit awkward when Dan asked the company name."

"It was. But I got out of it by quickly asking Lorna a question."

"Yeah, I picked up on that, but thankfully they didn't. He'll ask again though. He seems to be that type. You know, likes to know everybody and everything."

"I'll get in before he does, then. I'll tell him it's a company that likes to keep its assets confidential and the reason we do so well is because of it. Nobody spots us coming, that sort of thing, and give him a load of crap about how we work better this way, buying up properties covertly."

"Great. Do that before he questions me about it."

"If he does, just make a joke of it, tell him you'd have

to kill him if you disclosed it. He won't ask you though, I doubt it anyway. So, now all we've got to do is set up another meeting. How about a barbecue? I did tentatively mention we do them a lot."

"Did you?" she grinned, "And did you tell him pretty soon we'll have staff doing any barbecues we might have?"

"Er . . . no," he grinned back, "I think that might just give the game away somehow, don't you?"

"Just a bit. Anyway, you can forget the barbecue for now because you'll be pleased to know that while you and Dan were discussing golf, your loving wife here managed to get us a supper invite to theirs."

"Really?" he widened his eyes, "So soon. You are a clever girl."

"I know that," she pouted sexily, "how clever though?"

He took her face in his hands and kissed her hard. "I'll show you," he breathed, their kiss deepening and she met him hungrily. The future they were working towards had begun and once the plan he'd devised was sorted, he could concentrate on the life he'd always dreamt about. What did it matter if he had to promise Ingrid certain things? He definitely wasn't having the children she thought they were going to. They didn't figure in his plans at all. He had far too much living and spending to do once the final piece of the jigsaw fitted in.

And there wasn't long to wait now.

Chapter 8

Dan was driving to the Cairngorms to find his brother. He'd broken his journey with an overnight stay in a budget hotel, but following a lacklustre continental breakfast, he was keen to be out of there and on his way. The sat nav rebooted as he started the ignition and indicated another couple of hours' drive. He could have driven there without stopping off but he hated driving long stretches for endless hours. The memory of losing his parents in a fatal car accident still haunted him. The police evidence and the coroner's verdict had been his father had fallen asleep at the wheel. Because of that, he always tried to stop off when driving distances. As if his father was on his shoulder saying 'Don't make the same mistake that I did.'

The traffic was always busy on a Monday morning. Stop, start, stop start. No point in getting riled though. He still hadn't told Lorna what he was doing, that'd come later if he could persuade Connor to come home. Then he'd tell her. For the moment though, he didn't want anyone to know he'd found his brother. The fictitious seminar he was supposed to be attending, was only a white lie, Lorna wouldn't be that bothered anyway. Of late she seemed distracted but he couldn't put his finger on why. She was never the doting type, that sort of thing wasn't in her make-up. It could be the problems at work she was having. He'd patiently listened to her berating her new boss who she disliked, and while he sympathised and made the appropriate noises, he knew a lot of it would be Lorna. She had a bad attitude – a definite arrogance where authority was concerned.

Lorna had told him while he was away, she was going to stay in Leicestershire and visit her mother in the care home. She used to stay in a Premier Inn and see her mother for two consecutive days, but the tenants had moved out of Elizabeth Mann's house so Lorna had taken to staying there overnight. It was more convenient as well as being less costly, so she'd been spending more time there recently. He was keen to get the property on the market again as part of the rental income was support funding for her mother's care package at the residential home, and currently he was having to make up the deficit. But Lorna was dragging her heels, which he didn't understand. As far as he could ascertain, her and Elizabeth had never got on, so he found it puzzling that Lorna had been visiting more frequently. He tried to remember how long it had been since the trips had become more frequent, but with images of his brother at the forefront of his mind, and the task ahead of persuading him to come home, any thoughts of Leicester and a new tenant for his mother-in-laws house, were pushed to the back of his mind. He'd re-visit that later.

He put his foot down. The sooner he got to Connor, the better. It would be terrible if he got to the house he'd been hiding in, and he'd moved on. Connor was his family and the brother he'd always looked out for. Since his disappearance, he'd felt completely bereft. As he continued along the endless roads, passing only the occasional car, his thoughts drifted to the traumatic day in his and Connor's young lives. It had been a typical day at school, his English language lesson had just finished and he was packing up his text books when one of the older prefects had come into the classroom and told him he had to go to the headmaster's office. He hadn't been unduly concerned when he'd knocked on the imposing office door; he'd secretly hoped he'd been summoned because he'd heard the maths department were looking for students to enter the inter schools maths challenge and, because he'd excelled at maths, they might want him to take part. But once the headmaster had shouted for him to enter and he'd stepped in the office, he'd been surprised to see his brother there. At first, he thought it was because Connor had done something wrong, especially as a uniformed police woman was there also, as well as another female.

Sadly, it was a day that remained etched on his mind. The older woman had been a social worker accompanying the police officer. They were there to tell them both their parents had been killed in a head-on collision. They'd been given sweet tea and biscuits and once they'd finished them, they were taken to a children's home where they'd stayed for almost a year until they were eventually placed with foster parents. They had their elderly grandmother but she was ill with cancer so couldn't care for two boisterous teenage boys. Sadly, she'd died six months later, so the Lloyd family which once consisted of five, soon became two. And overnight, he became Connor's mother and father. It was he who had looked after his brother in the care home when he cried each night for their mum and dad, and it was him that worked hard waiting tables and studying well into the early hours each night to get into college and acquire his accountancy qualifications. And, once he'd qualified as an accountant, he eventually acquired a job that paid enough for them to move into their own accommodation; he laughed inwardly, remembering their absolute joy, eventually moving into what was described as a bijou flat, but in reality was a glorified bed sit. But they were together and that made Dan happy. Connor wasn't an academic, but he went to college, and once that was finished, got a job in the local council. Within months he'd met Ruth and before long they'd been living together, leaving Dan on his own until he'd met Victoria, the woman who'd shared his life for seven years before Lorna. But even though Connor had found happiness with Ruth, Dan continued to act as a surrogate father and bail him out of trouble time and time again, nothing serious, but there always seemed to be something. When Connor was made redundant, Dan had recruited him as manager of his accountancy practice. He knew he was filling the gap left by his parents. Lorna didn't like it one bit. She was always quick to point out that he over-indulged Connor, and she was right to a degree. It just irritated him hearing her say it. That's why he hadn't let on he was going to find him. She'd only tell him not to go and to let the police and

Ruth deal with it. But he couldn't do that. If anyone was going to persuade Connor to come home, it was him. They had a bond that went deeper than brothers. Ruth knew it and left them to it, it was such a pity Lorna couldn't.

The Cairngorms seemed endless. Arthur, who he'd been communicating with by phone, had given his postcode so Dan could find the way. He'd requested that Dan call on him first of all, so he could direct him to Connor as it was unlikely he'd find it, even with sat nav.

Eventually, Dan arrived at Arthur's isolated old house which stood on a hill, surrounded by overgrown wildflowers and trees with centuries old foundations that stood strong against a world that had accelerated since their onset. The old man, Arthur, must have been watching, he teetered out to meet him as he'd pulled up to the front of the house.

Arthur was a small man, leaning heavily on a well-used wooden walking stick. He had a ruddy, weather-worn complexion and a mass of unkempt long grey hair and beard to match. He looked to be about late seventies.

Dan exited his car and walked toward him, reaching out a hand.

"You made it then," Arthur said, taking his hand and shaking it firmly.

"Yes. You were spot on. It's certainly remote." Dan's gaze drifted around the backdrop of spectacular barren mountains dwarfing the tiny house, which probably wasn't that small, but it seemed so because of the landscape. "This place is pretty amazing."

"It is that," Arthur nodded.

"I can't thank you enough for helping me find my brother."

"Well, make sure you take him home, this isolation is no place for a young man. And especially since you told me he's got children, he needs to be with them, not hiding away here."

"I agree. And his family needs him."

Arthur scrutinised Dan's face. "You're a good man, coming for him . . . I knew that from the first time I spoke to you."

"Thank you, but I'd never have found Connor if it wasn't for you."

"You would have done. He'd have found someone else with a mobile phone eventually. He'd have got a message to you somehow, it was the only way he knew that you'd come and get him."

"Do you think so?"

"I know so. Here," he reached in his pocket and pulled out a piece of A4 paper folded in half.

"I've drawn you a map."

Dan looked down at the map. It was perfect, almost like a picture the way he'd sketched the roads and mountains."

"This is beautiful. You must draw and paint?"

"I used to, many years ago, but not now. Anyway, I'll not keep you. You get off and find that wayward brother of yours and take him home. Like I said, it's too quiet for a young man, here."

"It is isolated, that's for sure," Dan's eyes drifted towards the endless mountains, "but you're happy here?"

"I am, lad, very happy. This is where I'll end my days."

"Let's hope that isn't for a long time yet. And although this is goodbye, I'd like to think that one of these days in the future, I could be back. Maybe bring that brother of mine to thank you for your kindness."

"You could do," Arthur said, "but I doubt I'll be here, son. Pleased to have helped in some way, though. Now you go and talk some sense into him and take him home."

Dan opened the door to the back seat and reached in for the wooden box containing a bottle of whisky and handed it to Arthur. "A small gift of thanks. I'd imagine a tot in your tea would be welcome some days round here, particularly in the winter."

"You're not wrong there. That is generous of you, thank you."

"No, thank you," Dan nodded, genuinely warming to the gentle unassuming man, "it's the least I can do."

Dan got in the front seat and as he went to close the car door, Arthur put his hand on it to stop him. Fatigued, watery eyes peered into Dan's "Do you believe it spiritualism?"

"Can't say I've ever thought much about it to be honest. Why?"

Arthur paused for a moment, as if choosing his words carefully. "You need to take care of yourself," he cleared his throat, "make sure nobody takes advantage of you. You're an honourable man, I can see that. And there's nothing wrong with being honourable . . . but . . ."

"You've lost me now?" Dan said.

Arthur hesitated for a couple more seconds. When he did speak again, it was more a whisper "Maybe that's a good thing, son. Now, take it easy on these roads."

"I will do. And thank you again."

Arthur pushed the car door shut. Dan started the ignition and as he pulled away, raised his hand. He wouldn't see the stranger again. He knew that, as did Arthur. But he'd been exceptionally kind helping him and for some bizarre reason, he'd touched him deep within. An elderly man, living in a remote spot on his own, happily passing his days in God's waiting room.

He brought the car to a halt at a crossroads and glanced at the map on the seat next to him. The direction was left and he took the turning. *Make sure nobody takes advantage of you* the old man had said. It was an odd thing to say to a stranger. Maybe he'd been on the scotch already?

He accelerated to increase his speed and as he did so, he dismissed Arthur from his mind.

His focus now was reaching his brother and taking him home.

Chapter 9

Lorna was about to text her friend to ask where she was when Sarah's Citroen turned into the swimming pool car park and made its way towards her, pulling alongside her car.

"Better late than never," Lorna said as she exited her car at the same time as Sarah and closed her car door. "What kept you?" she asked, clicking the lock on the key fob.

"The usual chaos in the Parkinson household. Lilly couldn't find her blue top that she *must have* for the youth club and Harry had somehow misplaced his football boots." She opened the back door of her car and reached inside for her swimming bag. "The joys of parenthood, you're lucky to have escaped from it all."

"Too right, I'd be stressed to death."

"I am. And that's why I look like I've just got out of bed and you look fabulous."

"Yeah right," Lorna laughed, secretly pleased her friend had said she looked good. She linked her arm into hers as they made their way towards the entrance. Her new Stella McCartney navy blue gym kit which clung in all the right places had cost an arm and a leg, but it was worth every penny as far as she was concerned. Image was important to her.

She paid the entrance fee for them both on her credit card.

"No, I can get mine," Sarah protested.

"Don't be daft. I invited you."

"Still, you don't have to pay for me."

"It's only a couple of quid. You pay next time if you're bothered."

"Okay, I'll do that."

"I'm pleased I've finally got here and you're with me," Lorna said as they made their way toward the changing rooms, "it's great to have some company."

"It's nice to do something for me, but like I said last week, I don't often get chance to do that. What's it all in aid of anyway? I'm not buying this weight loss jargon. Your figure is perfect."

"What else could there be? I just want to get a bit fitter. In fact, I'm thinking of signing up for the swimming challenge they've got on. I rang and asked about it, it's one way to make sure I come each week." They walked into the communal changing room and found a locker each and started to undress.

"What's the swim challenge all about?" Sarah asked, discarding the clothes she was wearing over the top of her costume, folding them and placing them inside the locker.

"It's about gradually building up the distance you can swim. You increase the amount of lengths you do each time you come. You have a tracker and get it signed off each session depending on how many you do. The aim is to get to twenty-six miles."

"Twenty-six miles!" Sarah's voice went up an octave, "You can't be serious. That's a massive distance."

"Yeah, I know it is, but you build up gradually."

"Well, rather you than me, that's all I can say. I'm just here for pleasure, I can't be doing endless lengths, I'd soon get fed up."

"I'm looking forward to it. That's why I'm going to come two to three times a week from now on. The woman I spoke to said three times a week is good as you need rest days. She said our bodies soon get into the rhythm of exercise and I'll be surprised how quickly my stamina will build up."

"Honestly Lorna, you do surprise me," Sarah said looking down at her costume and attaching the locker key to her strap. "I can't believe you, swimming. You're sure it isn't going to be a ten day wonder?"

"Nope, trust me. I'm going to nail it in the next couple of months."

"Then what?"

"Then nothing. It's just to see if I can. I'm not a strong swimmer at all, so it can only do me good to push myself."

They started to make their way towards the pool. Sarah said, "But you told me yourself when you and Dan go on holiday, you don't even get your hair wet."

"Yeah, well that was then. Because I can't swim brilliantly, I tend to shy off. But not anymore, I'll be out-swimming Dan on our next holiday."

"Really? I still can't see it happening somehow. I tell you what, ten quid says you'll have given up by the end of the month."

Lorna smiled and reached out her hand which Sarah

took, "You're on."

Despite trying to do some lengths, Lorna's stamina soon ran out. It was obvious to her she had a long way to go before she became proficient but she was hopeful that the next time she came, she'd do better. She spotted her friend almost cowering in the shallow end. It was written all over her face she'd had enough. She swam towards her.

"Are you about done do you reckon?" Sarah said, her teeth chattering together, "It's getting pretty cold."

"That's because you're doing nothing. You haven't even got your shoulders in the water."

"I know I haven't, it's too bloody cold."

"Come on then, let's get out, shall we?"

They made their way to the steps and hoisted themselves out. Sarah was one step ahead as she made her way to her locker, not speaking again until she had opened it and wrapped a huge towel around herself. "Thank God for that. I'm not being awful but I don't think I can be your swimming buddy on a regular basis, I really am freezing."

"You'll be fine once you're out of your wet cossie. And you need to dry your hair, there's nothing worse than wet hair for making you cold."

"Aren't you cold?" Sarah asked easing her wet swimsuit down underneath her towel and kicking it off with her feet.

"A bit, yeah," Lorna said, vigorously rubbing her arms and legs, "but I'm okay. I kept swimming remember while you stopped. That's when you get cold."

Sarah wrapped herself up tightly again in the towel, still shivering.

"Are you going to grab a shower? Lorna asked, "that'll warm you up."

"I'll get one when I get home, or maybe even a bath."

"Yeah, me too. Put some clothes on then, you'll soon get warm," Lorna told her reaching in her locker for her own clothes.

"In a minute. Are you going to be okay coming on your own or can you drag someone else along?"

"Not sure, I'll have to think. There's no one that springs to mind who I know that likes swimming."

"What about Dan? He's exercise mad. He'd come with you."

"Nah, I don't want to ask him. Anyway, he doesn't even know anything about me doing the swimming challenge."

"Why not?"

"I want to surprise him when we go on holiday. He'll get such a shock to see how far I'm able to do."

"He will if he knows nothing about it," Sarah laughed, easing her pants on.

"Have you got time for a coffee in the cafe to warm us up?" Lorna asked towelling her hair.

"Yeah, definitely, with a brandy in it maybe."

"You'll be lucky. I don't think the cafe somehow does alcohol."

"Well they should, to cater for people like me."

Lorna was dressed first and hoisted her bag over her shoulder and Sarah followed as they made their way out of the changing room and headed for the cafe.

"So remember, whatever you do," Lorna said, "don't mention to Dan about the swimming challenge if you see him, will you?"

"I won't say anything but isn't he going to ask where you've been when you come home with wet hair and smelling of chlorine?"

"He's never home much before six. I'll be all showered by then if I go in the afternoons when I've finished work."

"Oh right, well don't worry, your secret's safe with me."

Chapter 10

Dan continued for another eight minutes from leaving Arthur's until he arrived at the cottage where Connor was supposed to be staying. He headed up the steep incline in a low gear until he reached the front of the house and brought the car to a halt. It was a ramshackle old place, in need of some urgent DIY judging by the faded and crumbling plaster frontage, the loose and discoloured shutters and the brown tiled roof with a dilapidated chimney. His heart leapt when he spotted his brother's face at the grimy window, peering out. He'd found him. All was well.

He made his way towards the weather-worn front door where his younger brother stood, thinner, dishevelled and with a desperate expression etched on his pale, pained face. As furious as Dan was at him, he grabbed him and wrapped his arms tightly around his scrawny frame. Whatever Connor was running away from, he would sort. He always did. For a few short seconds he savoured his dear brother and the fact he was alive.

As he eased himself away, Connor's weariness was evident. His forlorn expression and miserable remorseful eyes which had almost sunken into his face was proof of how traumatic the last few weeks had been for him.

"Now then, you silly bugger," Dan said, "of all the places to hide, you chose the middle of nowhere. It's taken me bleeding hours driving to get here, talk about the back of beyond."

"You'd better come in, then," Connor said, his voice faltering, "although I've not got much to offer by the way of Lloyd hospitality."

"Don't worry, I've not come for dinner." He followed Connor into the dimly lit hall and through to a small kitchen at the back. It was tiny from one end to the other. The house was musty, but nothing that opening the doors and windows wouldn't solve.

"Have a seat," Connor indicated to a small Formica table, a throwback to the sixties and just big enough for two. "Drink?"

"A coffee would be good."

"I haven't got any milk."

"Black's fine."

Dan made a show of staring at the view through the small window while Connor prepared their coffees, but surreptitiously he was watching him. As well as weight loss, he was scruffy. His filthy feet were evident in the flip flops, and his tee shirt and shorts hadn't been washed for days. And judging by his body odour, personal hygiene hadn't been a top priority either.

Connor placed two chipped mugs on the table and sat down opposite. Dan took a sip but it was too hot so rested it down. "Okay, bro, tell me what's going on?"

Connor's eyes brimmed with tears. "I've been a bloody fool, Dan."

"Tell me?" he urged trying to convey compassion as he stared directly into his brother's tortured face. He'd made a pact with himself not to chastise him. That would come later. For now he needed to find out what was going on and why Connor had upped and left.

"I'm up to my eyes in shit."

"What sort of shit?"

"How are Ruth and the girls?"

"Not good. But you'd expect that. What sort of shit?" he repeated.

"Debt."

The one word surprised Dan. It wasn't something he'd even considered. He'd thought about drugs but dismissed that as unlikely as he felt certain he'd have noticed. The likeliest explanation as far as he was concerned was that his disappearance involved a woman. And worst-case scenario, one he'd got pregnant.

"How much?"

"Too much." Connor raised his hands, "Everything's gone. I've remortgaged the house and borrowed money I can't pay back."

Dan stifled an urge to berate him. Right now he was too fragile. But he needed to know about work. His accountancy business was his life.

"What about the office?"

"Not there," Connor shook his head, "well, not really." His flat, monotone voice seemed resigned, "I've been dipping into the petty cash a bit, nothing major though. I knew you'd spot it if I did."

"Right, so . . . you're up to your eyes in a shed load of

debt. What have you been spending it all on?"

"Gambling." His voice began to break, "And before you say anything, I know I've been bloody stupid. You don't need to tell me anything I don't already know. If I could turn the clock back, I would. But I can't, I'm addicted, Dan."

"And that's why you're hiding away up here?" Dan said with a frustrated shake of the head, "Whose place is this anyway?"

"It belongs to Grange Wheeler."

"What, he's let you stop here?" Grange Wheeler was a wealthy client of the practice.

"Yeah, he never uses it. He knows I'm down on my luck and suggested I got away for a few days and said to stop as long as I needed to. He's out of the country anyway. Told me there was a hiding place for the key at the bottom of the garden under the gravestone of a pet. Seemingly, most of the time, this place is locked up. Can't think why he doesn't sell it really, something to do with it being his late grandfather's house and he can't bring himself to part with it."

"Well, at least you've had a roof over your head, we can be grateful for that. I had visions of you bedding down on a beach or something. The police said you hadn't used your cards or drawn any money out of the bank?"

"No, I brought cash with me," he winced, "withdrawn it from the girls' accounts. That's what sort of a dad I am . . . stealing off my own kids. I contemplated ending it all," his chin dropped to his chest, "but I couldn't even get that right. I kept thinking I'll do it tomorrow, but the coward that I am, I couldn't bring myself to do it."

"Don't be talking like that," he reached forward and squeezed his brother's arm, "whatever's gone on, we can sort. Nothing's worth killing yourself for."

"What, even though Ruth and the kids will be better off without me?" He shrugged, "The life we had has ended now because of me. She deserves better. The house and cars are going to have to go," tears threatened but he managed to swallow them back, "but what bothers me more than that is the girls' schooling. They're going to have to move and they love school. They're both bright and doing well, but there's no money left for school fees."

"Has Ruth got any idea of the amount of debt you're in . . . she hasn't said anything to me?"

"No. Well she hadn't, but she will have pretty soon when her cards are all declined."

"So what's your plan? You can't hide here forever."

"I know I can't. How did you find me anyway?"

"I followed up on the text you sent from Arthur's phone."

Connor nodded knowingly while his voice dropped to barely a whisper, "I don't know where to go from here."

"You need to come home," Dan said firmly, "and don't argue. I'm not leaving you here, you're coming with me and we're going to face this together."

"I can't," the threatening tears finally rolled down his cheeks, "the thought of telling Ruth kills me. She won't want me now, not after this."

"Ruth will be there for you. She loves you."

"Maybe she does, but there's nothing left. Why stay with me? The life she has is going to be taken from her. Her and the girls are going to end up in rented accommodation somewhere, and I'll be in a bedsit with Jack shit."

"It doesn't have to come to that," Dan took a sip of his coffee, "I'll help you get back on your feet."

"You can't help me. There's nothing left. It's all gone."

"I can help you," Dan said banging his cup down, "you love Ruth, don't you?"

"Course I do. But it won't be enough."

"How do you know? Come back with me and we can begin to sort things. I can't leave you here, not now."

Connor shook his head. He was going to take some convincing, Dan could see that.

"Look, I'm not saying it's going to be easy, but you can do this. You're not on your own. Apart from seeing Ruth and having to explain all of this, what's the worst thing you're going to have to face? What bothers you most of all?"

"The girls," his voice was barely a whisper, "losing their school places."

"Right, well, I can sort that. I'll pay until the end of the year. So that's one off the list."

Connor winced. "I can't let you do that."

"Of course you can. They're my nieces. If I had kids of my own, I'd be paying their school fees. You'll have to sell the house though to clear some of your debts."

"Ruth'll be gutted, she loves our house."

"Yeah, she will, but she loves you more, I'm sure. And you owe it to her to at least start to sort things out with her. She deserves that much. You can work through this, Connor. You won't be the first person to get themselves into debt, and I'm pretty sure you won't be the last. But you can't hide away for ever. You've got to stand up and be counted. You've made a mistake, now you've got to own it and start to try and put it right. And we can get you the help you need."

"Yeah, but what if she wants out?"

"What if she does? You'll have to deal with it if that happens. Right now she's worried sick, not knowing if you're dead or alive. She's owed an explanation from you at least. And she'll need some time. Don't be expecting her to take you back and everything be okay in the matter of weeks. It won't. You've hurt her."

"I know you're right," Connor ran his fingers through his greasy, unwashed hair, "you always are." His forlorn eyes met his, "How come we have the same parents yet you got to be smart while I'm useless? You're the one with the qualifications, the business, the stunning house, the gorgeous wife. You've got it all. I've always envied you that. I love you, you're my brother, but I can't help feeling bloody jealous sometimes. You'd never fuck up like me."

"Mate," Dan sat forward in his chair and rested his elbows on the table, "life's not all roses round the front door for me, you know. None of us have got it all, I've had my share of heartache."

"You mean Tommy?"

"Yep, and Victoria. I still miss them and the life we could have had, even after all this time."

"But you love Lorna," Connor tilted his head, "right?"

"Yeah, course I do," Dan smirked, "even if she is high maintenance." He thought about whether to discuss his marriage further. If it would help make Connor see that everyone had their share of troubles, maybe it was the right thing to do. He cleared his throat, "Our relationship was a bit of a rebound thing for me and for her. I didn't realise I was actively looking for someone, but I was and she fitted the bill after Victoria and I split up. She was sexy, stunning, and vulnerable. I had the mad urge to protect her and keep her safe after her previous partner had treated her badly," he took a deep breath in, "and the rest is history, as they say."

"But you're sound, aren't you? You're not heading for the divorce courts or anything?"

"God no, I'm just trying to be honest with you and spelling out I don't have the perfect life you seem to think I have. We all get thrown curveballs, you just have to play them the best you can."

For the first time Connor's face showed concern for him. "Lorna loves you though, doesn't she?"

"Course she does."

"So, what are you saying? Marrying Lorna was a mistake?"

Dan fiddled with the gold band on his left hand,

contemplating his answer. "We love each other and we're happy, but sometimes my mind strays to my life before I met her, with Victoria and Tommy and what might have been."

"It was a horrible time for you, but you never say much. I've never heard you talk like this since you met Lorna. Why now?"

"'Cause I'm trying to make you see that nobody's life is perfect all the time. We all have a cross to bear; it's just that some of us hide it better. I'm happy with my life, I'm not bleating on, but I'm trying to tell you so you don't measure your life against mine. I haven't got the answers, but I know we just have to get on with it, even during the hard times. Like when we lost Tommy. I had to keep moving forward. So, what you need to do now is come home, throw yourself at Ruth's mercy and hope she'll forgive you. That's all you can do. And if she can't, we'll tackle that as well. Hiding away here isn't going to help."

"I know you're right," Connor's eyes were slightly more vibrant than when he'd first arrived, "you're the best, you know. I don't say it often enough, but you really are my hero . . . sort of the wind beneath my wings."

Dan swallowed the lump in his throat, he loved his brother. He was all the blood family he had left. "I promised you when Mum and Dad died, I'd take care of you and I always will. You're my brother. I'll never let you down. Now shut the fuck up with the sentimental stuff or you'll have me crying in my coffee." He stood up, "I'll have a walk about outside while you give Ruth a ring and let her know you're safe and on your way home. Then we'll pack your stuff and get off."

Connor let out a huge breath as if some of the burden he'd been carrying had lifted. "I'm not bad-mouthing Lorna or anything, but I tell you this, it was her lucky day when you walked into her life. She'd never get anyone better than you. And if she can't see that, then she's making a big mistake."

Chapter 11

Lorna was visiting her mother in the care home out of duty and nothing more. She glanced at her watch. Ten more minutes and she was out of there. She'd played the respectful daughter for an hour and that was much longer than she deserved.

Her mother had nodded off, which was a relief. She resembled a corpse, dozing in the armchair with her head falling forwards and mouth wide open. Lorna gazed around the adequate but dated room. It was sparse with little by the way of furniture, the pink curtains at the window were no longer vibrant, and the patterned quilt on the bed faded from numerous washes. The chair her mother was sitting in had seen better days judging by the wear and tear on the armrests and the dirty headrest. Considering the amount of money they paid each month, it would have been nice to have had a more comfortable room, but it wasn't worth discussing with the manager. The one time Dan had mentioned it, they'd been told that the alternative if they weren't happy would be to move her to another care home, and Lorna definitely didn't want that. Why should she care how her mother spent her last days? As far as she was concerned, the basic room was karma. She'd been a horrible mother.

Her eyes focussed on three framed photographs which Dan had insisted she took in so her mother *has some family memories.* The once silver frames had tarnished and the prints appeared to be fading. There was one of her and Dan with her mum smiling broadly, taken at their wedding and a couple of her and Dan from holidays. Lorna stared at herself. She looked happy then somehow, or had the joyous smiles been just for the camera?

"Sorry," her mother opened her eyes, and wiped her mouth with one of the tissues she permanently seemed to clutch in her hand, "I must have nodded off. What time is it?"

"Just after three. I'm going to be making a move shortly."

"Can't you stay for tea? You've barely been here for five minutes."

"We've had tea."

"Have we? Are you sure?"

"Yes, I'm sure."

"Well, we can have another. What's the rush?"

"There's no rush as such. I've got a long drive home, that's all."

"Why don't you stay, like you usually do?"

Her mother's thoughts were drifting again. No doubt she'd be imagining they were at her small bungalow in the days when her and Dan used to stay over for a visit.

"I'm got someone coming round tonight," she lied, "so I need to go home and prepare some food."

"Suit yourself," he mother said, "where's Daniel anyway? Is he in the garden?"

"He's not come today."

"Why not?"

"He's working."

"Oh, right, well I guess he can be excused then. Why aren't you working?"

"It's my day off."

Her mother was silent for a few seconds. Sadly, the opinionated Elizabeth Mann could never keep quiet for long. "I can't believe you're still stuck in that shop," her lips pursed, "I keep telling you, you should go to night school and try and get some qualifications. Your problem is, your father indulges you and that's why you've ended up in a shop. You could have done so much better if you'd worked harder at school."

"I'm not in a shop anymore, I work in a doctor's surgery." And dad died ages ago she said under her breath.

"Doctor's surgery? Well," she pulled a disparaging face, "that's even worse than a shop. Fancy dealing with all those ill people every day. I hope they pay you well. I'd want danger money doing that job. That's the trouble though," she folded her arms, "no qualifications and you end up in dead-end jobs."

It was her cue to leave. Her mother had no idea that once she started her rants, Lorna had an overwhelming urge to stick a pillow over her head and shut her up once and for all. Never in all her thirty years had she a kind word to say about her. Even before dementia, she was a horrible woman. Every opportunity she could, she'd criticise her. And it still hurt even now. Whenever she reflected on her life, she blamed her mother for all the wrong decisions she'd made. Several bum relationships were retaliation against her mother's desire for her to conform. And her mother had disliked any one she ever brought home, until Dan. She loved him.

Lorna stood up, eager to be off. Once her mother started moaning on about her inadequacies, there'd be no let up.

"I really must be going," she leaned towards her mother to peck her cheek, always holding her breath. Her mother smelled old and familiar, of a time she liked to forget. She'd moved away from her oppression and thanked God every day that she had. "I'll be back in a couple of weeks to see you," she said, faking brightness as she picked up her handbag and flung it over her shoulder, "take care, won't you." She made her way to the door.

"Tell Daniel I missed him today, would you," her mother said, "and ask him to come next time."

For a split second it was almost as if her mother didn't have dementia as her eyes narrowed through her glasses as she gave an intense stare, waiting for her daughter to answer. Lorna's gut clenched. Anyone would make the old witch happy, anyone that was except her own daughter.

"Sure I will, bye," she said exiting the room and closing the door behind her. She eagerly made her way along the dismal artificially lit corridor to get to the exit, and with each stride, the lump in her throat thickened. She swallowed it away. She wouldn't cry.

The old bat didn't deserve her tears.

Chapter 12

"Leave Uncle Dan alone, you two," Ruth told her two eight year old daughters, "he's been playing with you long enough now. Go and get your iPads while we have a coffee."

"Aww."

"Never mind aw. Mummy and Daddy need to talk to Uncle Dan."

"But we want to play."

"I know you do, and you will in a little while. But the grown-ups need to talk first, so go on, shoo, the pair of you."

Dan watched them head off to their bedrooms. "I'll go up in a bit and have some time with them."

"Yeah, I know you will. Here," Ruth handed him a coffee and they sat at the kitchen table. Dan cared deeply for his sister-in-law. They'd always been close since the day he'd met her. Ruth was a small woman with a great big heart. Slightly overweight with short dark hair, she wasn't one for glamour, rarely wearing make-up and seemed happy in comfortable leggings or jeans. She certainly wasn't one for the designer labels Lorna favoured. She was devoted to Connor despite his previous infidelity. Dan had admired her loyalty at the time and, thought it was more than his brother deserved, although he never voiced that opinion.

"How you doing, buddy?" Dan asked Connor. It was early days and he was nowhere back to his usual vibrancy but his face was less etched with worry since his return home.

"Not too bad," he shrugged, "the bank have come up with a debt management plan and the estate agent is coming to photograph the house on Monday, and then it'll be going on the market. I was saying to Ruth yesterday, I ought to be coming back to work next week, I think I'm ready for it now."

"You're sure?" Dan asked, "Debbie's doing a terrific job in your absence sorting everyone out."

"All the more reason then, or I won't have a job to go back to."

"You daft bugger, you'll always have a job." He turned to Ruth who'd been nothing but compassionate since Connor returned home, "How are you doing?" he asked kindly, full of admiration for the way she'd handled things. As far as he could see, she was extremely supportive, which he was grateful for as Connor needed that. Although he'd been fairly confident she wouldn't be any less, there had been a tiny doubt in his mind that she might want out.

"Okay," she said brightly, "relieved he's home of course." As she glanced sideways at Connor, affection was evident in her eyes, but he could tell because he knew her so well, it was mixed with pain. "We're slowly working through everything," she squeezed Connor's hand, "aren't we, love? My parents have offered to help so we can hang on to the house, but neither of us is keen on that."

Connor's jaw clenched, "It's really good of them, but I want to try and sort this mess out myself. I got us into it, so I want to try and get us out of it."

Ruth nodded, "We're going to go into rented accommodation for about a year and then we might take Mum and Dad up on their offer and try and buy again. It'd maybe have to be in their name or something due to the debts we've now got."

"That's not such a bad thing though," Connor said positively. "If Doug and Angie are putting money into a house for us, it should be in their name."

Dan agreed but didn't say it out loud. It would be best for Connor to not have access to any mortgage rights. He might be tempted to remortgage again if he got into difficulty. He wasn't out of the woods yet, by any means. They needed to watch him carefully.

Connor ran his fingers through his hair, a habit he'd developed as a teenager when he was stressed. "I'm so bloody ashamed of what I've put you all through. I should have spoken up before it got to this," his shoulders sagged, "I know I keep saying it, but I am sorry."

"Look mate, we know you are. What's done is done. We can't undo it, so you have to move forward the best you can. You've got Ruth and the girls, and Lorna and I, so right now, you just have to give it time. The main thing is, you working on it and not letting things drift again. And you must tell us if you ever start to wobble, so we can help you."

"I will, I promise," his expression was pained, "but I'm never going down that road again, that's for sure. Anyway, on a brighter note, I had my first session with the counsellor yesterday."

"How did that go?"

"Okay. It seemed a bit of a luxury being able to offload with a complete stranger. I felt much better after the session. He seems a decent enough bloke."

"That's good. Did you come up with any answers as to why it all spiralled out of control so quickly?"

"Nothing concrete. It was all positive though."

"Yeah," Ruth said, "but remember, he did say not to discuss it at this early stage."

"I know. I'm just telling Dan so he knows. But you're right, so I'll say no more about it." His eyes focussed on Dan, "I don't know what we'd do without you," his voice cracked with emotion, "you've been an absolute brick and gone well above your big brother duties this time."

"Well," Dan said clearing his throat and trying to hide the tears in his eyes, "I'm sure you'd do the same for me."

"Definitely, but you'd never be weak enough to get involved with gambling."

"Too bloody right," he tried to lighten the mood, "as Lorna would say, I'm far too tight to squander money." They all chuckled at that, which was good. There hadn't been a lot to smile about in recent weeks.

"Lorna knows you too bloody well," Connor grinned. "Seriously though, I definitely owe you."

"You owe me nothing. All I want is for you to get yourself sorted and back on track, both of you," he smiled affectionately at his sister-in-law, full of admiration for the way she was sticking by Connor when she could have easily wanted out. "That's all I'm bothered about." Dan stood up, "I'll just pop up and see the girls and then I'd better get off."

Dan glanced at the clock on the dashboard as he headed home. He'd been at Connor's longer than he'd anticipated but they needed support right now and he wanted to be there for them. And with the girls it was always *five more minutes* which invariably turned into another half an hour, but he didn't mind as he loved them dearly.

The smell wafting from the kitchen as he opened the front door sent his senses into overdrive. He removed his jacket and hung it on the banister as Lorna came into the hall.

"At last!" her eyes flew to his jacket and she scowled, "Don't leave that there, take it upstairs with you. You're going to have to get a move on. They'll be here in less than an hour."

His vague expression must have spoken volumes.

"Ingrid and Perry, remember, they're coming for dinner." She scowled, "I did remind you yesterday."

"That's right, you did."

"Did you get to golf?"

"Yeah, but I only did ten rounds. I nipped to Connor's."

"What did you do that for?" Lorna's displeasure was evident as she launched into one of her tirades, "They need time on their own. You popping in every five minutes won't help; you'll be getting on Ruth's nerves."

"Oh, cheers. And here's me thinking they might need my support."

"That's half the trouble though, you're always there for Connor and that's why he takes advantage of you." She screwed up her face, "Anyway, we haven't got time for this. You better get showered and changed," she looked at her watch, "you've got forty-five minutes before they get here. And don't wear that awful beige shirt with the tiny diamonds on it."

He couldn't be bothered to answer. Lorna was always negative about Connor. He headed for the stairs longing to unwind with a few beers and crap TV. The last thing he wanted to do was entertain. He wasn't in the mood and couldn't understand why Lorna had even invited Perry and Ingrid. Okay, so they'd gone for drinks to their house, that didn't mean there was a need to reciprocate. They were hardly friends. But for some reason, Lorna had taken a shine to them and was keen to have them round. He'd have rather met them out somewhere for a drink and maybe a meal, at least that way they could slip away afterwards, but in his own home he couldn't. They'd be there until they decided to leave.

He increased the temperature in the shower and let the water cascade over him, trying to block out Lorna's negativity. It would be Connor's first day back at work on Monday and he'd devised a plan to set him on marketing and procuring new business. The clients they currently had were adequate, but expanding would provide Connor with some positive objectives, which he hoped would ensure his focus would be on success and achievement. Moving forward, his desire was the complete eradication of his debt problems.

Chapter 13

Bang on seven thirty, Dan opened the front door to let Ingrid and Perry in. If he'd thought Ingrid was attractive the first time he'd seen her, her appeal was even more apparent this time.

"Come in," he said with his best pleased-to-see-you smile. He shook Perry's hand, and was intending on clasping Ingrid's too but she leaned into him for a kiss. She was much shorter than him so stood on her tiptoes and placed her warm lips on his cheek. Her flowery, musky perfume was breath-taking. Totally unexpectedly and shockingly for him, he felt a twitch in his groin.

"So pleased you could both make it," he said easing himself away from her.

"We come with gifts," Perry handed him a bottle of wine and some liqueur chocolates.

"There was really no need," he took them from Perry, "but thank you. Come on through."

He led them to the lounge as Lorna come through from the kitchen, looking stunning in a fitted black dress exposing her delicate shoulders, and her shapely legs, lengthened by patent killer heels. He'd never seen any of it before, he'd have remembered if he had. And as he examined her more closely and absorbed the freshly highlighted hair, and the acrylic decorative nails, he knew without any shadow of doubt, Lorna's new attire would have severely dented the credit card. He could see the statement now with pound signs dancing before his eyes.

"Welcome," Lorna smiled warmly, "so pleased to see you." She gave them both an affectionate hug, leaving Dan feeling almost envious. She hardly ever spontaneously hugged him; he did all the initiating, even for a kiss. As he left the house each morning he would reach for her, and at night, he liked to kiss her before going off to sleep. But if he didn't bother, she certainly wouldn't. He couldn't remember a time when she made the first move to kiss him. Her explanation was that growing up, her mother had never shown any physical affection towards her, so it wasn't something that came naturally to her.

"Do take a seat," Lorna said directing them towards the sofa while Dan showed her the gifts. "These are from Perry and Ingrid."

"Thank you both," Lorna smiled, "that is kind of you."

Perry and Ingrid took their seats. "What a gorgeous house you have," Ingrid said, gazing around the room.

"It's stunning," Perry agreed, "Someone has good taste," he smiled cheekily, "now, which one. Eeny, meeny, miny mo," he said pointing his finger between the two of them.

Dan grinned, "Not me, I'm afraid, Lorna's the artistic one. Left to me, we'd still have the furniture from my student days."

"He's not joking, either," Lorna laughed. "Anyway, what can we get you both to drink?"

"I'll sort them out, love," Dan said still clutching the wine and chocolates, "you sit down and take the weight off your feet. You've been at it all day."

"Don't be silly, Dan," she scowled playfully, but he knew that look of hers. She was irritated with him even though she would have been at it all day. "I haven't gone to any trouble at all."

"Well, I hope you haven't on our account," Ingrid said, "cheese and biscuits would do us."

"I think I've managed to rustle up a little more than that," Lorna said, "Did you say something about drinks, Dan?"

"Sure." He smiled at their guests, "We've a nice bottle of champagne chilling if everyone is up for a Kir Royale, or would you prefer a beer, Perry?" He hoped they'd decline the champagne; it was way over the top as far as he was concerned, but Lorna had bought it as a Kir Royale cocktail was her favourite pre-dinner drink.

"I do like a champagne cocktail," Perry said, "I might hold you to a beer later on."

"Me too," Ingrid smiled, displaying her white even teeth with a tiny gap in between the two front ones.

He left them to it and went into the kitchen. He was completely flummoxed by his reaction to Ingrid who looked stunningly attractive in a lilac all-in-one pant suit. He'd have to keep his distance from her. An image flashed into his mind about how she would use the bathroom . . . would she take the whole thing off each time? His groin pulled again, imagining her wearing a tiny thong, so much so that he had to take his time before he went back into the lounge with their drinks.

Dan leant forward with the tray of cocktail glasses and let Perry and Ingrid take theirs first and then handed one to Lorna. Before he sat down, he raised his glass, "To friends," and reached to clink everyone's glass with his.

"That's gorgeous," Ingrid said taking a second sip, "thank you."

Dan took his seat in the armchair.

"How are you both settling in?" Lorna asked.

"Good." Perry turned to his wife who nodded, "I think we're pretty much sorted. It's work on Monday for us both so we've tried to get everything done in the time we've been off. Fortunately the house is in good order so we don't need to decorate or anything."

"It is a lovely house, there's no doubt about that," Lorna added.

It was nice enough, but not in the calibre of theirs. Lorna had an eye for fine decor and sophisticated living, but while she had grand ideas, she was clueless about what it all cost. Dan constantly had to rein her in with household expenses. Which reminded him, he needed to have a conversation with her about her credit card; she was spending far too much with little to show for it. Except of course the outfit and shoes she was wearing tonight he'd never seen before and God only knew what else she had hidden away.

"Did you say the last time we met that you both work for the same company?" Dan asked.

"Yes, that's right," Ingrid said, "although I don't quite

get the privileges Perry gets."

"What did you say the name of the company was?"

"I didn't . . ."

Lorna interjected, "Let's not talk about work tonight," she pulled a face at their guests, "I don't know about you, I hate thinking about it when I'm off at the weekend."

"Me too," Ingrid agreed, "we'll be back soon enough."

The pinging of a timer in the kitchen caught Lorna's attention. "Will you excuse me, I'll just check on dinner. I'll only be about five minutes and then we'll be ready to eat, if that's okay with everyone."

"Do you need a hand?" Ingrid asked.

"You can come and keep me company in the kitchen if you like."

Ingrid stood and followed Lorna out. Even her walk was graceful. Dan liked how petite she was. He realised that's why he found her attractive. Almost as if she brought out the cave-man in him with an urge to scoop her up and carry her off to bed. She was completely different to Lorna who was an extremely attractive woman, but she worked at it. Regular trips to the hair salon at seventy quid a time, nails at twenty quid a time, and eyebrows another twenty-five every few weeks. Dan wasn't fussed with his wife's eyebrows. They were too dark for his liking. She even went in for regular facials which she insisted were necessary and argued he was being ridiculous when he questioned what exactly where they doing for ninety quid. One look at Ingrid, he could tell she never indulged in tattooed eyebrows or bright red talons. She was a completely natural beauty.

"So," Perry said, taking a sip of his drink, "how's the old golfing going? I did have a quick look online at joining the club for six months, but it doesn't look likely. As you said, there's a waiting list."

"Yeah, it is a popular place."

"Lorna mentioned something to Ingrid about you inviting me to play a few rounds, or even endorsing me as a temporary member while I'm here, is that doable?"

He was stuck now. How he wished Lorna had kept her mouth shut.

"Er . . . yeah, sure. I can't say I've got any real influence though. I just pay my money like everyone else."

"What about a couple of rounds by way of an introduction if I promise I won't latch on to you every week?"

"Sure. Friday's usually a good day for me. I try and finish work early and unwind with a few rounds." He wasn't going to tell him he'd be playing Saturday and Sunday. He didn't want to give him options when he might be able to join him.

"Ah, that sounds great. Any chance of me joining you this coming Friday? Just say if I'm being too pushy and you have plans."

"No, it's fine. I could certainly give you the guided tour and introduce you to a few others and then we'll see about a round. Are you okay work wise? I mean are your hours flexible to accommodate a Friday afternoon?"

"Yeah, completely. I do pretty much as I want to. As long as the work gets done, it's fine. I sometimes prefer to keep my days free and work in the evenings."

"That sounds good. I wish I had that level of flexibility."

"You're your own boss though, aren't you?"

"I am, but I still need to be there each day."

"Didn't Lorna say something your brother working with you? Aren't you partners?"

Bloody hell Lorna, why don't you tell the whole street our business.

"That's right, he does. He's not a partner as such, but has been with me a long time."

"That's great. I'm an only child myself and would have loved a sibling growing up."

"Yeah, you must miss out. Lorna's the same, she's an only child."

Lorna's voice announced from the kitchen their starters were ready.

"Right, come on mate, I'll get you that beer, shall I?"

Chapter 14

After saying goodnight to Lorna and Dan, Perry and Ingrid made their way down the drive towards their own home. The security light came on in the driveway of the adjacent house and an old lady wearing a jacket over what appeared to be a dressing gown, approached the small wall dividing the houses.

"Good evening," she said, "you haven't seen a tortoiseshell cat with a red collar, have you? It's my Oscar. I've been calling him since teatime but he's nowhere to be seen." She looked anxious, "He doesn't usually venture far from home late afternoon until he's eaten. I just can't understand where he is."

"No, sorry," Perry said, "can't help, I'm afraid. We've been inside all evening and only just come out to walk home. We've just moved in actually," he gestured with his head, "to number six."

"I thought it might be you. I'm Phyllis Dixon, I'm a good friend of the Lloyds," her lips twitched, "well, more a friend of Dan's really."

"I'm Perry, Perry Hunter and this is my wife, Ingrid."

"Nice to meet you both," Phyllis nodded, "you aren't from round this neck of the woods are you. If I'm not wrong, you've a southern accent."

"That's right. We're from London."

"Are you? I used to live and work in Shepherd's Bush

many years ago, until I met my husband and we moved around the country and eventually settled here."

"It seems a nice area," Ingrid joined in.

"Oh, it is. I love it here. I've only just lost my husband earlier on in the year, but I feel safe. Dan keeps a watchful eye on me, which I do appreciate."

"That's nice," Ingrid continued, "he seems like a decent man."

"Oh, he is. A true gentleman."

"Sorry about your husband. Were you married a long time?"

"Thank you, dear. Yes, just short of fifty years when he died."

"Gosh, that is a long time." Ingrid smiled lovingly at Perry, "Let's hope we manage that long." She turned back to Phyllis, "Sorry we can't help with your cat, I hope you find him."

"Me too," she said wearily, "it's most unlike Oscar to not come back for food. I'll stay up a little longer I think and hope he comes back soon."

"I'm sure he will," Perry reassured, "he's probably been fed in another house tonight." His smile faded as he could see Phyllis wasn't amused.

"I do hope not," she said sternly.

Christ, he'd had too much to drink to be wasting time with an old dear and a missing cat.

"Well, it's getting rather late. We'd best be off. Good night, and nice to meet you."

"You too. Good night."

"Night," Ingrid smiled as they headed next door to

their own house.

Perry locked the front door behind them. "Nightcap?" he asked Ingrid.

"Yeah, why not."

They made their way to the back of the house and Ingrid flopped on the Chesterfield while he went into the kitchen to fetch their drinks. He came through clutching brandies for them both and sat down next to her, handing her a balloon glass.

"So that's the infamous Phyllis," she said taking the glass from him, "I don't think she appreciated you saying the cat might be eating somewhere else tonight."

"No, I don't think she did," he said, taking a sip of his drink, "but that's what cats do."

"Mmm, I know. Lorna can't stand her or that bloody cat of hers. Hey, maybe she's kidnapped it and locked it in her shed?"

Perry pulled back, "Really?"

"Nah, I'm only joking. Although she did tell me she has been known to chuck a bucket of cold water on it."

"God," Perry sniggered, "cats hate water."

"I know, and she hates that cat."

"Honestly, what's she like?"

"Fiery, that's for sure. While I was helping her with the desserts and coffees in the kitchen she was telling me about her new boss at work. The venom she spewed out made me feel almost sorry for her boss. And did you notice how she started on Dan's brother until he shut her up?"

"Yeah, I noticed that. He was a bit touchy. I thought there was an atmosphere after that. Good job it was the end of the evening."

"It'd be the drink."

"Yeah, she certainly loosens up after a few. Anyway," she stroked his arm lovingly, "tonight has confirmed to me that Lorna's definitely our woman."

"Don't you think I don't know that?" he said confidently, "I wouldn't have gone to all this trouble if I there was any doubt." Despite the alcohol-fuelled evening, energy flowed through him knowing he was close to achieving his objective. "What did she say to convince you?"

"All of it. I started asking random questions about where she was born and her parents and she spewed it all out, word for word."

"So, Inspector Hunter . . . do you feel better now that we have our woman?"

"Don't joke about it," she scowled, "I'm still worried . . . you know, when it comes to it," she bit her bottom lip, "but I try not to think about that too much. I'm just concentrating on the here and now."

"That's the best way. Leave everything to me. Remember, I'm not having you implicated in any way."

There was a slight tremor in her voice, "Promise?"

"I promise." He kissed her gently, "You are brilliantly clever, do you know that? I'm proud of you. Let's drink a toast to you."

"No, not me. How about to us and being wealthy beyond our wildest dreams."

"Sounds perfect."

He raised his glass. "To my beautiful wife Ingrid *and* being rich. Cheers, darling," he smiled lovingly as he clinked his glass with hers.

Chapter 15

Lorna leant back in her seat by the pub window and patted her tummy, "That lasagne was to die for, how was the chicken?" she asked her friend, Sarah.

"Bloody gorgeous," Sarah said screwing up her used napkin and tossing it on the plate, "I'm full now though." She eased herself back onto the velour, curved window seat. "I'm glad we came tonight, it seems ages since we've had a good catch-up."

"I know," Lorna agreed, "I have missed our suppers here." And she had. Normally she met with Sarah for a girlie catch-up out of work every second week, but her friend had been busy, visiting her mother-in-law in hospital following a stroke and sorting out short-term residential care in a local nursing home. "How's your mum-in-law settling in?" she asked reaching in her bag for a tissue.

"Okay, but she thinks it's only temporary at the moment. Neither of us have the heart to tell her that it could well be permanent. But what can you do? Her mobility is really bad and we can't look after her. Neil's upset, but we haven't the money to pay for her care and I can't see she's actually improving at all."

"It doesn't get any easier that's for sure," Lorna said, understanding perfectly. "My mother's care home isn't that nice to be honest but what's the alternative?

Thankfully she doesn't really know where she is half the time, so she seems fairly settled," she screwed her face up, "if you ever could be in those places."

"Does she complain about being in there?"

"Oh God, yeah, all the time. But that's my mother for you. If she lived in Buckingham Palace she'd say it was cold and draughty." She finished the dregs of her wine and placed the empty glass on the table.

"It's really sad, isn't it," Sarah sighed, "when they've worked hard all their lives and brought up families, yet they end their days in a care home. Both of them are too young really. I hope it never happens to me."

"No, me neither. They're awful places and that's what narks me. We pay a fortune for what I'd say was adequate care. Financially, we manage when her house is rented out, but we still have to top the fees up, to support the funding."

"Why don't you sell her house?"

"We might have to. Dan's not keen," she lied. He was actually desperate for her to sell it but she didn't want to. "He doesn't think it makes sense until the market picks up a bit. If it stands for a long time with nobody renting it, we may sell then. But we always seem to get someone to take it on. It's quite a central location so we're lucky there is always demand."

"That's good. Neil would hate that having to subsidise his mother's care. Doesn't Dan resent it, especially with it being his mother-in-law?"

"No, actually he doesn't. Well, if he does, he never says. I think because him and Connor lost their mum and dad and ended up in care, Dan thinks parents are really important and therefore need to be looked after."

"Aww, that's so nice. He's a good man."

"Yeah, I guess he is."

Sarah took a sip of her orange juice, "Why that sullen look, things are okay, aren't they? You're not still daydreaming about Mr New Zealand that got away?"

"Nah," Lorna grinned, "that ship sailed a long time ago. And it would be a bit far to travel for an illicit date."

"If he was closer, you wouldn't try and rekindle anything though, would you?"

"If I'm honest, I would be curious. He was once the love of my life, but the breakup was a bit nasty. I reckon that's why he took off to New Zealand."

"You said he's married with kids though, isn't he?"

"I believe so. Something like that anyway."

"So, what about you and Dan? Are you still *plodding along* as you put it last time?"

"Yeah. We seem to have turned into an old married couple overnight."

"Haven't we all?" Sarah smirked, "Neil's hardly jumping off the wardrobe naked to get to me on a regular basis."

Lorna laughed, "Crikey, I'll not get that image out of my mind now."

"So go on, tell me what's wrong?" Sarah urged, "'cause I know there's something."

"Nothing's wrong, honestly. It's just that a new couple have moved in next door to us. We've been round theirs for drinks and I invited them to ours for a meal. They are really nice, sort of dynamic but in an understated way. They have a vibrancy about them that maybe Dan and I lack."

"Are they our age?"

"A bit younger, but they're both really fit and attractive."

"So are you and Dan. You're an attractive couple."

"Yeah, maybe, but looking at those two has made me examine Dan closely, and he seems old, all of a sudden."

"Dan doesn't look old. He looks . . ."

"Go on, say what you were going to say."

"I think he looks . . . oh, God, I don't know, maybe what you'd expect an accountant to look like."

"Exactly. Like a boring old fart."

Sarah laughed, "Well, I wouldn't have put it quite like that."

"No, but I will. Even his persona is old. He's always nagging about the money I spend, even though I go out to work and contribute. Is Neil like that?"

"No, not really. Don't get me wrong, like most blokes he keeps an eye on things, but he's not in finance for a living. I guess for your Dan, working with money and accounts all day is bound to spill over. And if I dare say, you do have a tendency to spend."

"Yeah, that's true," Lorna grinned at her dear friend, the only one she'd allow to say that, "but that's what I like to do. It makes me happy. Anyway, enough moaning on about Dan, do you want a dessert or coffee?"

"Not for me, but you have one though. I'm pretty stuffed."

"Me too, actually. Shall I get the bill?"
"Great, I'll just nip to the loo."

As they reached their cars that were parked next each other, Lorna was about to hug her friend but Sarah hesitated. "I thought I'd leave it until the end of the evening to tell you," she pulled a pained face, "Elspeth's on the war path."

"Bloody hell, I've only been off a week. What now?"

"She found a referral in your desk drawer that hasn't been actioned."

Lorna knew exactly which referral. The one she'd purposely stuffed to the back of the drawer after she'd typed it. Before she'd gone on annual leave, a regular patient, Dawn Ellis attended the surgery. She was a young mother with three children under the age of five and always appeared dirty and grimy, with her skimpy clothes and cheap make-up. Dawn had kicked off big time in the surgery because she couldn't get an appointment that morning. Lorna had patiently tried to sort her one out for the following day, even though the temptation was to tell her to go and do one. Dawn became more agitated and verbally aggressive almost spitting she was a *jumped-up receptionist* and insisting she saw Elspeth who had been sympathetic towards her on a previous occasion, which irritated Lorna. Right on cue, Elspeth had arrived with her fluffed-up importance and took Dawn into the small office off the main reception, and when they came out, she had given her an appointment with a GP despite there being none available.

Lorna had waited until after Dawn's appointment with the doctor before checking her medical records. They gave an indication as to why she'd been so insistent on seeing a GP that particular day. She was pregnant and requesting a termination. As part of her job remit, Lorna typed the referral letter to the hospital the following day, and, after getting it signed by the GP, she was deliberately malicious and shoved it to the back of her desk drawer. As far as she was concerned, Dawn Ellis deserved to wait after kicking off and stupid Elspeth giving in to her.

"Sorry to be the bearer of bad news." Sarah's sympathetic expression disrupted her thoughts.

"Hey, don't worry, it's not your fault. I'll sort it. It's a pity Dame Elspeth doesn't understand that people do make mistakes from time to time."

"You know Elspeth, she runs a tight ship. She's not actually said anything to me as she knows we're friends, but Karen reckons she's going to see you in the office with Dr Varma."

"In the office! whatever for? Anyone would think I'd done it on purpose."

Sarah reached out and squeezed her arm, "I'm sure she knows you wouldn't do that. But it sounds like the girl might be over twelve weeks pregnant so a medical termination is out of the question, she'll have to have an anaesthetic procedure."

"Well, I reckon I've done her a favour, then. I'd much rather go off to sleep and it all be done than taking tablets and having to pass the . . ."

"Oh God, shush . . . I can't bear the thought of anything like that. Not when you think of how many women want a baby and can't have one."

"Sorry, you're right. Anyway, thanks for giving me the heads up. I still don't see how I can be blamed, though. If Dawn Ellis is late for a medical termination, then she should have visited the doctor sooner. Bloody Elspeth . . . she's definitely got it in for me. She's never liked me since she came to the practice."

"I don't think she's overawed with any of us if the truth be known. Anyway, I'd better get off. Let's hope you just get a slapped wrist." Sarah gave her a hug, "I'll see you Monday."

"Yeah, will do. Thanks for coming, Sarah, have a nice weekend."

"You, too."

Lorna got into her car and waited for Sarah to leave first and followed her out of the car park inwardly cursing. Bloody work. She hated it. It wasn't as if there was any point in confiding in Dan, he'd be on the side of Elspeth. He'd never do anything wrong in his ordered and meticulous life. She decided she wasn't going to let it spoil her weekend, she'd worry about Elspeth on Monday morning. That place took up far too much of her time. Pity they didn't sack her, then she wouldn't have to go to work at all. And no way could Dan kick off as it wouldn't be her fault.

After the short drive home, she pulled into the drive and stepped out of the car. As was predictable, the house was all in darkness; it was past ten thirty, so Dan would be in bed. She glanced at Perry and Ingrid's house next door with a huge lamp lighting up the hallway and a small lantern with a tea light in the porch. No doubt the house was full of life inside. Her mouth twisted in jealousy. She'd much rather be going in that vibrant house, than in her dull one. And come to think of it, she'd rather be in bed with Perry. He was certainly fit, anyone could see that. His scrawny wife with her flat chest wouldn't keep him satisfied. And not only in bed, intellectually too, as she clearly wasn't the sharpest tool in the box.

She closed the car door and pressed the fob to lock it. There wasn't even a small lamp on in the house to welcome her back as she opened the front door and let herself in. Dan couldn't sleep with any form of light. Despite this, she flicked the switch on that lit up the stairs and landing, not caring one bit if it woke him. As she wearily climbed each stair, she contemplated her future. There had to be more to life than a boring marriage and working at a GP practice? As always, she suppressed the memory of a previous time in her life which still had the ability to wrench at her heart, years later. It was always there, lurking, like a bad odour you just couldn't get rid of. The man she'd loved more than she loved herself. Was that even possible? Memories of their time together she'd constantly had to push to the back of her mind. He'd left her – and she'd never really come to terms with it.

So she'd married Daniel Lloyd.

And that's when her life became tedious.

Chapter 16

Dan discarded his tee-shirt as it was becoming too wet to soak up much more sweat as he pushed himself on the exercise bike in the garage. It was so hot, he'd left the door open to the back garden. The garage had two doors, the main one at the front, and another at the back which overlooked the house and kitchen. He glanced at his watch, ten more minutes and he'd jack it in. As he carried on pedalling, he heard the click of the side gate. He'd assumed it was Lorna back from town so was surprised to see Ingrid appear in front of him in tiny white shorts and a cropped tee-shirt, showing off her taught midriff. Just the sight of her had his mouth watering.

"Oh, hi," her expression was awkward, which matched his. With his bare chest he felt almost cave man. He suppressed an image of throwing her over his shoulder and carrying her into the house and upstairs.

"I'm here to see Lorna," she attempted to move towards the back door.

"She's not here," he said, grabbing his tee-shirt and pulling it swiftly over his head. "She's gone to Waitrose. Anything I can do?" He was conscious of how sweaty he was and embarrassed she'd seen him like that. He was minutes away from a shower.

"Oh, right, well you'll do nicely then," she smiled, her

perfect white smile, causing his abdomen to clench. He wished his body didn't betray him around her. Thank God his shorts were loose and nothing was visible.

"I'm trying to organise a surprise birthday weekend for Perry in York and I was hoping that Lorna and you could join us? I won't tell him though, I think it would be lovely for you two to be there once we arrive."

He'd taken quite a liking to Perry since he'd spent longer with him, playing a couple of rounds of golf, it would be hard not to fall for his charm, but the last thing he wanted was to go away with Ingrid, he couldn't think of anything worse.

She carried on, totally oblivious to his inner turmoil. "I thought it would be a really nice evening, the four of us having dinner together and actually being waited on for a change, and we could get up the following morning and have our breakfast together before heading back, what do you think?"

"Sounds great," he said, desperately searching for an excuse not to attend. "Haven't you got any friends closer than us to Perry, maybe family or something?"

"We have, yes, but none I'd want to invite," she giggled, "we aren't exactly close-knit, if you get my drift."

What the hell else could he come up with? He really didn't want to go anywhere with her. The lustful spasms he was having around her were alien to him. He'd woken up one night sweating profusely after a particularly erotic dream featuring her.

"Which weekend is it?" Whichever one it was, he'd be busy.

"The twenty-fifth, it's two weeks this Saturday. Please say you can make it. Perry would be thrilled, I know he would. The hotel I've been looking at has a spa, so I thought we could all relax in there for a couple of hours in the afternoon. What do you think?"

Jesus Christ, Ingrid in a swimsuit. He daren't allow himself to even picture an image let alone witness it in person.

"I can certainly run it by Lorna. I will have to check what I've got on though. I've sort of half agreed for a dinner with my brother and his wife, I just can't remember when."

It was feeble and he knew it. But what could he say? I'm sorry, Ingrid, if I see you in a swimsuit, I'll be walking around in a daze like a bloody hormonal schoolboy. There was no way he could cope with a weekend like that around her. It was so bizarre he felt that way. There was just something about her tininess that sent his libido raging. It was alien to him, especially as he loved Lorna and, since becoming friends with Perry and Ingrid, it had been full steam ahead in the sex department. Lorna was much more receptive lately than she usually was. So why the hell was he lusting after Ingrid?

"Okay," her expression was one of disappointment, "I'll let you get back to your cycling . . ."

The kitchen door opened. "I thought I heard voices," Lorna said as she walked towards the garage, "hi, Ingrid, how are you?"

"Fine," Ingrid said with a smile. "I came to see if you and

Dan fancied a surprise weekend away for Perry's birthday."

"That sounds great," Lorna beamed, "we'd love that, wouldn't we, Dan?"

"Er . . . yeah, but the thing is, I've sort of agreed to a meal with Connor and Ruth one of these Saturdays. I just can't remember which one it was."

Lorna scowled, "It's the first I've heard of it, but we'll reschedule if it clashes, Ruth won't mind." She turned to Ingrid, "It's not as if you can reschedule someone's birthday. Have you got time for a coffee?"

"Yeah, that would be lovely, as long as I'm not stopping you doing anything."

"No, not at all. Do you want a cold beer fetching out?" Lorna asked him.

"Nah, I'm fine. I'll be coming in for a shower shortly."

"Okay. Right, come on, Ingrid, I'll make us a drink and you can tell me all about the plan for the birthday weekend. I'm looking forward to it already."

Still sitting on his exercise bike, Dan watched them both walk towards the kitchen deep in conversation, his eyes on Ingrid's behind. Bloody hell. He might have to fake an illness or something. He hated lying, but what was the alternative? A weekend lusting after another bloke's wife when he already had a wife of his own? Lorna would be mortified if she had any idea.

As Ingrid followed Lorna through the kitchen door, she glanced back, smiled and gave a little wave. She knew he'd been watching her? His groin twitched in response.

He hated his body betraying him.

Chapter 17

Perry pulled out of the drive and they headed off for London.

"Are you sure you don't want me to come to the solicitors with you when we get there?" Ingrid asked.

"Nah, you enjoy your shopping, it shouldn't take that long."

No bloody way did he want her with him. The only details she needed to know was what he gave her and that's the way he wanted it to stay. No sense in her knowing any more than she had to. And it had taken that much coaxing to get her to comply in the first place, he couldn't cope with her having any more information than was necessary.

"Why have you got to go anyway?" she asked. "I thought you said the legal beagles were giving it until the end of the year?"

"They were, but seemingly they want to update me on a recent development."

"Aren't you worried?"

"Nope. Why should I be?"

"I don't know," she turned to look out of the window and her voice was almost a whisper, "it'd be an irony though if all this is in vain."

"It won't be," he said, confident he had every angle covered. He'd had to sort some things out as a teenager, ably assisted by his pushy mother. He'd done then what was necessary, that's why he wasn't concerned. The solicitors wouldn't have uncovered anything.

"Anyway," he said, "I'll text you when I'm done with all the legal stuff and come to you. We'll have a special lunch somewhere. You choose."

"That'll be nice. It'd be even nicer it we were staying in London and could go to a show."

"Yeah, but right now, we need to give the impression we've been out working all day. If we stay away overnight, the neighbours will only be asking questions where we've been."

"We could tell them though, couples do go away overnight."

"I know," Perry said taking a mouthful of water from the bottle he had next to him, "but I don't want them questioning us about London, where we stayed, what we did. Best to tell them we had a busy day looking round potential properties for the company."

"Okay," she sighed, "whatever you think. It's good though that I've cracked the birthday weekend, even if Dan was a bit hesitant. He was making out he already had something on, but, it all sounded a bit feeble to me."

"He's a bit cautious all round, isn't he?"

"Yeah, he does seem . . . careful." She took a packet of wine gums out of the glove compartment and put one into his mouth before taking one for herself. "Lorna's keen though, so I think she'll persuade him." She sucked on her sweet, "Do you reckon they're happy together?"

"What makes you think they aren't?"

"Because they're like chalk and cheese, she seems all glamorous and flighty, whereas he's the complete opposite. He always seems stiff around me somehow, almost awkward."

He raised an eyebrow, "Maybe he likes you?"

"Don't be daft," she hit his arm playfully, "what's made you say that?"

"Well . . . you're gorgeous for a start, any bloke can see that straight away. I did."

"That's different. We were both single. Dan's married and I can't somehow see him as the unfaithful type."

"You never know though, what if they aren't happy together? What if he does like you?"

"I'm sure he doesn't," she shook her head, "and if he did, I'd never be unfaithful to you, you know that."

"Course I do. No point in being married if you want to play around."

"Too right, let's hope you always think that way." She reached and stroked the side of his face, "Do you know, I used to be terrified when we first got married that someone would come along and pinch you off me."

He turned his head towards her and winked, "Not a chance."

"I know that now, but when we first got together, it was all so quick and we barely knew each other really. And your father was furious about us getting married, you said."

"Yeah well, he was furious about a lot of things. He's long gone now, thank God. And we didn't need his blessing anyway."

"I know, but he has made things hard for you. I think he did it just because you married me."

"It wasn't just because of that. He was always a bastard. That's what wealth does for you."

"Yeah, well as long as it doesn't spoil our relationship."

"It won't. Once this is all sorted, it'll just be you and me."

"And the children? Don't forget those."

"Course," he added quickly, "how could I?"

He could – quite easily. As he approached the motorway and indicated he was about to join, his thoughts drifted back to when they first met. She wasn't one bit interested in kids then. In fact, she was the complete opposite, that's what he found attractive about her. She adored him and made it seem like he was all she wanted. Their early days together were a bit hazy all round and he didn't want to particularly go there. He'd blotted them out, preferring not to think about the endless booze and drug-filled days. He could barely remember their wedding in Vegas, she always had to fill in the blanks. Thank God those times were long behind him and he'd have the life he'd always wanted, soon. He just needed to be patient a bit longer.

Ingrid's voice brought him back to the present. "I'm only doing this for our future and our children's future," the sadness was evident in her voice, "I wouldn't be contemplating any of it . . ."

"Hey," he reached across and squeezed the hand she had resting on her lap, "don't be going all morose on me.

It's all sorted. Our future is secure, or it will be shortly. So stop worrying." He leant forward and adjusted the air conditioning, "And getting back to Dan Lloyd and him finding you attractive . . . so what? Play along a bit, it won't hurt."

"What?" she scowled, "tell me you're joking?"

"Look," he stroked her leg, "you're a beautiful young woman. Be nice, that's all I'm saying. I'm not suggesting you fuck the bloke. We've got to do what we have to. We need to get them to Greece, you know that. None of it will work if we don't."

"Yes, of course I know that. But going on holiday together is a bit of a tall order. He might not want to come with us. And I get the impression he's in charge with decisions."

"I don't know how you've deduced that. In my experience the woman is always in charge."

"Yeah right," she said raising her eyebrows sarcastically, "you're in charge of our relationship. You'd have to be to have thought up this plan in the first place. I couldn't have."

"Because we want what's rightfully ours, so we have no choice."

"It's not without risks though," anxiety was back in her voice, "that's what keeps me awake at night. You know, worrying about anything going wrong. I'm terrified we end up in jail."

"You have to stop all this," he snapped. She was beginning to irritate him going over and over it, every few days, about how worried she was. He'd given her ample opportunity to back out. Even on the day they drove to Nottingham, he'd asked her if she was sure. And she'd assured him she was. As far as he was concerned, they'd come this far and he wasn't about to quit now. He was too close.

"I've told you hundreds of times, there's no risk to you at all," he said, "I'm the only one taking risks."

"But can't you see, that's what frightens me. I don't want to live a life with you locked up and me visiting you in prison."

He sighed heavily, "That's not going to happen, we've been over this time and time again. It's all sorted. I've got everything covered. All you have to do is work on Lorna, who seems to me as if she's up for anything, and be *nice* to Dan, and let's get them both to Greece. I'll do the rest."

"But what if they won't come? To be honest, half of me is hoping they won't."

"Don't say that," he couldn't help the irritated tone that crept into his voice, "I'm working bloody hard for this," he slapped the steering wheel, "for us. I'm not going to allow our future to be compromised. So stop going on about them not coming to Greece. We'll have to make sure they do. I'm relying on you to persuade them. Be nice to her, but *nicer* to him. And remember, he's an accountant. The promise of a free holiday will be the incentive he'll need. He'll come, I'm sure of it. We just need to take our time and not rush things."

"Okay, okay. There's no need to be so irritable, I'm doing my best."

"I know you are. But you harping on about risks, isn't helping."

"Fine, I'll shut up then." She turned away to look out the window.

"Look, I'm sorry for being sharp. We're so close now and I just want to get the job done."

"I know you do, but there's not much time between now and August to get them to Greece, is there?"

"Yeah, I know that. We can't be too pushy though. We're on track. We'll woo them at my so-called birthday weekend, give them a great time, and let's hope they'll be up for a full week abroad. I can tell Dan's warming to me."

"That's good." She lifted his hand and kissed the back of it. "Sorry if I've made you cross. I do love you, you know. I hope you realise how much."

"Of course I do. But give all this pessimism a rest would you, eh."

"I'll try," she said, nervously biting the side of her mouth. "Have you got a villa sorted for us yet?"

"I have actually. It's luxurious and completely isolated, so it'll be a perfect."

"Is it in Fiscardo?"

"Yep. And it's ideal for getting the boat and taking them out in it. I'll show you some pictures online of the villa, then when we're with them in York, we'll sell the holiday to them. Who wouldn't want free a break in Greece? When are you next seeing Lorna, did you invite her out for a girlie lunch like I told you?"

"I mentioned it, but seemingly she's got some sort of

swimming challenge going on for the next couple of weeks after she finishes work. I did suggest joining her, but I got the impression she goes with a friend and two's company, three's a crowd."

"Maybe go out somewhere for dinner, just the two of you. I'll take you both and pick you up, then you can have a drink and butter her up some more."

"Okay, I'll text her and ask her. I think she mentioned Dan was away overnight next week so that might be a good time to go out rather than lunchtime."

"Perfect. Now, tell me when you need to stop for the toilet and I'll pull in."

She rolled her eyes. "You mean, you want to stop for food."

"Not at all, I'm only thinking about you." He moistened his lips, "That's not to say that I might pick up a snack though if we do stop. I'll see how I'm feeling."

"Which de-coded means you want junk food at some stage."

"Only if you want to stop."

"Oh, shut up," she laughed playfully, "stop whenever you want. I'm not bothered."

"That's better," he said, "keep smiling and doing what I tell you to, that's all you have to do.

And leave everything else to me."

Chapter 18

Lorna arrived at work earlier than usual on the Monday morning after her week off. If Elspeth was on the warpath, she didn't want to give her an excuse to add timekeeping to the list.

As she entered the medical practice through the automatic doors, Elspeth, with her stiff, hair-sprayed bob and dated blue eye shadow was visible behind the reception desk. Waiting for her, no doubt. As she wasn't supposed to know anything about her wanting to see her, she needed to play dumb. The last thing she wanted to do was drop Sarah in it for telling her.

"Morning," Lorna greeted her boss. Being nice took effort. Normally, she only spoke to her when she had to.

"Good morning, Lorna. I'm glad you're early. Doctor Varma and I would like to see you before surgery starts."

"What, right now?" she feigned confusion, "Can I get rid of my jacket and bag first."

"Yes, but quickly please. Then make your way to Dr Varma's office."

"Is there a problem?" she asked, injecting a level of anxiety into her voice.

"I'll see you shortly," Elspeth said as she walked away.

Lorna nipped to the toilet to stall a bit longer. Let them wait. They were being ridiculous.

Five minutes later, Lorna tapped on Dr Varma's consulting room door and went in.

"Good morning," she smiled brightly at him, "I understand you wanted to see me."

"That's right, Lorna, come in and take a seat would you."

She took the chair adjacent to his desk that the patients would use. She'd wasn't keen on any of the four GP partners at the practice, but Dr Varma was perhaps one of the better ones. He was a small, Indian man with a big girth, sort of cuddly, with a kind manner towards the patients. But as for the others, as far as she was concerned, they saw themselves as superior human beings. Okay, so they'd studied at medical school which might be a bit challenging for a few years, but after that, it was a meal ticket for life. It didn't necessarily make them special. What it did do was pay them an inflated salary for little effort. And this particular consortium of GP's had a pharmacy in the building which she knew was lucrative. They all had pots of money, and listening to the practice nurses, they didn't pay massive wages, and they certainly didn't pay over and above for admin staff either. She always joked to the girls in the office that if she was single, she'd have made a beeline for one of them if only for the prospect of a lavish lifestyle.

Elspeth was sitting to the left of Dr Varma. Her eyes narrowed, staring intensely. Lorna could almost feel the heat of her displeasure.

"Is everything alright?" Lorna asked clearing her throat and forcing a concerned expression.

"Not really," Dr Varma said sternly. "Seemingly there has been an altercation in reception between a patient of the practice, Dawn Ellis and yourself. Do you remember that?"

"I do, yes. She was demanding an immediate appointment as per usual, and was quite aggressive towards me. Elspeth sorted it out in the end and gave her an appointment," she looked at Elspeth who didn't acknowledge it even though that was the case. All Elspeth did was continue to stare. Probably trying to unnerve her . . . as if.

Dr Varma peered over the top of his glasses. "Do you know why she wanted to see a GP urgently that morning?"

"Yes. I typed the referral letter the following day to the hospital."

"But prior to typing the letter, did you access her records to see why she was demanding to see a GP that morning?"

Lorna had done exactly that and knew that both Dr Varma and Elspeth would have checked SystemOne; the computer holds records that log everyone who accesses it.

"I did, yes. I wanted to know why she had been kicking off that morning in the surgery."

Elspeth interjected, "So you logged into someone's records without a reason to. You know that is completely against policy."

Lorna knew exactly that.

"As I said, I wanted to know what had caused her to

make such a fuss. And," she glared at Elspeth, "you completely overrode my decision to give her an appointment the following day. So I was curious, that's all."

"But her medical condition is nothing to do with you," Dr Varma reminded her.

"I know it isn't. But I was upset. And I'm not likely to be discussing anything relating to patients with anyone. I am bound by confidentiality."

"That isn't the point," Elspeth snapped.

Dr Varma shuffled the papers on his desk. "Let's move on shall we and look at the next reason you're here." He lifted up a letter, "This is the referral letter you typed for Dawn to attend hospital. It was found in your desk drawer under a pile of other papers. Can you explain how and why it was there when it should have been posted?"

"No . . . I can't really." Lorna screwed up her face, "The only thing I can think of is, it may have been on my desk and I've inadvertently picked it up when putting papers in my drawer. That would explain why it was underneath other stuff."

"I see." He didn't see, she could tell that, but he couldn't really argue. Mistakes happen.

"It isn't good enough, Lorna," Elspeth interjected, "this is a medical practice. Because of this, Dawn has missed the time frame for a medical termination and will have to have an anaesthetic procedure now, which was completely unnecessary. And all this is due to your sloppiness."

"I'm sorry about that, but I didn't do it on purpose," Lorna couldn't help raising her voice. "You can't think I did it deliberately, surely?"

Neither of them answered.

"Oh, for goodness' sake, what do you take me for? Do you think it matters to me whether a woman with three children gets a termination? Why would you even think I'd try and prevent that happening? It makes no odds to me how many women have terminations, I just type up the referral letter. This hasn't happened before. It has been a genuine mistake."

She stared at Dr Varma willing him to agree. He was a decent man and she was confident he would see it as that, not Elspeth though. She had it in for her, anyway.

He placed the papers he was holding on the desk. "You better go back to work. For now, I'll accept your apology and urge you to try and learn from this."

She was about to nod in agreement, until Elspeth chipped in, "Yes, please make sure you do. Any more of this sloppiness and we may have to take things further."

"Sorry," Lorna frowned, "what do you mean, further?"

"I mean an official warning about your employment here."

"Now, hang on," Lorna protested, "this isn't fair. I've apologised and explained it was a mistake. I can't see how it even warrants a discussion like this. You're making me feel like a naughty child, when I haven't done anything wrong."

"But you have," Elspeth's jaw clenched. "You've

accessed a patient's records which you shouldn't have done unless you had a specific reason to do so, and you didn't have. You looked because you wanted to see what her consultation was about and that is in breach of practice policy."

"But I was asked to type up the referral letter to the hospital."

"Yes, but prior to that, you had no idea why Dawn Ellis was attending the surgery yet you took it upon yourself to find out. So I need to reiterate to you that you do not access a patient's records unless you are specifically asked to do so, and, if you are speaking to a patient, you have their verbal permission. Do you understand?"

"Yes."

"Very well," Dr Varma said, "I think we'll leave it at that for now."

Leave it at that for now – they must be joking. She wasn't going to let either of them off that easily.

"I must say," she held her head high for maximum effect of her displeasure, "this has been completely punitive and intimidating to say the least. You can see it was a genuine mistake, so to make threats of a formal disciplinary action is grossly unfair. I'd like it documenting that the next time you wish to see me on a matter relating to my work, you give me formal notice, so I can bring representation."

"I'm sorry you feel like that, Lorna," Elspeth's tone had altered to a more conciliatory one, "we'll say no more on the matter for now and let you get back to work."

Not a chance. She couldn't waste all the bumf on bullying and harassment she'd been reading up on over the weekend. She was certainly looking forward to Elspeth squirming some more.

"I'm not sure I can, to be honest," she faked nervousness by nibbling her lip. She was actually enjoying herself. "I feel rather shaky. You've made me feel completely worthless when I'm trying my best for this practice." She raised her eyebrows at Elspeth, "This isn't the first time you've questioned my work, yet before you came to work at the practice, I hadn't been scrutinised before. My record is exemplary. I've never had a development review that has indicated any concerns. So this feels to me almost like bullying and harassment and I believe there are employment laws against it."

"I beg your pardon . . ." Elspeth was nearly choking on her spit.

"Now, now," Dr Varma interjected, holding a hand up. The tone of his voice changed too. "Go to the staffroom and have a cup of tea, Lorna, take your time and hopefully after that, you'll feel a little better. And as I said earlier, just be mindful of what I've said and we'll say no more about it."

He stood up which indicated the meeting was over. Lorna did too but Elspeth remained seated. Good. Right now there was nothing more to say. As Lorna walked slowly to the door, she had to suppress two urges – one to skip out and shout yippee, and the other to slam the door behind her.

She filled the kettle in the staffroom and waited for it to boil. Her lips twitched at the edges in half a smile. No need to rush back to work, that's what Dr Varma had said, take your time. She opened the biscuit tin and selected two chocolate digestives.

Stupid bloody practice. She was intending to leave anyway – that confrontation had just expedited it.

And it would certainly be good riddance to the lot of them.

Chapter 19

Dan looked up from his desk as the office door opened. "Have you got time for this?" Connor asked, clutching two coffees from the machine in the staffroom."

"Yep, come in and have a seat. How's things?"

"Okay," Connor placed the coffees on the blotter and sat down opposite. "I just wanted to let you know, we've got a buyer for the house and we've got the asking price."

"Brilliant. I thought you would, or at least pretty close to it. It's a lovely house."

"Yeah, it is." A shadow passed across Connor's face. Dan knew it'd be hard selling it, they'd lived there since the twins were babies.

"How's Ruth taking it?"

"She's good. You know Ruth, pragmatic is her middle name. She'll have everything packed and in boxes by the weekend."

Dan nodded. He never understood why Connor let Ruth down the way he had with his debts. She was a wife in a million. He'd always felt that his brother was punching above his weight with her. But she clearly loved him and he was grateful for that. Connor needed her and the kids now, more than ever.

"So you'll be on the lookout for a rented place, I guess?"

"Yeah. Ruth's got her eye on a couple which she's going to try and get viewings for. That's why I'm here really, to ask a favour."

"Ask away." He had an inclination what it would be. He always knew with Connor.

"If we see something we like, would you be able to help us with the deposit until the house sale goes through? We'd give you it back as soon as we have the money."

"Yeah, no problem." Didn't he always bail him out?

"Are you sure? What about Lorna, will she be okay about it? I know I'm not her favourite person right now."

"She'll be fine. Don't think too harshly of her, she's still cross about you disappearing. She had visions of something terrible happening to you. We all did, and I'm afraid she's not the forgiving type." He gave a wry smile, "You said Ruth's middle name is pragmatic, well, I'm afraid Lorna's is *hold-a-grudge*." Although said in jest, it was most definitely the truth. "She'll eventually come round, I'm sure. She wouldn't want Ruth and the girls struggling."

"I hate what I did to you all. I just somehow lost it, you know . . . I wasn't thinking straight."

"We know that. It'll take time to work through everything. And you're lucky. You've still got a wife and family standing by you."

"Yeah, but for how long?" Connor started nibbling his thumb-nail, a habit which had started when their parents had been killed.

"What, you think Ruth wants out?" Dan frowned, surely not now? At first maybe, but Connor had been back a while now and they appeared to be okay.

"I dunno. Things are pretty strained right now," Connor said quietly.

"But that'll get easier. It's bound to be hard initially. You're going through a massive upheaval."

"I know, and I'm really trying. I hate what I did to her."

"Ruth's a good woman, she'll come round, I'm sure of it."

"I hope you're right. She's still pretty rigid in the bedroom department, though. I'd kill for some action right now but she's having none of it. Women eh, why do they always hold you hostage to that? It's like I'm being punished, you know, no sex until you've complied."

"Yeah, well, they all play that card."

"I can't imagine Lorna would."

Dan didn't want to be discussing Lorna and their sex life, he never had done and he wasn't about to start. And certainly not now he had no worries on that score. Lorna was more receptive to him than ever. But he felt sorry for Connor, a no-sex ban was tough for any bloke, he'd been there himself. A thought struck him, like a light bulb going on in his head.

"Hey, you don't fancy a weekend away with Ruth, do you? Some quality time when all you have to do is eat, drink and sleep?"

"I'd love it, mate, but I'm afraid finances won't run to

that."

"I can pay for you to go somewhere, maybe as an early birthday present?"

"I can't let you do that. You have done more than enough already. And there are the girls as well."

"Don't you worry about the girls, Lorna and I could look after them. They'd love a couple of nights at ours."

"Nah, honestly Dan, I can't let you do that. Ruth would go ape shit at me taking a freebie from you."

"But what if I booked something and give you both it and say it's a joint birthday present? A nice break, before you have the upheaval of moving house?"

"God, it sounds tempting. If I could just get that part of our marriage back on track, I'm sure the rest would follow."

"We'll do it then, leave it with me. There's just one thing though. Do you think you could go away a week on Saturday, the twenty-fourth and twenty-fifth?"

"Yeah, I'm sure we can. Why though?"

"Don't even ask. Suffice to say, if we are looking after the girls, then we can't go away to York for a weekend, which Lorna's after."

Connor grinned, "So this freebie's helping you too?"

"Something like that, yeah."

"Well, in that case dear brother, if you put it like that, you're on. Thank you."

"Don't thank me yet until you can see what I choose. It might be a B&B in Blackpool."

"As long as it's got a double bed, I don't care."

Dan laughed. "Okay, leave it with me and I'll sort it.

But keep that weekend free whatever you do, it has to be then."

"Will do. Thanks Dan, you're a good man. I'm lucky to have you."

"Go on, you bloody softie, get out of here. I'll see you tomorrow."

Connor got up and walked towards the door and smiled affectionately. "Cheers, bro."

Dan messaged Lorna and said he'd be half an hour late, brought up Booking.com on his PC and keyed in Norfolk. Once he found a suitable hotel, he called them to make the booking rather than online. He'd stressed it was a special weekend and he wanted some flowers in the room for Ruth and a bottle of prosecco to hopefully set the mood. Once it was all confirmed he texted Connor and told him the name of the hotel and reminded him of the dates again explaining it was all sorted and booked.

He switched off his PC and reached for his jacket. Lorna was not going to be happy. She would protest as she'd want to go to Perry's birthday party in York. He gave a wry smile, pleased he'd made sure that wasn't happening. No way was he ever going to be in a hotel all weekend with Ingrid who was invading his sleep on a regular basis, which was bad enough. At the end of the day, he really needed to keep temptation out of his way. He'd done the right thing. Lorna's displeasure would be a better price to pay than actually going to York. And even she'd get over it.

***

They sat opposite each other at the kitchen table. She knew Dan had purposely finished his dinner before dropping his bombshell.

"What! You can't be serious. We've already said we'd go to York for Perry's birthday."

"That's not strictly true, you said we'd go. I did point out that I'd already agreed to something."

"Dinner you said, not babysitting the girls. That's why I said at the time we could easily change a dinner."

"Yeah, well we can't now. I've already agreed."

"You had no business doing that. And how can they afford it anyway with all their debt?" She glared at him. "Please don't tell me you've paid."

"I have actually. It's a joint birthday present for them both."

"A weekend away? Why don't you give them a couple of bottles of wine like you usually do?"

"Because they've been through a lot and they need a break together."

"And whose fault is that? If your stupid brother hadn't gambled all their money away, they wouldn't be in this mess."

"Look, we've been over this loads of times, give it a rest would you. It's all sorted and booked, so there's no point in going on about it."

"No point to you, you mean. It's ridiculous enough that you've been as extravagant as to pay for a weekend away, but you've no business saying we'll take care of the girls, not when we've got something on."

"We haven't got anything on. Nothing definite anyway."

"Yes, we bloody have," she snapped, "and, since Perry can't change his birthday, Connor and Ruth will have to change their weekend away. And, if there's any cost involved," she glared, "Sugar Daddy Dan can pick up the bloody bill."

"There's no need to be so mean. I don't want to go on Perry's bloody weekend away, anyway."

"And their lies the problem. I wouldn't put it past you to have organised this to get out of going away with Perry and Ingrid." She glared, "I bet I'm not far wrong, am I?"

"What does it matter? I'm not asking them to change the weekend, so we can't go to York. End of!"

"That's the trouble with you. You think we live in a world where your word is gospel, well it isn't. I've already agreed we're going away for Perry's birthday, so Connor needs to change his weekend either to this coming one, or the week after. I'm looking forward to York. I've bought a new dress and already got Perry a birthday present. End of!"

"What sort of present?" Dan scowled, "I hope you haven't been throwing money around."

"What like you, you mean?" she huffed, "I haven't bought him and Ingrid a weekend away, that's for sure."

"I would hope not, considering Perry's a neighbour and Connor and Ruth are family."

Lorna got up from the table. "I'm going to get ready to meet Sarah. Ring the hotel and get the weekend you've organised changed."

"I'll have to contact Connor and see if they can change it first."

"Well do it then. They'll have to anyway if we can't take care of the girls, and I'm telling you now, I'm not, so you'd be on your own."

The kitchen door slammed behind her.

He sighed heavily. He knew Lorna would protest, only not so badly. Wouldn't it have been great for her to have complied for once? He'd been foolish to think he could get away with backing out of the weekend with Perry and Ingrid.

When Lorna made up her mind to do something, she always followed through.

Chapter 20

Dan was joining in the banter around the dining table at the hotel in York for Perry's birthday. They'd enjoyed pre-dinner drinks and a delicious meal of seafood and steaks. Perry appeared to have a penchant for fine wine, insisting he chose, which Dan wasn't bothered about. He could tell Perry was showy. It was going down well though and he felt light-of-heart and suitably inebriated. Lorna looked stunning as usual in a burgundy dress he'd not seen before. During the afternoon they'd made love slowly and sensually in the large king bed in their room. Lorna knew exactly how to make him feel good. That's why lusting after Ingrid was alien to him. Why would he do that when he had a fabulous wife who pressed all the right buttons?

The volume of Lorna's voice brought him back into the conversation. It always became louder the more she had to drink.

"And the silly old bat actually stood on the doorstep clutching a book for Dan and wouldn't give it to me. Said she wanted to discuss it with him. I told her he might be a while on his zoom call and can you believe, she wouldn't let me have it to give to him. She took it away with her and said she'd see him another time. Honestly . . . what is that all about?" She shook her head playfully at Dan, "I'm wondering if I should be worried."

Perry joined in, "Sounds like you've got a secret admirer to me, mate. You read about these lonely widow types. Maybe you need to give her a wide berth." The others laughed but Dan didn't find it one bit funny. Phyllis was a nice old lady who he liked and respected.

"Yeah, right," Dan grinned, playing along, "I should be so lucky. I'm sorry to disappoint you all, but the only thing Phyllis is interested in is book reviews. She's a prolific reader and just likes to share the good ones with me."

"And of course Dan reads each and everyone," Lorna said, loving her audience around the table, "I swear, the day of his funeral, he'll be in his coffin clutching a paperback."

Dan rolled his eyes good-naturedly, wishing she'd shut up. He decided to move the conversation away from Phyllis. "So, Perry, you've not told us yet what delights Ingrid has bought you for your birthday. Let me guess, socks, underpants and a wallet."

"No, not at all." Ingrid's eyes twinkled and she pulled a cute disparaging face which caused a heated flush to creep up Dan's neck. He reached for his glass and gulped down some cold water to dampen it. She's only being playful, he told himself.

Ingrid carried on, "I was much more creative than that, thank you very much. I got him two new golf clubs and a weekend circuit racing, which he'd been going on about doing for ages. Although," she frowned, "there were a couple of mundane presents. He loves chocolate and biscuits; he's a sugar junkie, so there are a few of those."

Perry squeezed her hand, "They're all brilliant presents, darling, and this hotel break, it's all been great." He turned to him and Lorna, "Thanks guys for making today special, I am grateful to you for coming."

"We've loved it," Lorna said, "haven't we, Dan?"

"Yeah, it has been great, it's made a nice change."

"We'll have to do it again sometime," Ingrid said, looking directly at him again as she spoke. He broke their eye contact. Surely he'd imagined that?

"Oh, yes, we must," Lorna said enthusiastically, knocking back the last of her wine.

Perry turned to Ingrid, "Are you going to ask them, babe, or shall I?"

"You do it," she said, "you're more a salesman than I could ever be."

"Okay, but let's get another bottle of wine first to butter them up." Perry winked at Dan, "And I'm paying for the meal tonight, no arguments."

"Don't be daft," Dan protested, "you don't need to do that. We can split it."

"Of course you can't pay," Lorna touched a hand to Perry's on the table. "No one pays for their own birthday meal."

"Nope," Perry shook his head and patted Lorna's hand. "I'm paying, no arguments. Ingrid invited you, and I'm picking up the bill. Now, where's that waiter?"

"Let him pay," Ingrid chipped in, "it'll make him happy."

Again, she was looking directly at Dan. He wasn't

imagining it, nor the cheeky smile.

"So what is it?" Lorna said to Ingrid, "now I know you've got something to ask us, I can't wait to hear what it is."

Perry shook his finger playfully, "No, no, no. You're gonna have to wait for more wine. I want to soften you up first, so you can't say no."

"Excuse me for a moment would you?" Dan said standing up, "And don't start without me whatever you do. I'll only be five minutes."

Perry imitated zipping his lips, "Not a word until you're back."

Dan made his way toward the bathroom. It had surprisingly been a pleasant afternoon. Despite his anxieties regarding Ingrid in a bikini, he'd circumvented it all quite well. Once he'd seen her wearing the tiny red bikini, it was hard to get the image out of his mind. So, he'd come up with an idea. The pool, sauna, steam room and Jacuzzi were all together in the basement of the hotel, and while Perry, Ingrid and Lorna alternated around each, he swam endless lengths of the pool trying to think of anything other than taking that tiny bikini off Ingrid and exploring what was underneath it. Lorna had at one stage called him over and insisted he joined them in the Jacuzzi, but he'd sat on the edge and dangled his feet in, saying it was too hot for him after the swimming.

The women had spent their time relaxing and chatting on the loungers, in between flitting in and out of the Jacuzzi and steam room. Perry, like him, was more into swimming lengths. There wasn't an ounce of fat on

Perry, so he must work out, and Dan knew he ran regularly as he saw him going out each day in his running gear. He found himself wondering if Ingrid was into running. Then imagined her running in that bikini. He shook those thoughts away, finished washing his hands, and splashed his face with cold water.

When Dan returned to the table and took his seat, his wine glass was full.

"First of all," Perry lifted his glass, "here's to fabulous friends."

They all clinked their glasses.

Dan swirled the wine around the glass for a few seconds to release its natural aromas before taking a sip, swishing it around his mouth and swallowing. "Mmm, this is rather nice," he said, glancing at the Château Pape Clément label on the bottle. Perry certainly had extravagant taste. It'd easily be more than a hundred quid with corkage.

The waiter appeared with the menus and handed one to each of them. "Can I leave these with you to select your desserts?"

"Thank you," Perry said, "can you give us ten minutes, I don't know about everyone else, but I'm pretty stuffed."

"Yeah, a breather would be good," Ingrid said patting her perfectly flat tummy.

"That's absolutely fine, sir," the waiter said and walked away.

Dan loved Ingrid's compliance with Perry. It was

evident she adored him. Despite fighting against the urge to look directly at her for most of the evening, his eyes strayed to her tiny wrists adorned with numerous silver bangles. They were so petite, as were her hands with delicate fingers and natural nails. How would they feel on his chest and digging into his back?

"Have I got your undivided attention?" Perry asked, interrupting Dan's fantasy.

"Yep," Dan said, urging himself to get a grip, "we're not going anywhere." He wondered if Ingrid might be pregnant but then dismissed it. Perry had said he wanted to ask them something and gave the impression he might have to persuade them to join in with whatever it was.

"Then I shall begin," Perry said playfully. He cleared his throat. "Each year, usually in August, Ingrid and I go to Greece for a holiday. We've got the use of a villa that's in the family and we wondered if we could persuade you two to join us for a week or so, this year?"

Lorna's face lit up. "You want us to come with you? To Greece?"

"Yeah, don't look so surprised," Perry smiled, "we'd love to have you both."

"You'll love it," Ingrid chipped in, as if they'd already agreed to go, "Fiscardo is where the villa is. It's stunning, so traditional and typically Greek. It's quite secluded, we don't like touristy."

Although Ingrid was talking to him and Lorna, her eyes seemed to linger on him. Was he imagining her batting her eyelashes in a flirty way? She couldn't have any idea how he was lusting after her, surely? Nothing could possibly be obvious, yet he could almost swear she was different with him this evening as opposed to other evenings they'd spent together. It was as if she was watching him closely for something. But what . . . he had no idea.

"Ingrid's right," Perry carried on, "we hate the tourists, even though that's what we are. We're just in love with our little piece of Greek heaven and I know you both will fall in love with it too. It's just a harbour village, but we do plenty of exploring and rent a boat while we're there so we can visit the neighbouring islands."

"They're all gorgeous," Ingrid said, "Ithaca, Lefkas and Meganisi are my all-time favourites. We'll take you to them," she said excitedly, "we can just put the anchor down, swim and snorkel and either eat on the boat, or call into one of the beachfront restaurants."

Dan wondered how many bikinis she owned. He pictured her in a white one. White would really suit her.

"It doesn't have to be busy every single day though," Perry said, "we have some days just lounging around the villa, walking to the harbour for lunch and maybe barbequing in the evening. It's just a fabulous place to unwind. And if you can't make a full week, come for a few days at least. You'll love it, I'm sure."

Lorna's eyes were alive with excitement, "It sounds amazing, doesn't it, Dan?"

"Yeah, it really does," he agreed, trying to join in with all the enthusiasm.

"You don't have to say yes right now," Perry said,

"have a think and let us know. We're going anyway, but we'd really like to have you with us." He turned to Ingrid, "We enjoy having company, don't we, darling? It adds to the joy of going away to our perfect place."

"Yeah, definitely," Ingrid responded, "and I just know we'll have a fantastic time, all of us together. Please say you'll come, Dan."

There it was again. Her eyes directly on his. And hearing her say his name had his groin twitching all over again. He needed time to think. The last thing he wanted was a full week away in her company. Short bursts of her he could just about manage, but no more than that.

"It sounds amazing," Dan said, "but before we get too carried away," he rested his hand on Lorna's arm, "I'd need to check how things are at work. I have a part-time accountant that works with me. He's semi-retired, but I'd need to make sure he was around if I was away. I'll find out when his holidays are, if that's okay before we commit?"

Lorna pulled a face, "I can't imagine he'd be going in August when children are off school. Anyway, I'm sure you told me that he'd booked a cruise on the Queen Mary in October. I don't reckon he'll be off in August as well as that. And, as Perry says, there's some flexibility. I think it's a fabulous idea." She grinned at Perry and Ingrid, "I'm definitely in, even if Dan isn't."

Typical Lorna. Dan put on a fake smile, despite the overwhelming urge to strangle his wife at that precise moment. "She means it too, she'd go without me."

"Too right," Lorna laughed, "of course I would. Who

wouldn't?"

"We'll keep everything crossed you can *both* come," Perry said, "let us know. If you can, we'll give you more details. But suffice to say, you'll love it, I know you will."

"I know we will, too," Lorna replied eagerly.

Ingrid's smile made him feel there was only her and him at the table, "I'm keeping everything crossed you can join us," but it was fleeting and he wasn't entirely sure if he'd imagined it. She turned her attention to Lorna, "You'll need plenty of sun cream, it gets pretty hot in the afternoon round the pool."

"Oh, the villa's got a pool?" Lorna asked which encouraged Ingrid into a description of it.

As Ingrid talked, his eyes seemed to have a will of their own and strayed towards Ingrid's small cleavage, enhanced beautifully by her tight-fitting cream top, which was sheer and showed off her undergarment. She wasn't wearing one of those camisoles that Lorna favoured, so her white lacy bra was visible. Her breasts weren't massive by any means, she was like a little doll, but he imagined taking that bra off her. Those pert little breasts in his hands. How would she feel underneath him? Or on top?

Jesus Christ. He reached for the water jug on the table and topped up his glass. No way could he spend a week in Ingrid's company, seeing her each day and imagining her in the bed next door.

He just couldn't.

***

"So, what do you reckon?" Lorna asked Dan as she climbed in the hotel bed next to him. "How lovely, being invited to Greece."

"Yeah, it's really nice of them," he said in a matter-of-fact tone as he flicked through the channels on the TV, "can't say I fancy a full week away with them to be honest. Nice as they are, I think it'd be too much."

She reached for the remote control and put the TV on standby. She wanted Dan's full attention and she so wanted to go to Greece.

"Why would it be too much? We wouldn't have to spend every second with them, we can do our own thing and maybe meet up for dinner in the evening."

He shook his head, "I can't imagine they'd go for that. By the sound of things, they want to show us around the island. I wonder who exactly owns the villa, Perry was a bit vague."

"He said it was family-owned. Anyway, does it matter?"

Dan ignored the question. "August isn't good, anyway. Connor will be away with the kids and I don't like leaving the business without one of us there."

"But he's not going to be taking them away for the whole six weeks of the school holidays." She raised an eyebrow, "And right now, can they even afford a holiday with everything that has gone on?"

"They're talking about visiting Ruth's parents in Cornwall."

"We can work round that, I'm sure," she said,

squeezing some hand cream on her hands and rubbing them together. "Perry said they're flexible too. And did you hear him saying they'd go the week before to get everything ready and then come and pick us up from the airport when we arrive."

"Mmm . . . I did. But I'm still not sure."

"Why ever not? They're great fun, and we deserve a holiday. It's not as if we've got anything booked."

"No, I know we haven't. I was getting round to it. I have had a lot to sort out these last few weeks."

"And whose fault's that?"

"Don't start on that now. Connor and Ruth are working hard to move forward."

"Yeah, well don't ask me to be sympathetic. I still can't forgive him for what he did."

"I see, so . . . I'm guessing from that response, a break away with him and Ruth for a long weekend, to say Disneyland Paris, is out of the question?"

"You are joking," she scowled, "as if. That'd be like rewarding him for all he's put us through."

"Yeah, but they are under a lot of strain. I thought a holiday might be nice, for all of us. And the girls."

"Well, you thought wrong. I'm not going away with him or the girls. I want an adults only holiday, thank you. And Greece sounds perfect to me. What is it really? Don't you like Perry and Ingrid?"

"Of course I like them. I just don't want to be stuck in a villa with two people I don't know terribly well for a week."

"But you do know them and you've said yourself they're

nice people. We've had a great time with them here."

"I know we have, but that doesn't mean I want a week's holiday with them, though."

"What about what I want for a change? I'd like to go. I've had a crap time lately at work, I could do with something to look forward to."

"What's been happening at work?" he frowned, "you haven't said anything."

"Cause it's nothing major. Just the usual Elspeth stuff that's all, getting on my nerves."

"You really should try getting on with her you know. Work would be much easier if you did."

"Trust you to be on her side." She wouldn't expect any less with diligent Dan. That's why she'd said nothing.

"I'm not on anyone's side. I just don't like to think of you getting a hard time at work."

"I don't. I can handle jumped-up Elspeth. But I still would like a holiday and Greece is perfect. And you're shutting the door without even considering it. I can't believe you're turning down an almost free holiday either. We'd only need the flights and some spending money. I would have thought that would really float your boat."

"What the hell is that supposed to mean?"

"It means you don't like spending money. You're always the accountant, watching every penny we spend."

"Yeah, well maybe someone has to the amount you spend each month."

The conversation hadn't gone anything like she'd hoped. She knew he would initially be hesitant to the idea, but she thought the cost savings might sway him. But right now he had a determined expression on his face. One she knew well. It was resolute, he didn't want to go. She needed to change tack and give him a push. And she knew the way to do that. If sex got her to Greece, then that was easy currency.

"Look," she stroked his arm, "it's a great opportunity for us to have a break together at very little cost. And I'm sure we'll have a lovely time. Think about it, nothing but sunshine and plenty of afternoon siestas, not to mention the amazing food . . . and the sex." She touched a hand to his chest, leaning into him.

"Okay, I'll have to check first of all when Connor's away. So don't whatever you do tell them a definite yes, right now." He let out a huge yawn, "Just give me some time."

"Great, long as it isn't a no." She ran a hand over his stomach and reached up to kiss him. "I really do want to go," she nibbled his bottom lip, "how tired are you, exactly?"

"I'm not," he breathed, pushing her hand further south and deepening the kiss, "I'm wide awake."

Chapter 21

Dan was already harassed by the time they'd arrived at East Midlands airport. Lorna had delayed him leaving the house so he'd had to put his foot down which he hated doing. That combined with endless road works, hadn't made for a pleasant journey. He and Lorna were total opposites. His preference was to leave plenty of time if driving anywhere, whereas she was always last minute.

He smiled as they approached the heavily made-up stewardess who'd called them forward to the check-in desk. "Good morning."

"Good morning," she replied, "you're heading for Cephalonia?"

"That's correct." Dan handed over their passports.

"How many bags are you checking in?"

"Two."

"If you could put the first one on," she indicated to the scales and he hoisted the first case on. The digital reading took a few seconds to calibrate. It was well within the allowance. He knew it would be, it was his case. Lorna's, he doubted very much would be within the twenty-three kilogram limit. The stewardess diligently attached the relevant label and stickers to his case and gave it a gentle push along the conveyer belt.

"Next one," she said. Dan lifted the much heavier case onto the scales. He watched the digital number closely as it swiftly increased and passed the twenty-three kilogram mark and registered at twenty-eight. No surprise there. Despite telling Lorna to be careful, she'd have packed as if she was a fashion designer with her whole portfolio in her case.

"I'm afraid that one's over the limit. It'll be an extra forty pounds."

He grimaced as he handed over his credit card. Lorna didn't even have the grace to look awkward; her expression was smug, almost as if she'd done it on purpose.

"What the hell have you packed, for Christ's sake?" he snarled as they made their way towards passport control. "It's week in a villa, not a bloody world cruise."

"Oh, for God's sake, it's only forty quid. I'll give you it, if it bothers you that much."

"It's not the forty quid. You've no need to go over the amount you're allowed in the first place. Why can't you ever stick to the rules? Every single time you flout them, it's as if you take a delight not conforming."

"Maybe I do it so I don't have to live a life governed by Dan Lloyd's rules. Just relax will you. At the rate you're going, you'll be dead before you're fifty. Remember we are actually going on holiday. Surely even you can stop counting the pennies for one week."

His wife had a cruel way of putting things. If she didn't fritter money away all the time, he wouldn't be as rigid as he was. Despite working and keeping all her own money, he'd checked the joint account they used for household bills and grocery shopping the previous day, and was irritated to see on the statement, she'd started using the card linked to that account too. And as far as he could see, it was hardly for essential items. After the holiday, he was going to have a serious talk with her. Her spending was getting totally out of control. But for now she had a point. It was their holiday and he needed to try and relax. Quite how that was going to work out in the company of Ingrid he wasn't sure. Just thinking about her caused him tension. And how ever much he tried, he couldn't get the images out of his mind about how she could relieve his tension.

Once on the plane, he stowed their hand luggage, sat down and fastened his seat belt. Lorna was already flicking through the duty-free magazine, no doubt itemising the load of rubbish she would be expecting him to buy her. He reached in his pocket for his phone to put it on flight mode. There was a recent text from Victoria. She rarely messaged him, just a Merry Christmas or Happy Birthday, but it was neither of those occasions.

> *Hi all, just to let you know that Mike and I have separated. It was mutual so no big drama – it's fair to say it's been coming a while. We both are fine and decided it was easier to send a generic text rather than contact everyone individually. Xx*

He wasn't surprised, the last couple of times they'd met up on Tommy's birthday, she'd been vague about her husband when he'd asked. Nevertheless, he was sorry. He wanted her to be happy. She'd been a huge part of his life, his first love and she was still special even though they weren't together anymore. He thought about her far more than he should, but the way he saw it, it was harmless. Nobody knew, only him. The stewardess's announcement about no further use of electrical devices prompted him to put his phone away. He'd text Vic when he landed to say how sorry he was.

After a couple of gin and tonics, he started to unwind. Lorna was right when she'd told him that he was older than his years. He knew he was. Not in his fitness though. He worked at that. His whole fitness regime was regimented by gym workouts and golf. His body could easily pass as ten years younger.

Lorna had dropped off to sleep and was leaning into him. She was beautiful; there was no doubt about it. Almost angelic with her eyes closed. If only she was more touchy-feely with him, maybe then he wouldn't be lusting after Ingrid quite so readily. Affection wasn't in Lorna's make-up. She was fiery. As soon as the basket was open, the Cobra poked its head out. He took another swig of his gin and tonic and made a pact with himself. This holiday, he was going to concentrate on her. No more mentioning money, or nagging on, he'd make her the whole focus of his attention. And somehow he needed to stop the ridiculous lusting after Ingrid and make love to Lorna, daily. She was receptive currently and he was going to capitalise on that. During their marriage, he'd often day-dreamed about the delight of trying to get her pregnant, but the pain of Tommy's numerous health issues and losing him, was always there. It never left him. The fact Lorna didn't want children made her a great match for him. But he couldn't deny, he'd have liked the physical trying for a baby and ultimately succeeding. That joy him and Victoria had shared when they'd discovered she was pregnant, was a joy like no other.

He placed the empty nut packet in the plastic cup and tilted his seat back to rest. As he closed his eyes, he thought back to first meeting Lorna. Connor had told him he was going to ask Ruth to marry him and he'd seen a ring he'd liked and wanted him to go look at it with him, despite Dan telling him women's rings weren't his forte. But Connor insisted and they went into town, had hearty, cholesterol laden breakfast and headed for House of McIvor.

They browsed for a while in the window and Connor excitedly showed him the red ruby he'd chosen. He was not intending to make any suggestions other than it was just perfect, but that all changed when he went inside the shop. Greeting them both was the lovely Lorna, according to her badge, who worked there as a jewellery assistant. He was immediately taken with how beautiful she was. Her hair was thick and lustrous, fastened back, and her slender figure enhanced by the tight black skirt, piqued his interest. As she produced the tray from the window, his eyes were drawn to her ample breasts with the black shirt encasing them and the top three buttons left undone delightfully displaying a glimpse of olive skin.

"So, what do you think," his brother's voice brought him out of his admiration trance, "do you think Ruth will like it? I think it's just her."

"Yeah, I'm sure she will. Who wouldn't be pleased with it?" He had no worries that Ruth might turn his brother down, they were deeply in love, anyone who came into contract with them could see that.

Lorna smiled, "I think it's a beautiful ring, and quite unusual for an engagement ring."

"Unusual?" Connor asked, "in what way?"

Dan should have spotted Lorna's cunningness at the time, but he was so entranced by her that he got sucked in, just like Connor.

"It's just that the most popular engagement rings we sell are solitaire diamonds. We have a range I could show you." She proceeded to take the ruby away, reached into the window for a display of diamonds and put them on the black velour mat which, under the light, showed off their vibrancy. But of course diamonds came with a price and Dan could see Connor was torn now she'd said that, which was exactly why she'd done it. But he could forgive her. She was probably on a commission anyway so it was in her interest to get a potential buyer to spend more.

The single solitaire Connor selected had a much higher price tag than the ruby. He lifted it up to the light which only made the brightness of the diamond sparkle more.

"This is rather nice," Connor twiddled the ring between his fingers. "What do you reckon, bro?"

Dan never made hasty decisions, his thought process was always to take his time.

"Yeah, it is nice, but I think the ruby is too. That's the one you originally wanted."

"The ruby is lovely," Lorna agreed, "but personally speaking," she rested her hand on her chest which accelerated the feeling that he so would have liked his hand there, "as a woman, the diamond would be my choice for an engagement and maybe a ruby later for an anniversary or something. An engagement ring is so special, you wear it for ever."

Dan noticed her slender fingers with the delicate manicured nails were bare of rings, which was good. He wanted to ask her out.

"I tell you what," Dan said, "why don't we go grab a coffee and have a think? Then we can come back."

Connor looked puzzled, "If you want." It was obvious he wanted to get the ring right there and then and be done with it.

"Before you go," Lorna dazzled him with her smile, "if you'll excuse me for a moment. The manager is in today. Let me see if I can get you some discount."

"You're sure you don't mind?" Connor asked as Lorna took the tray of rings and locked them up.

"Not at all. I won't keep you a minute."

Dan knew it was a ploy. He'd been on the receiving end of a slick car salesman only the previous week who told him that by luck, the manager was in the office that day and he might be able to get him a reduction in price on a particular car. Funny how these managers just happen to be *in that day* when in fact they were in every day. Just a sales ploy to make you think you were getting a personal discounted price.

"What do you really think?" Connor whispered, "the diamond or the ruby?"

"I'll tell you when we get out of here. Don't buy it yet, whatever you do. We need to come back. And he did need to come back. He wanted to return to ask Lorna out.

Connor eventually chose the diamond for Ruth which meant he'd had to lend his brother more money, but he didn't mind as he'd got the date with Lorna and lending his brother a few hundred quid was a small price to pay.

Lorna wriggled beside him but didn't open her eyes. A wry smile passed his lips thinking about that day and meeting her. She'd certainly meant what she said about the diamond, he'd ended up having to fork out considerably more for her engagement ring than Connor had for Ruth's. And it hadn't stopped there. She'd badgered him for a diamond eternity ring for their first anniversary too. He loved Lorna but she was high maintenance in the spending department and despite his gentle warnings that her spending had to stop, she took no notice whatsoever.

The tannoy announcement from the captain telling the passengers to return to their seats and fasten their seatbelts as they were beginning the decent, woke Lorna.

"I'll just have to nip to freshen up," she reached in

her handbag for her make-up bag.

"I don't think you're supposed to go now the announcement's been made," he said.

"I've got to," she stood up, "I can't meet Perry and Ingrid looking like this."

He moved out of the seat to let her pass. No point in arguing. If she was stopped by the stewardess, she'd have an excuse like she had a weak bladder or tummy ache. Nobody would be able to prevent Lorna getting in the toilet, she was quite adept at rule breaking. It's one of the things he found infuriating about her because integrity ran through him like words through a stick of rock.

Chapter 22

"There they are, look." Lorna pointed to Perry and Ingrid as they entered the arrivals lounge. They swiftly made their way towards them, pulling their cases. Lorna threw her arms around Ingrid first of all, while Dan leaned into Perry and gave him a brotherly hug, then they swapped. She hugged Perry, who looked strikingly hot in his designer tee-shirt and shorts, and smelt absolutely heavenly. All crisp, aromatic and clean. She liked it. Dan rarely wore aftershave even though she bought him some for birthdays and Christmas. He said it made him sneeze.

Lorna pulled away from Perry. "Have you been waiting long?" she asked, as Dan eased himself away from Ingrid. A glimpse of awkwardness passed across her husband's face. Why was that? It was just a hug.

"No, not at all," Ingrid answered totally oblivious to Dan's stiffness, "we've been here about thirty minutes and grabbed a coffee in Costa."

"Here," Perry reached out for one of the two cases, "shall I take one?"

"Cheers mate, do you want to wheel mine, it's lighter than Lorna's."

"That's a dig at me," Lorna said to Ingrid as she fell in step beside her while Dan dragged her case alongside Perry.

"Don't tell me," Ingrid said, "he reckons you've packed too much."

"Spot on," Lorna laughed looking sideways at Ingrid in her skimpy shorts and tight halter neck top. It was evident she was braless which did nothing for her flat chest. Thank God she was lucky enough to have nice breasts. She'd hate to be tit-less.

"It's good you're both finally here, we've lots to show you," Perry said, "we want you to have a great week with us. I hope you're prepared to be busy, as we've loads planned."

"Sounds great," Dan answered him, while Lorna chipped in, "we're in your hands. Quite happy to fall in with whatever you suggest. We're just delighted to be here. Neither of us have been to Greece before."

"Then you're in for a treat," Ingrid said, "it's a beautiful island, you're gonna love it."

As they made their way through the airport exit and away from the air conditioning, heat blasted them.

"Oh, God, how fabulous is this," Lorna cooed reaching in her bag for her sunglasses.

"It was hotter yesterday, I'm glad it's cooled a few degrees," Ingrid said putting her sunglasses on too.

They wheeled their cases along the tarmac to a parked Hyundai SUV. It was a relief to Lorna that it had a sunroof.

"You'll perhaps be best in the front with Perry, Dan," Ingrid said as the men loaded the cases into the boot. "Are you okay in the back?" she asked Lorna, "you don't get travel sick or anything?"

"No, that's fine."

"Are you sure?" Dan said, "I don't mind sitting in the back."

"Don't be daft, "you ride shotgun with Perry. You'll be doing me a favour," Ingrid pulled a playful face, "I'm not a lover of his driving out here. At least from the back I'll not see the traffic coming towards me as he overtakes."

"In that case," Dan grinned and climbed in beside Perry.

"Do you have this level of confidence from your wife?" Perry asked fastening his seat-belt, "listening to Ingrid you'd think I was a risk taker. Despite me telling her time and time again, she doesn't get that we Brits have to drive differently on the continent."

"Yeah, so you keep saying," Ingrid chipped in, "but I don't notice others driving like you. So please, can you for once take it steady so we all get to the villa in one piece?"

"Yes, dear," Perry replied cheekily as he started the ignition and manoeuvred the car out of the car park. "When we get to the villa, we thought we'd have a welcome drink, then let you unpack and maybe have a siesta, before tonight's barbecue round the pool. How does that sound?"

"Sounds pretty good to me," Dan replied keenly. Lorna was pleased he sounded enthusiastic. She must remember to ask him later why he was stiff when Ingrid hugged him. One thing she was certain about was, he wouldn't be attracted to flat-chested Ingrid. Loyalty was

Dan's bag. She'd never had any concerns on that score. He berated Connor often enough for having a brief affair that had threatened his marriage in the early days with Ruth. Although it was a long time ago, Dan had a memory like an elephant and stored every little detail in his accountant's brain and brought it up often when he deemed necessary.

"We can start the sightseeing stuff tomorrow," Perry looked in his mirror at the girls in the back, "if that's okay with you guys?"

"It sounds perfect," Lorna said addressing Ingrid more than him. "You'll have to tell us if you want us to hire a car for a day or two while we're here. We don't want you to feel you have to ferry us around all week. It's your holiday too."

"We wouldn't hear of it," Perry said, "we'll still be here for a while after you leave so we've plenty of time to do anything we want to."

"And we love company," Ingrid smiled.

"Yep, that's why we bought the villa, so we could have family and friends here with us often."

"It's yours, is it?" Dan asked, "I thought it belonged to your family."

"We all have a share in it," Perry corrected, "all the family put in a bit each."

"Ah, I see. You never say much about your family. Do you have a large one?"

"Not really." Perry pointed at the windscreen to a huge hill looming up. "Lorna, you see up there, what looks like an old church right at the top."

"Yeah, I can."

"Well, that's run by Trappist monks and they brew beer."

"You're kidding me. Monks brewing beer?"

"Yep, I know. But I tell you what, it's the most wonderful tasting beer, we can visit one day, if you like and try a few samples. You and Dan might like to take some bottles home."

"Oh, we'd love that. Thank you so much for inviting us. This week's going to be fabulous, I just know it is. But, as I was saying to Dan, we can't have you doing all this without us contributing. You must let us pay something towards our keep."

"Don't be silly," Ingrid said, "it's no extra cost you two being here. You can treat us to a meal out if you like."

"Definitely. In fact, we'll pay for all the meals out while we're here, won't we, Dan?"

"Yeah, sure."

"Stop worrying about stuff like that," Perry smiled kindly in the mirror again. "You're here as our guests and we want you to have a great time. So relax and no more talk about money."

Dan was nodding in agreement in the front. Perry couldn't have said anything better to him. It would delight him having little to contribute to their holiday. She was just relieved he actually liked Perry, if he didn't, she'd never have been able to persuade him to come along. He wasn't exactly overawed about it, but she'd got him there. And as she looked out the window at the majestic mountains and hillside hamlets, nobody could fail to be enchanted by the country. Not even Dan Lloyd.

The villa was stunning in itself, but it was its location that set it apart from many. It was perched on a secluded hillside with breath-taking views of the glistening sea, surrounded by mountains. There was a feeling of much needed coolness as they entered the stone building through the front door. The white-washed walls, exposed stone work, and tiled floors were obligatory, as was the air conditioning. It was a great relief from the outside heat.

Perry and Dan wheeled the cases into the spacious hall.

"How are you fixed for a quick look round, a drink and some nibbles?" Perry asked.

"They might want to have a siesta after their journey," Ingrid said to Perry but looking at them both.

"No, we don't need a siesta," Lorna shook her head, "a drink would be lovely first of all and then we'll have an hour or so to unpack."

"Sounds good to me," Perry said, "let's show you round."

Lorna was amazed at the beauty inside the villa and knew Dan would be too. It wasn't massive by any means, but it was spacious and minimalistic. It had three bedrooms, all en suite with wooden beds which looked to be hand-made, and painted beautifully in soft, clean colours. Their room had a small sea-view window with two chairs so they could leisurely sit and enjoy the vista.

The villa had a fully equipped kitchen with oak cupboards, and even a small games room with a pool table and a large TV.

After the tour and depositing the cases in their room, Perry guided them to the outside terrace area. "Take a seat and I'll be back shortly. Ingrid, do you want to give me a hand?"

Lorna sat next to Dan on the wicker sofa and they both stared at the view from the pergola-shaded terrace. It was warm but not oppressive. Alongside the comfortable outside seating area, there was a long dining table and a secluded barbecue area. The array of deep pink hydrangeas contrasted beautifully with the turquoise water from the private swimming pool. Surrounding the pool was wooden decking, wicker sun beds and three large parasols.

"Isn't this just perfect," Dan's voice was the most animated she'd heard for ages.

"It certainly is. We are going to have such a great week, I know we will."

Dan leant forward and kissed her. "I'm looking forward to our siesta," he grinned cheekily, pulling away as Perry and Ingrid approached.

"I've bought a great wine which the ladies will love," Perry said, as Ingrid placed some cheese, crackers, crisps and olives on the coffee table, "but never thought to ask mate, is wine okay for you? I've got beer if you'd rather."

"No, wine is absolutely fine."

"It's quite dry but refreshing I find." Perry passed her and Ingrid a glass first, before handing one to Dan, "Try it and tell me what you think?"

Dan took a sip. "That is rather nice. Is it Greek?"

"No. It should be Greek while we're here but I'm a bit of a traitor. It's Italian."

Lorna downed a gulp of hers. Perry was right, it was refreshing. "It's lovely. Funny isn't it how wine always tastes better in a hot climate?"

"It does, you're right," Ingrid said reaching forward and offering a plate to her and Dan. "Help yourself to nibbles."

"Not for me thanks," she shook her head, "I'm fine with the wine."

Dan reached forward and selected some food and rested the plate down at the side of him. He winked at her as he munched an olive and took another sip of wine. She grinned back lovingly, pleased to see him relaxing into holiday mode. Just what she'd hoped for.

Perry's phone pinged, "Excuse me, I just need to check this. I'm waiting for confirmation from the boat hire company. I've booked a particular boat I like for a couple of days so we can take in some of the islands." He reached for his phone and looked at the screen as Ingrid peered over his shoulder. "What have they said?" she asked him.

Dan squeezed Lorna's hand, "Are you okay? You seem miles away."

"I'm just soaking up the atmosphere." She smiled and lifted her glass, "Here's to a fabulous week together."

"Absolutely," he clinked his glass with hers, "Cheers, love."

Chapter 23

Ingrid sat with Perry at their bedroom window overlooking the bay. It was the fourth evening of their holiday. They'd kept their guests busy with something different to explore each day.

"It was nice of Dan to offer to drive to the winery today so you could have a drink."

"Yeah, it was. We've been," he did quote marks with his fingers, "good hosts showing them round. I've had enough now, though."

"Me too. I want it all to be over, but I still feel . . . you know . . . really anxious about it all. They're decent people."

"I keep warning you not to get too close to them. Yesterday at the Drogati Caves, you were far too nice to Dan."

"Because you told me to be," her voice went up slightly, "it wasn't real. And I could say the same about you. Today at the beach, I saw you eyeing Lorna up in her swimsuit."

"Shush, keep your voice down and stop being stupid. Why would I do that when I've got you?" He reached for her hand and kissed it. "You're all I'll ever want, so don't talk like that. And all this is false anyway."

"Are we definitely going ahead tomorrow?" she asked lowering her voice to a whisper again. Although Dan and

Lorna's room was further down the corridor and they couldn't possibly be overheard, their conversation was for their ears only.

"Yep, absolutely. I've checked the weather and it's going to turn at around four o'clock."

"So what time are we setting off?" She wrapped a strand of hair around her finger nervously.

"About two thirty, I thought. We'll have a full day with the main objective of plying them with drink. We need to keep busy though as I don't want them having a siesta tomorrow. I want them pissed."

"How are we going to stop them? Lorna told me that Dan looks forward to it each afternoon. I think being here has perked their sex life up."

"Yeah, well it isn't happening tomorrow. The main thing is keeping them occupied. We'll get up late, have some salmon and champas for breakfast, go out for a walk around the bay and stop off for an early lunch with plenty of wine. The market's on so take Lorna with you for a look round. I'll stay with Dan for more drinks. When we get back to the villa, the boat will be ready. I've spoken to Nikos and he's leaving it at the jetty for us. We'll load up with the drinks and set off."

"What if Dan checks the weather, you know how anal he is. He'll probably say it's too risky to go out in the boat."

"By the time I've finished plying him with drink, he won't be able to even see his phone. You need to keep the pressure on though as he might be knackered, and as you say, try and lie down. So keep both of them going."

"I will."

"And once we set off, I'll serve the drinks and give them generous measures."

"Okay. Hey, Lorna can certainly knock the gins back, can't she? She's taken a real liking to it while she's been here."

"Yeah, I noticed."

"What about you? You can't be pissed. More than any of us, you need your wits about you."

"Don't worry about me. I'll watch what I'm having. The main thing is keeping them fed and watered, especially out in the boat. And remember, as soon as I give you the nod, make sure you get them both to the edge of the boat. Can you remember what I said to get their attention?"

"Yeah. Get excited about some parrot fish or other."

"That's right. If they're hesitant, really lay it on about how gorgeous they are in the water. Once they're leaning over the edge and looking downwards, I'll do it."

"What if . . . you know, hitting them with the boat hook doesn't work?"

"It will work. Stop worrying. It'll be over quickly."

It would most definitely work. The molly would be taking effect by then. No need to mention that though. The less Ingrid knew the better."

"What if one of them turns around and sees you?"

"I'll be too quick for that. First Dan, and then Lorna. And then I'll shove them into the water. Leave it all to me. Remember, you won't have been taking part in anything. It's all me. That would always be your defence.

I coerced you. You were terrified but daren't say no."

"But you said the plan was foolproof and we couldn't get caught."

"It is. It's just going to look like a drowning accident. As long as you stick to the story we've rehearsed from the beginning, it'll be fine. By the time they've retrieved their bodies, they'll be black and blue from the coral so it won't be evident they've been hit. And when they check for alcohol, they'll have way too much in their system."

"What about the boat explosion though, you've never told me exactly what you're going to do."

"Cause I purposely don't want you to know. Remember, afterwards we're going to be questioned about it all. The less you know the better."

"But I wouldn't breathe a word."

"I know you wouldn't. But what you don't know, you can't say. You'll stick to the story as to exactly what happened. We were all blotto, and there was some sort of explosion on the boat. I shouted to get in the water which you're going to do. You don't need to ever say any more than that. When you're questioned, just keep focussing on Dan and Lorna asking if they've found them. At all times appear vague and upset. They'll speak more to me. They'll want to know about the explosion."

"How do you know what to do with the boat to make it look like an accident?"

"Because I've been around boats since I was a kid. Whenever I visited my father in the school holidays, he'd take me sailing along with whichever woman he had in tow at the time. That's how I earned my sailing qualifications. He was a complete arsehole but insistent about boat safety."

She still looked uncertain, which was understandable. He was on edge too, despite being on the cusp of everything he ever wanted. That's why he'd planned things so meticulously. It had taken an age to get to where they were right now. He'd got his explanation ready for the police – the cloths wrapped around the boat engine as he suspected the engine was leaking – a vagueness with the police that he hadn't thought about it getting overheated – yes, he may have had a cigarette in his hand – yes, once the flames started to rise up, he tried the extinguisher but in the end it appeared futile and he'd abandoned ship. He was well sorted with the plan. He'd rehearsed it that many times in his mind.

"Hey," he squeezed her hand, "It's going to be alright. Trust me."

"I do," she swallowed, "it's just the realisation of what we're going to do."

"We've been over this. One more day and then it's done. Don't go all weak on me now. After tomorrow we'll have all we ever dreamed of and there's nobody to stand in our way."

"I know that but I'm still terrified. How in God's name I'll sleep tonight, I don't know."

"Do you want something to help you?"

"Like what?"

"A sleeping pill."

"Where from?" she frowned, "we haven't got any sleeping pills."

"Yes, we have. They gave me a few at the hospital when I injured my knee."

"I didn't know that. You never said."

No, he hadn't said because there were no tablets from the hospital. He'd bought them on the internet along with the molly he was going to use to spike the drinks. If the authorities tested their bodies, and found evidence of the drugs, they are a recreational drug anyway, so wouldn't arouse suspicion.

"I forgot about them. They are good though, I must say. Knock you right out, so you get plenty of shut eye."

"You took some, then? This is the first I've heard of it."

"Just two one night, that's all. That first night when I was in so much pain."

"Aren't they addictive though?"

"Course they're not, not if you take them ad hoc. If it helps you get through tonight, take a couple. I'll get you them. Do you want a night cap as well?"

"Not with tablets, I don't."

He walked to the wardrobe and found his soap bag to retrieve the tablets he'd hidden from her and headed for the en suite for a glass of water.

"Here you go."

She swallowed the tablets with water. "Thank you."

"Now just relax and sleep tonight. Do exactly what I've told you and this time tomorrow, we'll be all done."

"Promise?"

"I promise."

Chapter 24

Dan was sat at the back of the boat, a bottle of beer in hand, enjoying the warm breeze as the cabin cruiser sailed along the water, ably skippered by Perry. Both him and Ingrid were brilliant hosts. Perry had put his iPad on and all the familiar tunes he was playing were related to water, sunshine and holidays. The rhythmic beat throbbed throughout the boat. They were all on a high from a full day of boozing. Dan couldn't remember being so half-cut, it must have been way back in his uni days. Lorna was well-oiled too – she kept kissing him and sticking her tongue down his throat.

The sun was beating down, so he was bare-chested, wearing just his shorts, but it was the girls, alluring in their bikinis and shorts that had his full attention. Lorna's breasts were spilling out of her top and at that precise moment, if they didn't have an audience, he'd have ripped the bikini and shorts off her in a second. And as if that image wasn't enough to have him bulging, there was Ingrid, with her cute breasts barely covered with a tiny white bikini that outlined her hard nipples. He was beside himself each time he caught sight of the decorative navel ring peeping out teasingly from her shorts. What he wouldn't give to kiss his way down there. The women, alongside the booze, gave him an overwhelming urge to fuck the pair of them both together. Right there on the deck, naked with the sun beating down on them and the momentum of the ship enhancing their writhing bodies, as he took each one of them in turn.

The boat appeared to be slowing down. "Just putting the anchor down for five," Perry called as the boat juddered and eventually stopped. Seconds later, he appeared in front of them clutching a small tray with 4 shot glasses.

Perry handed Dan a glass first. "Here you go, mate. This should liven the party up. On your feet everyone."

"What the hell is it?" Dan asked eyeing up the pink liqueur.

"A sort of tequila shot, the first of many."

Dan hesitated, "I might stick to beer . . ." He didn't want to make a fool of himself and throw up everywhere.

Lorna wrapped herself around him, "Don't be daft, it's a party. You have to join in. I love this new, relaxed husband you've become this holiday." She reached for a shot glass for herself and Perry handed one to Ingrid, "There you go, babe."

Perry put the tray down and raised his glass. "Okay, shipmates, down the hatch after three. All together now . . . one, two, three."

In unison they all downed their shots.

As Dan knocked his back, the liquid burnt the back of his throat. He screwed his face up,

"Bl-oo-dy-hell . . . it's like rocket fuel."

Perry put an arm around him and patted his shoulder,

"You drink rocket fuel regularly do you, mate?" he laughed.

"Christ," Dan's eyes began to water, "leave me out of anymore of that."

Lorna was giggling hysterically. "What the hell is it?" she wiped her tongue on her teeth, "I've never had anything like that in my life. I feel like my head's coming off."

"Plenty more where that came from," Perry said, heading back up the two steps to the bridge, or cockpit as he called it.

Lorna grabbed hold of Dan's arm. "Hold onto me before I fall down." She went all limp and floppy, so he eased her into the seating area around the back of the boat and lounged against it himself, before his own legs gave way.

What the hell was in that shot?

***

Perry watched it all from behind his shades. Dan was hopelessly pissed, exactly how he wanted him. Lorna was all over him, and while Ingrid was putting on a showy, happy, carefree face, he knew she was terrified. And he wasn't exactly calm himself. What they were about to do was abhorrent. But he knew precisely what he was doing. And he also knew, lots of people each year lose their lives in swimming and boating accidents. He'd rigged the ship ready for the explosion so nobody would be able to prove it wasn't an accident. All Ingrid had to do was lure them to the edge of the boat and he was going to do the rest. He was fairly confident the Greek authorities wouldn't do extensive investigations into the accident. Of course they'd have to establish how two people had died, which would mean examining the bodies and the boat, but that would be about it. He knew the authorities well. His father used to be disparaging about them, cynically saying if he wanted to murder his wife, he'd do it at sea in Greece. The investigation would be over before it'd begun.

Lorna was shrieking with laughter. "We should go for a swim, all of us. Hey, I know, why don't we go skinny dipping?" Perry watched as she started to nibble and lick Dan's bicep. "You'll come in with me, won't you?" Dan had a stupid grin on his face, one he'd never seen before. The man was permanently measured. But right now, he was probably considering getting Lorna in the water and swimming off somewhere secluded. Fat chance of that though, they were purposely in the middle of nowhere. The shore was miles away.

Ingrid looked in his direction in the cockpit. He couldn't see her eyes as she was wearing sunglasses, but he knew exactly what she was thinking. The same as he was. She wanted it over. And he did too before Dan realised he'd been slipped a molly. In preparation for what he was about to do, earlier, he'd pushed the heavy-duty boat hook along the floor of the boat with his foot. He'd wrapped the tip in a rag and taped it up to make sure there wasn't any forensic evidence on the bodies when they were found. Not that he thought there would be. He would sling the rag in the water afterwards.

All Ingrid had to do now was exactly as he'd instructed. From her sitting position at the back of the boat, she removed her sunglasses and looked directly at him. She looked nervous. Perry felt a twitch of sympathy but pushed it aside. Lorna was all over Dan and they were laughing hysterically. Perry nodded. The nod Ingrid was expecting. It was time.

She was hesitating. Hands on her thighs, glued to her seat and getting the cold feet he feared she might. He moved forward to the steps, took off his sunglasses and gave a firm nod with a smile.

Ingrid nodded back and relief flooded through Perry when she turned and leant over the edge of the boat, peering into the water, "Oh, my God," she said, her voice shaking a little, "have you ever seen anything like this? Quickly, come and look at these parrot fish. They're absolutely huge."

Lorna swayed her floppy body towards Ingrid and placed a knee on the seat and leant over the edge of the boat.

"Where?" she slurred, . . . "I can't see anything?"

"Hang on," Ingrid said peering intently into the water, "they were there a second ago. You have to see them, they're stunning. I wonder if they've gone underneath the boat maybe. Keep watching right there," she pointed.

"Dan, come and have a look," Lorna said, "can you see anything?"

Dan, docile as a baby, turned sideways and glanced over the side of the boat.

"Kneel up, Dan," Ingrid urged, "you'll see better then."

Perry watched Dan's movements. They were cumbersome as he brought himself up onto his knees and leant forward, resting his arms of the edge of the boat.

"Where are the li'l shits?" he said, staring into the green-blue water, "I can't shee anything." His words were becoming more slurred – the molly had well and truly kicked in. The regimented man who earned his living balancing figures had long disappeared and in its place was a stoned bloke, off his happy head. He probably wouldn't resist if he clobbered him right at this moment. But he wasn't going to do that.

Ingrid had successfully got them in position, just as he'd told her to do. Perry's abdomen tightened seeing all three of them hanging over the edge of the boat. He moved silently towards them, like a leopard stalking its prey, and reached down for the boat hook. He was ready. He took a huge breath in but Dan glanced his way, his drugged eyes looked surprised to see him there.

Perry changed tack. "Let me have a look," he said, stepping up behind Dan and Lorna and peering over their shoulders, brandishing the boat hook as if he might harpoon the elusive fish.

"There!" Ingrid said, pointing.

Dan and Lorna's attention went back to the water.

It was now or never.

Perry's heart was racing, his palms clammy with sweat as he raised the boat hook high.

Just do it, he told himself, tightened his grip and brought the boat hook down on the back of Dan's head with such force that he slumped like a sack of bricks.

Ingrid moved to one side in anticipation of him hitting Lorna as planned. A look passed between them, a flicker of . . . fear, or horror in her eyes, as if she suddenly knew the truth. She glanced to Lorna then. Lorna that was no longer drunk, and certainly not screaming for her poor husband.

Ingrid opened her mouth to speak, but Perry brought the boat hook down a second time, directly on his wife's head.

Two figures lay motionless.

Ingrid and Dan were slumped side by side, both unconscious. The rise and fall of their chests indicated they were still alive – they had to be.

Perry, still clutching the boat hook, stared at Lorna.

They'd done it.

All that was left now was to hoist Dan and Ingrid's bodies into the water and set the explosion. They had to be alive as they went in. It had to be a drowning accident. It was the only way their plan would work. The plan formulated meticulously during the past year. During their clandestine meetings at Lorna's mother's house in Leicester, where they'd vigorously made love and plotted Dan and Ingrid's deaths. Now there wasn't anyone to complicate their life. Exactly as it should have been all those years ago when he'd fled to New Zealand and Lorna, the only woman he'd truly loved, had married Dan Lloyd. And stupidly, as a consequence, he'd hastily married Ingrid.

But now, they could finally be together as they should have been ten years earlier. Dan and Ingrid were gone. All that was left was for them to quickly finish the last part of the plan of making the whole thing appear as an accident. That was vital.

Getting caught wasn't an option.

Chapter 25

Lorna took Dan's legs while Perry had his torso and they hoisted him over the edge and into the water. Lorna stared at her husband's body, expecting it to sink straight away. But it didn't.

"Look at me," Perry snapped pointing two splayed fingers toward his eyes, "not him." She watched as he effortlessly picked his wife up and dropped her into the water. Lorna scanned the water again for any sign of Dan, but he'd gone. The blow to his head had rendered him unconscious and despite her fear he might wake up when he hit the water, he clearly hadn't. The warm Aegean Sea had sucked him in, quickly followed by Ingrid. They'd done their research and established both of them had to be alive when they entered the water. Seemingly a post mortem examination of lung contents and tissue could establish if a person was dead before they went into the water.

Despite Perry's instruction, her eyes frantically scanned the water again, as if both Dan and Ingrid would emerge and attack them for what they'd done. But there wasn't a chance of that. The sea was calm and it had taken their bodies – exactly as her and Perry had intended. Now the final part of the plan had to be executed. Quickly – they had no time to waste.

"You ready?" Perry asked.

She nodded, completely compliant with the man she loved.

"Here," he handed her the boat hook, "Do it. Not too hard, mind."

She pulled the boat hook back and wacked him across his forehead. She winced as the blood started to ooze above his eye.

He grabbed her arm and pulled her towards him. "It's okay. You did good, darling," his lips found hers and he kissed her hard. "Get as far away from the boat as you can. Remember everything I've told you."

"I will. I love you."

"I love you too. Now go."

The time for talking and being together would come soon enough. She purposely moved away from where they'd pushed Dan and Ingrid in the water. Standing on the edge of the boat and without a backward glance, she dived into the water. The next part of the plan was the distance she might have to swim. And she had to keep going all on her own. They were miles from anywhere. But she'd prepared herself with the swimming lessons she'd pushed herself to do. She could easily swim twenty miles or so now. Perry had insisted on the regular swimming sessions to increase her stamina. He wasn't sure how long it would take for the rescuers to get to them following the mayday he was intending sending out, before he detonated the explosion.

She glided forward into the abyss, the buoyancy of the saline water and her even breast strokes propelled her away from the boat. It was essential she put as much distance between herself and the boat. Perry had taught her well. The next few days and weeks would be hard. They had to play the grieving spouses, especially when Dan and Ingrid's bodies were found. She thought about the times he'd play-acted with her about certain scenarios. He'd posed tricky questions and told her how to answer. He'd been a good tutor – she knew exactly what to expect.

The explosion came minutes later. She screamed, even though nobody could hear her. It would be the adrenaline Perry talked about. He'd said she had to go through the motions and behave as if she was a victim, for when she would have to repeat the story. Perry would have made sure she was a safe distance away. He'd set it all up. She didn't fully understand the engineering jargon, but Perry did. He talked about the fuel leak and the errant spark from a cigarette which would ignite the fumes. All she cared about was his reassurance that he wouldn't put himself in any danger. So even though she couldn't see him, she knew he was out there. He'd said they must swim separately until they were picked up.

A second explosion blasted through the air.

She turned her head to look back at the boat in the distance. The hull was still intact, floating on top of the water amongst lots of debris. Although a little sluggish from the alcohol in her bloodstream, she'd been careful and not drunk as much all day as Dan, but it was essential she drank some. Neither her nor Perry could predict whether they'd have to give blood samples when they were found. The sudden liking to gin and tonic had ensured Dan and Ingrid hadn't been aware she was drinking less than they were. All the frolicking had been playacting. Even though Ingrid had been careful with her measures, Perry said he was slipping something into Dan's drinks to relax him. Purely recreational for when his body was tested.

Time stretched on until she finally heard a boat engine. She started to drink seawater as Perry had told her, and lots of it before flaying her arms around to draw attention to herself.

"Help," she screamed, "help, someone help me." She continued to call out over and over, "help."

A male voice in the small rescue boat coming towards her shouted. "You're okay, we're going to get you out. I'm going to throw this ring to you, grab it and keep a tight hold."

She did as he'd instructed and reached for the safety ring. "My husband is in the water somewhere," she called, "I can't see him."

The boat came up closer to her. By now the engine was barely running as it eased alongside her.

"Here," the young Greek man was leaning out of the boat and extending his hand, "take my hand. You're safe now. Let's get you out of the water."

As he and another rescuer reached to hoist her into the boat, she babbled on, almost screaming. "My husband and our friends, they were in the boat. There was an explosion. Please, you've got to help them."

While one of the rescuers put a foil blanket around

her, the other one spoke to her, "What's your name?"

"Lorna Lloyd. My husband's in the water . . ." she exaggerated scanning the endless stretch of water . . . "somewhere. You have to find him."

"We have another boat out searching," he reassured, as one of the other crew members was checking around her head and neck for any signs of a head injury. "My name is Andreas. We're Sea and Rescue and we're going to get you to the hospital. How many of you were on the boat?" he asked.

"Four of us," she started to sob and raised the pitch of her voice, "please, you've got to look for them," she pleaded, "my husband's out there."

"Try and take some deep breaths. We are looking, I promise. Did you see your husband go into the water?"

"Yes . . . I don't know . . . I think I did. He was trying to put the fire out with Perry, our friend. He shouted at me to get in the water." She sobbed, "I'm not sure . . . I never saw who got into the water . . . I just kept swimming away from the boat . . . I was scared . . . scared it would explode. God, if anything has happened to them . . ." she sobbed louder.

"Was the other passenger female?"

"Yes," her teeth chattered. "It's Perry's wife . . . my husband's a good swimmer . . . he has to be alright."

"One man has already been picked up," Andreas told her.

"Who?" she asked, piling on the anxiousness, "Is it Dan, Dan Lloyd, my husband?"

"I haven't got any more details. Try to keep calm and

we'll get you to shore as quick as we can and then to the hospital to get you checked out."

"I don't want to go to hospital . . . please can you go back . . . they could still be in the water . . . they might be hurt."

They'd expect her to be in shock and babbling. They were just the rescuers, it would be the police she needed to be on her guard against.

As the boat swiftly moved towards the shore, she pulled the foil blanket around herself, looked up at the sky and started to pray. "Please God, let them all be okay."

At the hospital, she continued with the tears, but didn't say anything verbally, she just stared at the wall as the nurse put a probe onto her finger and a cuff around her arm before attaching her to a monitor. A doctor had been in and told her the other person that had been rescued was Perry.

"I'm just going to put something in your ear to take your temperature," the nurse said. As a device bleeped, she removed it and discarded the tiny cover in the bin.

"Please, you said you'd take me to see Perry. Can I go now?"

"Yes, all your observations are fine. I'll fetch a wheelchair and take you to see him."

Minutes later, she was taken to Perry's room by the nurse. He was sitting in bed, propped up on several pillows, with a dressing on his forehead where she'd hit him with the boat hook. He was wearing what looked like a surgical gown and delicate white gloves.

She jumped out of the wheelchair and ran towards the bed and wrapped her arms around him.

Perry held her tightly. "Thank God you're okay."

She pulled away and looked directly into his eyes. "Have you heard about Dan . . . or Ingrid? Nobody's telling me anything."

"Nothing." His eyes filled up . . . "I'm so sorry."

"I don't understand what happened." She wiped her tears away with her wrist. "How come they've found us? Did you see them go into the water?"

"I don't remember." He screwed his face up, "I'm trying. Everything is hazy and my head hurts."

The nurse interjected, "Stop trying to remember right now. You'll only make your head worse. Your recollection will come back, but right now, your brain has been traumatised. It really does need to rest."

"What's wrong with your hands?" Lorna asked staring down at the white gloves.

"Burns."

"Oh, Perry."

"Hey, it's okay. Don't worry about me. They have to find Ingrid . . . and Dan. That's the most important thing."

"Yeah," she nodded forcing down more fake tears, "Dan's a really strong swimmer. He'll be on land somewhere, it's just a question of finding him."

"I know."

"He'll be looking after Ingrid as well. Is she a strong

swimmer?"

"No, not really."

"Oh, God Perry," she sobbed, "I can't believe this is happening."

He pulled her into his arms again. "Shush, they'll find them. They'll have swum to safety. We have to stay strong."

Chapter 26

It was after midnight when two Greek police officers escorted Lorna back to the villa. Her nerves were in tatters having been quizzed at the hospital by the police. Just as Perry had instructed, she feigned confusion explaining they'd all been drinking and on a high at the time of the accident. She'd been asked if she'd taken any drugs, which she hadn't. They'd taken blood samples from Perry to check for drugs, which was only to be expected with him being the skipper of the boat. He hadn't taken anything, though. The conclusion of the authorities had to be a boating accident. Any drugs in his system and they could consider manslaughter for Dan and Ingrid's deaths. They'd only find drugs in Dan's system when they retrieved his body. The molly Perry had slipped into his shot.

Perry was to remain in the hospital overnight. Lorna would have preferred to have stayed too, but it didn't appear to be an option. She'd been allocated two support liaison officers, Arina and Georgios. They would remain with her overnight while they waited for news. Perry had reminded them at the hospital of a spare key in the soil of a small plant pot on the terrace. All their personal possessions had been on the boat.

Arina was seated alongside Lorna in the lounge area overlooking the terrace. They were sipping the obligatory pot of tea Arina had made. Georgios was sitting in the corner of the room and using a small console table to set up a laptop.

Lorna was heeding Perry's advice and only speaking when spoken to. He'd told her the authorities would expect her to be in shock and there would be quiet periods as well as moments of babbling away randomly. But such was the level of her anxiety, she could almost hear her own heartbeat drumming away, and her tongue was dry, leaving a bitter taste in her mouth. Her overwhelming desire was for a warm bath and to clean her teeth, but she daren't suggest it. Maybe they would?

The once vibrant villa felt chilly and detached. She felt almost like an interloper being there without Perry and the others. Each second dragged as she stared into nothing, desperately trying to forget what really happened on the boat. Although Perry had prepared her by going over and over every eventuality, it was completely different in reality. It felt almost like a nightmare she'd wake up from and all four of them would be enjoying drinks and a barbecue on the terrace.

She tried not to, but her eyes were systematically drawn towards Georgios' phone he'd rested on an adjacent chair arm. If willing it to ring had any effect, it would have done so, announcing that Dan and Ingrid's bodies had been found. Once she'd been told that, she could focus on her grief. Perry had expected the bodies would be found quite quickly after the accident and they'd planned for that. So the length of time she had to spend waiting, she hadn't anticipated. Nor being on her own at the villa with the liaison officers. She'd expected Perry to be there. Her anxiety was burbling away inside, almost ready to explode. Not only for Dan and Ingrid's bodies to be found, but she was anxious about Perry also. The one thing she'd feared was him getting injured and the fact the hospital were keeping him in was worrying. Did he really have memory loss? He'd certainly never told her he was going to use that as a ploy.

"Would you like to go to your room to try and rest?" Arina's voice interrupted her thoughts. "I'll wake you if we hear anything."

"I can't rest," Lorna protested, rubbing her hands up and down her arms to keep warm. The hospital had given her a zip-up jump suit which was nylon and itchy. Tears threatened. She was becoming quite adept with the fake tears as the ramifications of their actions were truly vile. "I just want Dan to be found . . . and Ingrid."

Arina touched her hand, "You're bitterly cold." She turned to her colleague. "See if you can find some brandy, would you?" Georgios retrieved his phone and headed off to the kitchen.

"You should try and rest. Even if you don't sleep, lying down is better for you. You might find you doze a little."

"I don't want to doze," Lorna snapped, "I want to wait for my husband."

"I know you do. Sea and Rescue are doing their best to find him and Ingrid. But they've lost the light now, so will have to wait until dawn."

"What do you mean, lost the light? They're still searching, aren't they? Don't tell me they've stopped."

Georgios returned, preventing Arina from answering. He was carrying a thick throw over one arm and a brandy schooner in his hand. Arina took the throw from him and wrapped it around Lorna's shoulders, before taking the brandy goblet and handing it to her.

"Sip it slowly," she instructed.

Lorna savoured the burning liquid as it flowed through her. Her body felt almost as if she had ice running through it. She felt cold inside and out.

"Surely they have searchlights. They can't have abandoned the search. Dan and Ingrid could be anywhere."

"They haven't given up looking completely," Georgios said, sitting down in the corner, "they've just scaled down the number of boats until dawn. It's difficult without light. But I can assure you, they're doing everything they can to locate them, I promise you that."

Lorna wrapped her fingers around the glass and took another sip of the brandy. The warmth seemed almost to kick-start the blood seeping around her veins, easing the internal storm. An image of Dan's face as they hoisted him into the water to his death was hard to erase. Although they'd prepared for it, the fact her and Perry were now murderers was truly abhorrent. It was completely different plotting the murders to actually carrying them out.

Arina cleared her throat, as if she had something

difficult to say and wanted her attention. "We need to think about contacting someone to be with you. A family member, maybe?"

Christ, not a chance. She wasn't having Connor sniffing around, even though she did expect him at some stage. But not right now.

"I don't have anyone. I only have Dan. My mother's in a care home. Oh, God . . . Connor."

"Connor?"

"Dan's brother. They're really close." She looked pleadingly at Arina, purposely creating more drama, "How am I going to tell him? I can't."

"He will need to know."

"Dan could be found soon, though . . ."

Arina would no doubt have her own police agenda and part of that would be to have a relative to support Lorna, and possibly one for Perry too when the bad news came.

"The media have got hold of the story and while they don't have names or anything yet, with it involving Brits, it will be on UK television."

"I don't know what to do for the best," Lorna whined, shaking her head.

"I think you should call him and explain what has happened. It might be better coming from you. We can of course speak to him if you don't feel up to it."

"I can't." Lorna screwed her face up. "He's going to be devastated."

"Yes, I'm sure. But it is best you inform him now rather than . . . rather than later. You can then give him updates when we know anything, maybe tomorrow."

"I can't ring him. I don't have his number. It's in my mobile . . . was in my mobile, on the boat."

"They don't have a landline?"

"I guess so." Lorna frowned, "I'm not sure, we use mobiles."

"I see. We could ask the police in the UK to go to the house."

"Oh, God no, please don't do that. They have children."

"We are going to have to make contact at some stage."

"Why? Do you know something?" Her eyes darted in Georgios' direction, "Have you heard anything?" she asked, injecting fear into her tone.

"No, sorry. No news yet."

Lorna considered for a few minutes before imparting further information. Connor would have to know at some stage. "Erm . . . my husband has an address book he keeps telephone numbers in. He always says if we lose our mobiles, we'd be screwed." She rubbed her forehead, "He's right, of course," the corners of her mouth twitched affectionately at her own comment, but she purposely didn't break into a smile, "he always is. The book will be in Dan's hand luggage, in the wardrobe in our room."

"Do you mind if I go and get it?" Arina asked.

Chapter 27

Perry was being discharged from the hospital and returning to the villa that morning. The hospital had provided him with some jogging bottoms and a sweatshirt and some sort of foam concoctions for his feet. He was sitting in a chair beside the bed he'd been resting in all night, with a probe on his finger attached to a monitor. The incessant bleeping from the machine was grating on his nerves. He hadn't slept. He daren't, despite the fact the high adrenaline levels had levelled out and he was completely exhausted. But he'd forced himself to stay awake. It wouldn't be a good look to be asleep when his wife was still unaccounted for. And he was positive the news would come through soon. He'd even considered they'd actually been found and there was a delay in telling them for some reason. He'd dismissed that though on the grounds they couldn't carry out the required post-mortems without telling next-of-kin.

A tap on the door made him turn his head. A police officer he'd spoken to the previous evening came in. Perry looked hopeful, silently asking if Ingrid and Dan had been found.

The officer shook his head. "I'm afraid not." He reached for a small wooden chair, placed it in front of Perry and sat down.

"They've retrieved the hull and engine and brought them ashore."

Perry nodded. It was to be expected. He was confident that whatever investigations they carried out, the eventual findings would conclude it had been an accident. He knew boats, and he knew engines. And with gasoline engines, fuel vapour build-up is one of the most common causes of fire or an explosion. Faulty fuel lines that were once flexible and properly sealed can grow brittle over time, often developing cracks and leaks. And he'd certainly been able to install a faulty one, carefully. The leaked fuel and fumes build up in the engine compartment, and once mixed with seawater in the boat's bilge, it creates a situation that would be disastrous once a spark or match was lit. He rigged it all, but the more difficult part for him, was the risk to himself of the boat exploding before he got off it. But he'd pulled it off perfectly. Timing was everything.

"Early indications are, that it could have been a faulty fuel line and a spark, possibly from a cigarette, which caused the initial explosion. I know you said your recollection was vague, but it appears the fire extinguishers had been discharged."

"Maybe Dan and I?" Perry shook his head. "It's like a dream. I can't quite get every detail."

"You'd probably smelt burning of some sort, or there could have been a small fire. That would explain Mrs Lloyd telling us her husband had almost screamed at her and your wife to get off the boat and swim away from it."

"Yes. Our priority would most definitely be their safety. And Dan's. I'd have shouted at him to get off the boat as well, I'm sure I would." A wave of forced hopelessness passed across his face. "It's not looking good, is it?"

"I'm afraid not, no. There's always hope, but I think by now, it's highly likely we would have picked them up if they were alive."

A nurse came into the room, followed by a male medic. The officer stood and moved his chair back against the wall. "I'll leave you to it, Mr Hunter. There'll be a liaison officer at the villa when you get there."

"Thank you." Perry nodded.

Wrapped in a blanket, Perry was pushed in a wheelchair to the ambulance. He was transferred to the stretcher inside and, after securing him with a belt, the medic tapped on the dividing space to the driver. Seconds later the engine started and they were away.

After an initial conversation about his comfort, Perry closed his eyes. The last thing he wanted was small talk for the duration of the journey. The ambulance was taking it steady, there'd be no need to rush, he was a patient being discharged, not an emergency. He wasn't under any illusion that the next weeks and months weren't going to be difficult. He couldn't be with Lorna yet, but he would be eventually, brought together by their respective grief at losing their spouses. That would be the easy part of the plan. Right now, it would be torture for them not being able to be together. They'd waited long enough. But they were closer now than ever and couldn't afford anything to undo their hard work.

His heart rate accelerated at the thought of seeing Lorna again. He had no doubt at all she'd be playing her part well. Lorna was like him. If she wanted something, she went for it. That's what he loved about her. Unlike Ingrid, who he'd never really loved, lusted after, yes, but never loved.

His thoughts drifted back ten years earlier to him and Lorna. Their relationship had been volatile, largely due to him. He was the son of a wealthy man and behaved accordingly, not always for the better. He'd loved her though, and she him. But they'd been young and he'd not always been kind. She'd wanted commitment, he hadn't. And he'd foolishly let her go, intent on a desire to go to New Zealand and experience freedom for a few years before he settled down. It had been a mistake once the novelty wore off. And when he heard Lorna had married Dan Lloyd, he'd been devastated. His ego had assumed when he returned to the UK, she'd have been waiting for him. Once that was no longer an option, it was easy to fall into a relationship with Ingrid. She was beautiful, kind, compliant, and loved and doted on him. Every man's dream woman.

"Are you okay?" the medic asked, "You keep wincing. Are you in pain?"

"My head's throbbing a bit, but everywhere aches. They did say at the hospital to expect that."

"Would you like something for the pain?"

"I think I'll wait. This is nothing compared to . . ." he

let out a heart-wrenching sob . . . "compared to my wife's suffering. I'm sorry. It just keeps coming in waves."

"I do understand. Maybe close your eyes again and see if that helps. If not, just say and I'll give you something."

"Thank you."

This time when he closed his eyes, his parents came to mind. Although his mother and father divorced when he was a teenager, his father had provided well for them and he'd always known upon his death, he would inherit his immense fortune and the opulent Gayton Manor, the mansion in Buckinghamshire that had been in the family for generations. Not bad for a child who'd started life in an orphanage run by catholic nuns.

Throughout his life, he'd experienced a constant elephant in the room which came in the guise of his father's genetic daughter. Seemingly, as a young man, his father had an affair with an eighteen-year-old woman employed at the house in the kitchens. She eventually became pregnant and his grandfather paid her off to leave the house and never contact the family again.

Perry's mother and his father had married but could never have their own children. Investigations concluded his father had a low sperm count, so although not impossible to father a child as he'd already proven he could, it seemed unlikely it would happen again. As a result, Perry had been adopted by them both and lived a privileged lifestyle until his mother's excessive drinking habit culminated in alcoholism and his father divorced her. Perry had been packed off to boarding school. It wasn't an option, it was a necessity. His mother could barely look after herself, and the old man didn't really want his twelve-year-old son cramping his lavish lifestyle. During school holidays, he was able to visit Gayton Manor and spend time with his father and whichever latest floozy he had in residence, but there had never been love or affection from him. Only discipline.

The old man died almost a year ago. The delay in the estate being settled was a source of frustration. By now Perry should have it all, but it wasn't to be. His father, in his infinite wisdom, had left part of the estate to his illegitimate daughter, if she could be found. It was an impossible task, which his father knew only too well as he'd spent years trying to trace her with a great deal of money being spent on investigators in the UK and overseas, all to no avail. Nobody had any idea where the young pregnant girl had disappeared to once she'd left the house. And, as single women tend to marry and change their names, it was like trying to find a needle in a haystack. But his father never gave up and he'd left instruction in his will that the search for his daughter must continue for one year and, if found, she would be awarded a share of the estate. And it was for that reason Perry's inheritance was on hold.

But Perry had a secret. One he'd shared with no one. He knew categorically there was no way his father's genetic daughter would ever be found. And for that reason, in less than four months, he'd inherit the whole estate. And, due to their ingenuity and tenacity, he and

Lorna would spend the rest of their lives together . . . for ever this time. And they would take pleasure in his vast inheritance now there was no Ingrid to claim her share as a legitimate wife.

Chapter 28

After hours of no sleep whatsoever, Lorna opted for the shower for quickness even though the bath was more appealing. She was anxious it might appear decadent to be laid in a bath while waiting for news as to whether her husband was dead or alive.

As she stood in the shower, allowing the hot water to cascade down her body, she thought of Perry. How she longed to wrap herself in his arms and for him to tell her she'd done well. She had, she knew that, but she so needed some comfort from the man she adored.

She remembered the first time he'd contacted her out of the blue, begging for a chance to meet with her. He'd returned from New Zealand for good. His father had been terminally ill so he was forced to return, and once his father died, he'd have to oversee his vast estate. Or sell it; he had options. Much as she knew it was wrong to meet with him as she was married to Dan, and Perry was married too, she hadn't been able to resist. When had she ever been able to say no to him? Never. He'd been the love of her life . . . the one that got away.

That first meeting led to a passionate all-consuming affair, almost a year in duration. They met when she visited her mother in Leicester. It was hard for them both, being married to others, and it didn't help that Dan was constantly droning on about renting out her mother's house to support the care home costs. But how could she? It was the only place her and Perry could meet after both realising rather quickly, they'd made mistakes and married hastily. But the cost of Perry extracting himself from his marriage to Ingrid was a mountain he didn't want to climb. With the help of a slick divorce firm, she'd take him to the cleaners, which could mean the estate could take years to settle. He'd still be wealthy, but why should he lose so much to her?

Lorna stepped out of the shower and vigorously rubbed herself dry with the coarse towel, hoping it would put some zest into her. Despite the warmth of the water, she still felt cold. It had been a relief to eventually go to her room, supposedly to lie down and rest for a few hours, and have some much-needed space from the scrutiny of the liaison officers. She'd resisted initially, but eventually gave in to their coaxing. Perry was being discharged from the hospital and returning to the villa that morning, Arina had told her. Lorna was beside herself with anticipation. All would be well once Perry was there.

Georgios and Arina were sitting together with a tray of tea in front of them on the coffee table as Lorna entered the sitting room after her shower.

"Would you like some tea?" Arina asked, attempting to stand up.

"No, thank you . . . please, don't get up," Lorna said, sitting down on the ornate wicker sofa opposite. "Any news?" she asked Georgios, just for something to say.

She knew there hadn't been. Arina had been up to her room an hour earlier with yet more tea and had said as much.

He shook his head. "Nothing."

Lorna met Arina's eyes, "It's not looking good, is it? Surely they'd have been found by now . . . if they are . . ."

A car door banged. Lorna turned her head towards the door with a level of expectancy on her face. Arina got up from her seat and made her way into the hall.

"It's Mr Hunter returning from the hospital," Georgios informed her.

Lorna painted on a forlorn expression before closing her eyes and bowing her head. All for Georgios's benefit.

***

Perry was unsteady as he entered the sitting area of the villa, with the medic holding onto his arm and guiding him towards a chair. His head wound was exposed now where Lorna had hit him with the boat hook. Ten stitches held the wound together, which was more down to him aggravating the cut as it wasn't as big as that initially.

He could see Lorna's eyes had clocked it, and he could tell she was unsure what to say. He knew her as well as he knew himself. She'd be thinking what exactly was appropriate.

The medic made sure he was comfortable and left him with details of who to contact if he became unwell. Georgios went with him to show him out.

The female liaison officer smiled at him. "I'm Arina

and my colleague is Georgios. We're leaving shortly, as soon as our replacement arrives as we've been here overnight. Our job is to ensure you have support and everything you need. Can I get you anything?"

His overwhelming urge was to tell her he'd like some coffee, so he could have just a moment with Lorna alone, but it wasn't appropriate. "No . . . I'm fine. Thank you."

Lorna approached him in his sitting position and leant forward to hug him. Not too tightly though, just a supportive hug. Briefly he inhaled her freshness. She'd showered and smelt all lemony and citrusy.

"I'm okay," Perry reassured, desperately damping down the overwhelming urge to hold her in his arms. He could feel her anxiety with the female liaison officer present. "How are you holding up?" he asked as she pulled away and returned to the sofa.

"Not terribly well. I don't understand why they haven't been found."

It was all playacting, but completely necessary.

He nodded, forcing a pained expression. "I'm beginning to fear the worst."

"There are teams out searching still," Lorna said in a voice that indicated she was saying the words, but didn't really believe them, "there must still be hope?" She looked at Arina but no comforting words were forthcoming.

Perry gave a resigned stare at the police officer too, as if asking the same question.

Lorna reached for a tissue from the coffee table and

blew her nose. It was amazing how she could cry real tears. Only Lorna could pull it off.

"Can you remember anything at all?" Lorna asked him, appearing desperate for answers, "Did you see Dan go in the water?"

"I don't know. I'm sorry. It's coming back in flashes. The doctors say it might take days if not weeks to remember everything. I can't . . ." his voice cracked . . . "I can't remember seeing Ingrid either."

Lorna rushed over and knelt down beside him, reaching for his hand.

"It's okay. They'll come back to us," she squeezed tightly, "they have to."

Chapter 29

Day three at the villa was the same relentless drag, waiting for news. Lorna and Perry were in the presence of police liaison officers day and night, so were never alone together. A medic came each morning to attend to Perry's hand dressings and that particular morning, a doctor had visited to check on them both.

Lorna was on her bed in her room, being examined by the doctor. He did a blood pressure check and looked in her ears as well as listening to her chest. She knew it was all about water inhalation. She buttoned up her top while he sat down on the bed next to her and jotted down details of her examination.

"How are you feeling?" he asked, "I know the stress must be enormous while you wait for news."

"It is. I'm starting to fear the worst now after all this time. I know Dan would have been found now if . . ."

He nodded knowingly. "You turned down my offer of medication previously, but it's still there. I can give you something to help over the coming days."

"No . . . thank you," she shook her head, "I'd rather not. Tablets make me ill at the best of times. I don't want to feel any more nauseous than I already do."

"If you're sure," he said sympathetically.

"Is everything else alright?" she asked, biting the side of her mouth to give the impression of anxiety.

"Your blood pressure is a little high, but that's to be expected right now. It should settle. I'll ask the nurse to check it again tomorrow when she comes to do Mr Hunter's dressings." He placed the notes inside his bag. "If there's nothing else, I'll go check on Mr Hunter's hands myself."

She shook her head, "No, I don't think there is."

His compassionate old eyes met hers, "I sincerely hope you have some news soon, Mrs Lloyd."

"Thank you," she smiled meekly as he collected his bag and made his way towards the door. No wonder her blood pressure was up. The constant burden of having to play a part was taking its toll. Neither of them had prepared for this eventuality. Both had assumed they'd be on their way back to the UK by now as grieving spouses, preparing for both funerals.

It was afternoon when Lorna heard a car approach the villa and she rushed to the front door. Connor had flown out to be with her and the police had sent an escort to the airport to collect him.

Dan's handsome younger brother appeared expectedly weary as he exited the car. It had only been a few days but it was evident to Lorna he'd lost weight. His shorts hung well below his waist. He hadn't shaved either, which was unusual for him, he was normally pristine. As the police officer went to the back of the car to open the boot, Lorna ran towards Connor and threw herself at him. His arms tightened around her as she buried her face in his chest, loathe to break away. Not because she found his arms comforting, it was the part she was now forced to play, stretching her nerves to capacity. It was constant.

"Thank God you're here," she sobbed, "there's no news . . . on either of them."

"I know," he eased her away from him, holding firmly on to her forearms, "they're still looking, though. We have to keep strong."

His eyes mirrored hers with tears, only his were genuine. The sound of someone clearing their throat interrupted them and they turned to see Perry stood in the doorway. She took her brother-in-law's arm and led him towards Perry. It struck her how much Connor walked like Dan.

"This is Connor, Dan's brother," she said to Perry, and turned to Connor, "this is Perry. Perry Hunter."

Perry's bruising around his head had turned yellowish giving him the appropriate injured victim appearance, he'd not shaved either but it was impossible with his bandaged hands. A young auxiliary medic came each morning to the villa to assist him with personal hygiene and Perry had refused the offer of a shave.

"Pleased to meet you," Perry raised his white-gloved hands, "I can't shake your hand."

"Not a problem. I'm sorry about everything, and that your wife is still missing."

"Thank you."

"Have you got anyone here with you for support?"

"No. I don't want to trouble any family members, not until . . . well, you know."

"Yeah, sure, I do understand."

The police driver approached them with Connor's holdall in his hand. "Would you like me to take your bag inside?"

"No need," Connor said, "I can take it. Thank you for picking me up from the airport."

"You're welcome. There's an officer in the house who'll keep you updated and answer any questions." He nodded respectfully at her and Perry, "I hope you get some news soon."

As the officer made his way to the car, Perry said to Connor, "Come in. I'm sure you're ready for a drink."

The latest female liaison officer, Zoe approached them in the hallway and introduced herself to Connor. "I'll let you catch up with your sister-in-law and then I can update you on the search and rescue."

Connor nodded, "That'll be helpful."

"I'll make some coffee for you all."

"Thank you, that'd be nice," Lorna said, holding onto Connor's arm and guiding him towards the outside terrace. Coffee, coffee, coffee. It was exasperating the amount of times she was offered refreshments. And they were having food brought in. But she barely touched any of it. How could she possibly eat?

Perry followed them both outside. She wasn't sure if he would join them but she was pleased he had. It was comforting to have him close as she spun more lies to Connor.

"Please, take a seat," Perry said, "I'm sorry we're meeting in circumstances such as these."

“Absolutely,” Connor said sitting down in the chair shaded by an overhead canopy. “I’m sorry but I’ve got a million questions,” he rubbed his forehead, “I’m struggling to understand it all.”

“Yeah, me too,” Perry said taking his seat, “It’s all a bit vague, I’m afraid. I’m still trying to piece it together.”

“Perry’s got a head injury,” Lorna felt the need to clarify, “so things aren’t terribly clear.”

“Can you remember anything?” Connor asked.

“Bits. I’m starting to get flashbacks.” He cleared his throat, “From what the police have told me so far, there appears to have been a fuel spill on the bottom of the boat. I can’t remember doing so, but I’m told Dan and I may have reached for the fire extinguishers, but I guess the flames just took hold. It’d be very much a case of getting off the boat before it exploded.”

“So you all dived in? You weren’t thrown off with the explosion?”

Lorna interjected. “Dan and Perry did go and deal with the fire, I remember that. Dan screamed at me and Ingrid to get in the water and swim away from the boat . . . I can’t believe I did. I was so scared. I just swam and swam until I heard the first explosion.”

“What about you and your wife? And Dan?” Connor stared at Perry, “Can you remember getting in the water?”

“That’s what’s so difficult, I can’t. I’m confident we will have done though. Once I’d realised how bad things were, I’d have said to abandon ship. I’m sorry, I know this must be hard.” Perry said.

"What I can't get my head round is, Dan's a strong swimmer," Connor said, "If he'd got in the water, like Lorna did, he'd have made it. So that's what I'm struggling with." His eyes fixed on her, "Did you see Dan go into the water?"

She sighed. "I didn't see him. But like I said, I just kept swimming. It sounds selfish I know. We'd all been drinking, so things aren't clear for me. I just remember swimming and calling out for Dan, over and over. Then I was picked up."

"Did you two see each other in the water?" Connor asked.

Perry shook his head, "No. To be perfectly honest, it was a blur. I found myself in the water and thought maybe I was the only one that made it. I checked round, of course, but couldn't see anyone so I swam like fury to get to shore and get help."

"I'm sure you did your best. Sorry for the endless questions. It hardly seems real right now. I've asked if I can be taken out to the search area today."

"Is that wise?" Lorna asked, "It'll be terribly painful for you."

"I know it will, but it's what I want. I still can't believe any of this is happening. I'm expecting to see Dan's," he paused and then had a crack at lightening the moment, "ugly mug to come waltzing through the door. You must both feel like that too, every time the door opens?"

Lorna gave a compliant nod. As if. There'd be absolutely no future for her and Perry if that happened. They'd be locked up for the rest of their lives.

The door from the villa to the terrace opened. Zoe stood there with a pained expression on her face, minus the tray of coffee she was supposed to be bringing.

"I am really sorry to have to tell you, they've pulled a body out of the water."

Lorna's hand flew to her mouth.

"Who . . . Who is it?"

Chapter 30

The police escort vehicle collected Lorna and Connor from East Midlands airport to take them to Lorna's home. They were all silent in the car. What was there to say? They were returning with the certainty in their hearts that Dan was no longer alive. But unlike Ingrid, the sea hadn't given up Dan's body yet, so officially he was missing, presumed dead. Perry had headed back to London two days earlier, and would now be in the process of organising Ingrid's funeral.

The car pulled up outside Lorna's house. Ruth opened the front door and rushed out as they exited the vehicle. She flung her arms around Lorna first of all and held her tightly. "Aw, love, I'm so sorry. Poor, poor Dan."

Lorna pulled away, forcing the tears, "God, Ruth, it's a complete nightmare."

"Come on, let's get you inside." Connor reached for his wife and kissed her. The police escort assisted them with their bags into the hall.

"Would you like me to stay for a while?" he asked.

"I don't think so," Connor said. "We just need some time alone right now . . . as a family."

"Of course."

"You will let us know as soon as . . . if you hear

anything, won't you?"

"Yes. We're in direct contact with the Greek authorities. As soon as they know anything, they'll inform us and an officer will come round. We won't call."

Lorna followed Ruth through the house to the kitchen and left Connor seeing the policeman off.

Ruth took a tissue out of her sleeve and dabbed her eyes. "I can't imagine how terrible it's been for you. Come and sit down, I've got the kettle on. And I don't want you to worry about anything, Connor and I are staying tonight."

"What about the girls?"

"It's okay. A friend of mine has them and is taking them to school tomorrow. I'll have to leave to pick them up in the afternoon, but Connor can stay. Or, we hope you'll consider coming to ours for a few days. You can't be on your own."

"Thank you, it's a lovely thought, I'm not sure though."

"A few days might just help. You've been through such a lot."

Lorna gazed around the contemporary kitchen, "I feel closer to Dan being here."

"I'm sure you do. We'll sort something out, even if it means Connor staying with you."

No, I don't want Connor or you staying. I want to be on my own so I can speak to Perry.

After an afternoon of tea and sympathy, rather than setting up the dining room to eat dinner, Lorna sat with

Connor around the kitchen table attempting to eat the chilli con carne, rice and salad that Ruth had prepared for them. It was a sombre meal, what was there to say? Connor and Ruth were grieving, they loved Dan and would be struggling to come to terms with the fact he was gone and they weren't going to see him again. Although she'd thought about nothing else but life after Dan's death, in reality she was barely coping since the accident. Constantly being under scrutiny by the watchful eyes of the police in Greece had taken effort and vigilance, and now she was home, she yearned to be alone to escape from the part she had to play. Not once since the accident had she been alone. Keeping up the pretence was much more difficult than she ever imagined.

Determined to get rid of them both the following day, she had to speak up. After another mouthful of food she forced and tried not to gag on, she rested her fork down and directed what she wanted to say to Connor. "You've been an absolute brick coming over to Greece and bringing me home, and," she smiled at Ruth, "you too for being here. I am truly grateful. You asked me earlier about coming to yours for a few days, but seriously, I want to stay here. Even if I come to yours, I will eventually have to come home on my own. And being here feels closer to Dan somehow, while there's still, you know, a grain of hope that he might just . . . " the tears came easily.

"I understand," Connor rested a hand on her shoulder. "If you're sure, but you're welcome anytime.

And ring if you need anything. Even if it's the middle of the night and you just want to talk."

She reached and grasped Connor's hand, "I promise if I can't cope, you'll be the first to know."

"And if there's any news, you'll ring, won't you?"

"Of course. But what about you, how are you holding up?"

"It still hasn't sunk in yet. I keep expecting him to walk through the door any minute." Connor loved Dan, he was like his father and mother rolled into one. He was really going to struggle over the coming months without his brother in his life.

"It's made worse by them not . . . you know." He reached for the water carafe, filled his glass and gulped down a mouthful of water, "Finding him would make it more final."

"It would," Lorna said wearily, then, after a suitable pause, "but he's not coming back, is he?"

Connor didn't need to answer. He looked down at his untouched food and pushed the plate away.

Lorna placed her knife and fork together and pushed hers away, too. Clearly neither of them had an appetite, him because he was mourning the death of his beloved brother, her because she was responsible.

"He'd have hated causing this much inconvenience," Connor smiled, "he was a sorter, wasn't he? He'd have had this lot put to bed by now."

"Too right he would," she agreed, painting a loving expression on her face.

"I'm going to be here for you," Connor said fighting

back the tears, "we'll get through this together. It's what Dan would have wanted. I've let him down on too many occasions, but this time I'm going to make sure I don't. I'm going to do everything right by him."

"I know you will. You've already done so much. Coming out to Greece was so supportive of you. Dan would have been proud. He loved you so much, you know that, don't you?"

"Yeah, he did. And I loved him. Still do. He means . . . meant everything to me."

Her gut clenched. Connor and Dan had a strong bond. Connor was hurting terribly and she was responsible for that. What had she done?

Before things got any more morose, Ruth interjected. "Why don't you two make yourselves comfortable in the lounge, there are a pile of messages and some cards to open. I'll load up the dishes and bring some coffee through."

"I'm sorry I've not eaten much," Lorna said, "it was lovely though."

"Don't worry about that, although you must eat to keep your strength up. You're thin enough as it is. Now, you get yourselves into the lounge and get comfortable. Go on, both of you. I'll be there in a minute."

Lorna was trying her best to join in and respond appropriately as all three of them huddled together in the lounge reminiscing about Dan. All she really wanted was to go to her room, remove the new pay-as-you-go phone from the back of her wardrobe that she'd bought in preparation, and to call Perry. She was desperate to hear his voice. It had only been two days since he'd left the villa to fly to his home in London to make arrangements for Ingrid's funeral, but it felt so much longer. The distance between them for now, was too much. She could barely cope with the ramifications of their actions. Without him, she was bereft.

The shrill of the front doorbell ringing interrupted the melancholy atmosphere as Lorna opened each bereavement card and passed it to Connor to look at. Ruth was busying herself placing them on the mantelpiece, hearth and windowsills.

"I'll go see who it is," Connor said standing up and heading for the door.

"Don't let anyone in, love, as well meaning as they might be," Ruth said, "not tonight."

"I won't."

Lorna listened carefully to hear who Connor was politely informing that it was too early for visitors. It only took a second for her to recognise the voice of the female protesting, "Just for a minute. It is important and will help, I promise."

"Oh, God no," Lorna muttered. Nosy parker Phyllis from next door was the last person she wanted to see. The nerve of the woman imagining she'd want to see her.

The lounge door opened and Connor came through with Phyllis following. "The lady from next door insisted on having a quick word," he rolled his eyes as if to say he'd tried to get rid of her.

Lorna scowled at Phyllis and didn't get up from her seat. "I'm sorry, I really don't feel up to seeing anyone right now. Maybe in a day or two."

Anyone normal would instantly know they weren't welcome, but not Phyllis. "That's all right, dear," she carried on, totally oblivious to Lorna's stern glare, "I won't stop. I've brought some cakes for you all to have with a cup of tea. I've left them on the hall table."

"Thank you," Lorna nodded, being intentionally rude and not introducing Ruth. The old bat could get lost. She didn't want her lingering.

Ruth did it for her. "I'm Ruth," her sister-in-law said, "Connor's wife. We've met before."

"That's right," Phyllis smiled, "the twins' mother."

"Yes."

Jesus bloody Christ. Get lost, Phyllis.

"They're lovely girls. You must be very proud."

"We are," Ruth said, "but it's a difficult time for us right now."

Phyllis wouldn't get subtle, Ruth.

Phyllis eased herself down into the spare sofa seat next to Lorna despite nobody offering her one. "I'll say what I've come to say and then I'll be off."

Nobody answered.

"I have some news," she turned her head towards Ruth and Connor, "for you all really. You won't know this as I don't broadcast it, but I'm a psychic, I've been that way all my life." She turned back to Lorna, "That's why I wanted to see you all as quickly as I could to reassure you that Dan isn't dead. My late husband has passed over to the other side and he tells me Dan isn't there. He's very much alive. That's what I wanted to come and tell you to put your mind at rest."

The room was silent. All three of them stared at Phyllis in shock.

Connor's expression darkened with rage, "I must ask you to leave right now. This is too distressing . . . for us all. We're trying to come to terms with my brother's . . . passing, and talk like this isn't going to help. So please," he stood up, "you need to go. I'll show you out."

"I'm sorry," Phyllis looked indignant. "I haven't come here to upset you all. I thought you'd want to know." She got up from the sofa, "I'll leave you to it, then. But I promise you, Dan is still alive. Please take comfort in that." Connor ushered her towards the door and still she droned on. "I'm sincerely trying to help. I'm just next door when you do want to talk."

Connor closed the lounge door behind them both. He'd be no doubt giving her a firm talking to on the way to the front door.

Ruth's eyebrows came together. "What the hell just happened? For God's sake, the woman's crazy."

"She is. I can't stand her. Why Dan liked her, I really don't know. The pair of them were like a mutual appreciation society. I'm used to her, but even I'm shocked at her coming round and saying that. If ever there was a reason for selling up and moving away, it'd be getting rid of her as a neighbour."

"God, don't say that. Moving away should be the last thing on your mind. We need you here were we can keep an eye on you."

Lorna clasped her hands together to stop them shaking; Phyllis had rattled her. "Course I'm not moving. I meant more when . . . when Dan was alive."

Connor came into the room and threw himself in the armchair. "The cheek of the woman, who the hell does she think she is?"

"She's a nightmare, honestly," Lorna said feeling sick to the pit of her stomach, "how dare she come round spouting that rubbish."

"The bloody nerve. As if we don't have enough to deal with." He looked at his empty coffee cup, "I don't know about anyone else, but I could do with something stronger than coffee right now."

"There's plenty of brandy in the dining room cupboard. Do you want me to go and get it?"

"No, I will."

Connor stood up and made his way to the door. He paused, half in the lounge, half out of it with a woeful expression on his face.

"If only she wasn't such a crackpot and it was true."

Chapter 31

The journey to the hotel to meet Perry had taken for ever. Lorna had gone by train rather than drive as she didn't want her car appearing on CCTV. It was ridiculous taking so many precautions, but she was more scared now than ever, even though neither of them were under suspicion for Ingrid and Dan's deaths. And it wasn't as if she couldn't legitimately meet a friend, especially when they shared such a traumatic experience. She'd managed to hold it together somehow the last few weeks since returning from Greece, but only with regular telephone conversations with Perry from their secret second phones.

Connor had sorted her out with a new iPhone and even though she did have Perry's new number in as a contact, they didn't use those. Perry advised caution and sticking with the pay-as-you-go phones until such a time as they could begin the charade of meeting up, supporting each other and eventually becoming a legitimate item, drawn together by the deaths of their spouses. But she knew that was a while off yet, at least until Dan's body was recovered.

As soon as she'd closed the door of the hotel room, her and Perry had practically ripped each other's clothes off. They made love frantically. It had been weeks since they'd been intimate. During the time of Perry and Ingrid living next door, they'd managed once to meet up at her mother's house in Leicester, she on the pre-text of visiting her mother in the care home, and Perry supposedly returning to London to sign some papers relating to his late father. She recalled the irony that Ingrid had moaned about being on her own while Perry was in London, and did she fancy a girlie day out? The other time they'd actually made love was by meeting in woods and behaving like two teenagers in the back of the car. Both of them had to return to their respective spouses, but the closeness between them helped the momentum of their plan moving forward.

Their lovemaking today had been intense, passionate and deeply satisfying. It was the first time they'd been alone together since the boating accident. Fully satiated in the king bed, Lorna pressed her naked body into his. He lifted her hand to his lips and kissed it. "God, I've missed you."

The difference in their skin colours always fascinated Lorna. Due to Perry's mixed-race heritage, his honey brown skin made a sharp contrast to her milky white colouring.

"Me too. How are your hands?" she asked looking at the healed skin on his palm.

"Fine. Still a bit tender, but I'm okay."

She reached up to his forehead and stroked his scar. "I can't believe I did this to you."

"You didn't. Your cut was tiny, I aggravated it."

"Gosh," she winced, "I thought you must have done.

Don't tell me how you did that, nor how you burnt your hands. I can't bear the thought of it."

His kissed her head. "You are lovely."

She could hear his heart beating as her head rested on his chest. "I've missed this. I've missed us. It seems for ever since the last time. I'm really struggling right now with all of this."

"I know, but you have to keep strong. We knew this bit would be the hardest."

"It's much worse than I envisaged, though. Can't you visit me or something? We're both grieving so it's probable we will be comforting each other."

"I don't know about that," he rubbed his forehead, "maybe a chat on the phone, yes, but not meeting up. The plan was always to keep apart. It'd look odd if I came visiting now."

"But you've got to come and empty the house, haven't you?"

"I've organised a firm to pack the stuff up and bring it to London. It looks better that way."

Her heart plummeted. She'd been so looking forward to him returning next door. She knew he wouldn't be there long, but to have him close by even for a day or two would have helped.

"I need to see you," she said firmly, "I can't carry on like this."

"Hey," he leant on his elbow so his face was close to hers. "It's hard for me too. But we have to hold tight for a while yet. Remember, I've only just had Ingrid's funeral. I'm supposed to be grieving."

"This isn't how it was supposed to happen though. My nerves are shredded to bits without Dan's body. Connor's going on about some sort of memorial now."

"That's not a bad idea, if it helps."

"How can it help," her voice went up an octave, "a coffin without a body in it?"

"Hey, come on now, they don't have coffins at memorial services," he must have spotted the genuine tears in her eyes, "don't get upset. I was just thinking a service might give you closure."

"What closure? There is no closure. Without Dan's body I'm in limbo. It's torture."

"I know, I know. Come on, shush, we've come this far, just a bit longer now. You've done so well. I need you to stay strong."

"But how can I? I can't move on. I thought by now we'd have had a funeral and I could be tentatively looking at a short break away. Right now, I'm stuck at home with Ruth and Connor suffocating me. I just want Dan to be found."

"I know. I do too."

"If he isn't found, I'm stuck. I can't do a single thing. I can't sell the house, the business. I can't even access his bank accounts. I need him to be found. Why is it taking so long?"

"I don't know. I never expected this either. But don't worry about money, I've told you, I have money."

"It's not about the money. I have money. I just want it all sorting. I'm scared."

"Scared about what? We've got through the hardest

part."

"You have you mean. I haven't. Ruth's on my case suggesting I need to see a doctor now."

"What do you need a doctor for? You're fine."

"I'm not fine. My nerves are in shreds. I can't eat, I can't sleep, I feel sick all the time. I'm climbing the walls. If I could see you, I'd be okay. It's the being apart that's torture. I ask myself some days if it was all worth it."

"Course it's bloody worth it. You want us to be together, don't you? I love you."

"I know you do and I love you too. I thought the hardest bit was over, but not being with you is even worse."

"You just need to hold tight for a couple more months. Then we'll be together for the rest of our lives. I'll have the inheritance and we'll start our new life together. We'll want for nothing."

"I can't wait, though." She lowered her voice to almost a whisper even though nobody was nearby. "If they could just find Dan's body, I'd be able to settle everything. I can't believe none of the insurances will pay out without it. I'm even fighting the banks as I have no death certificate and he's currently still missing. Can you believe it?"

"No, I can't."

He extracted himself from her and threw the covers off. She gazed at his naked body as he made his way towards the dressing table and reached for the bottle of champagne on ice. As he opened it and poured two glasses, the tummy butterflies fluttered as she admired his toned limbs and bronze skin. If a man could be beautiful, then Perry was. She was overwhelmed with love for him and the fact he now belonged to her. But occasional days in hotels weren't enough.

He placed the glasses on the bedside table and reached for his pillows to put behind her so she was sitting up. He sat down on the bed next to her and handed her a glass.

He raised his. "To the clever, gorgeous, desirable Lorna, the woman who makes my heart beat a tiny bit faster every time I see her. I love you, you know that don't you?"

He was trying to lighten the mood and she loved him for it. "Of course I do. And I feel exactly the same. That's why it's so hard not being with you."

"I know. But I need you to hold on, just for a bit longer. We're almost there."

He was right. She knew that. Perry was sharp and intelligent and so far, everything had gone according to plan. Except Dan not being found.

"Do you think it's karma?" she asked taking a sip of her drink.

Perry frowned, "What's made you say that?"

"'Cause this isn't what we planned." She ran her tongue around her lips, "I just wonder sometimes if it's karma getting one back at me."

"Course it isn't karma. You'll get that call about Dan soon enough and then you can start sorting stuff out. But if not, you don't need to worry. I'll have all the old man's money soon. And there's no Ingrid to make a claim, so you and I can be together through our grief, just as we planned."

"I want that more than anything."

"Me too. We haven't done all this for nothing. We will be together, we just have to take it steady for now. We can't have any suspicion whatsoever pointing at either of us. We have to keep apart."

"But for how long? I'm going out of my mind not being with you."

"Look, I think a memorial service for Dan would be good first of all. That way you'll be able to start moving forward. Maybe then start back at work . . ."

"I'm not going back to work," she snapped, "no way. I can't," she shook her head, "I just can't. I need to move away as soon as I can. I'll tell Connor and Ruth I'm going to stay at Mum's house."

"That's silly though, for the sake of a few months."

"I can't stay in the house, everywhere I look I'm reminded of Dan. And every day, from going to bed at night, to getting up each morning, I think about what we've done. I feel like I'm going mad."

"But won't your family think it's odd? The last thing we want is them questioning anything. Surely you can see any grieving woman who loved her husband would want to be in the marital home where she'd been happy?"

"And some would have to get away for a while and I'm going to be one of them. I'm not staying there a minute longer than I have to." She took his drink off him and placed it on the bedside table with hers and took his hands in hers, "Don't make me stay there, I want to be with you," she pleaded with her eyes, "I need to be with you. You said we'd be together."

"I know I did, but I never expected that Dan wouldn't be found. Surely you can see it changes things."

"No, I can't. He's still gone and not coming back. I'll give it a few more weeks and have this memorial, but then I'm leaving. I'll get something temporary. But I'm not staying there any longer. I need to be close to you."

"Okay, calm down. You're right, have the memorial, that's step one." He reached for his drink and walked back round to his side of the bed.

"Will you come?" she asked as he got back in beside her, took his pillows back and lay down.

"I guess so," he turned towards her and tucked his arms underneath the pillows, "if you want me to be there."

"I do. I can get through it then if you're there."

"Okay, then I'll come. But I won't be near you though, it'll have to be respectful and I'll leave as soon as it's appropriate."

"That's fine. Just knowing you're there will help."

"Right, so that's sorted. How about I book us another hotel somewhere and we meet up again after the memorial? You can visit your mother at the care home and then come and meet me and we'll have some time together. Then we can plan our next steps."

Her mood was lighter. She stroked the side of his handsome face. "It's sounding better already."

"Good. Now," he kissed her gently, "what next? Do you want to go downstairs to the restaurant to grab something to eat," she felt his hardness against her leg, "or do you fancy something else?" His lips kissed their way down her neck. "You decide."

She took his head in her hands and brought it close to her face. "I'll go for the something else," she breathed, kissing him deeply.

Chapter 32

"Morning, Connor," Lorna put her iPhone on speaker while she loaded two days' worth of wine glasses and coffee cups into the dishwasher.

"Hi," he answered, "I was going to ring you later."

"Can you talk now or shall I ring back?"

"No, it's fine. It was to tell you I've had a word with Nigel and he's agreed to work up to four days to help out, but he doesn't want it permanently."

"I didn't expect he would, he sold the business to Dan so he could semi-retire."

"Yeah. I'm relieved though, even if it is only temporary, as it gives me a chance to try and get another accountant to help out. I'm going to put an advert out."

"You're a brick, you really are. Thanks for sorting that."

"Don't thank me yet until I've got someone. There aren't an abundance of qualified accountants looking for work."

She sighed heavily, "It's such a mess, isn't it? I wish we could just sell the business as a going concern."

"Me too, even if it does put me out of work. It's not an option though, sadly."

He was right. There were no options. Not unless Dan's body was found. They were stuck in limbo and the best they could do was continue to keep going. Each night she would go to bed praying news would come the next day, and each morning she woke up willing it to be their last day of torment. Surely the sea had to give him up soon?

"Dan would be really proud of you looking after the business."

She heard Connor's intake of breath. He was struggling emotionally. Ruth had told her that much. Her mission now was to move on and extract herself from the past. Only then might she get closure. Coming to terms with what they'd done was becoming more stressful each day, not easier as Perry had said it would.

"How was your mother?" she heard the crack in his voice as he changed the subject.

"Okay," she lied. Supposedly visiting her mother had been a good cover for seeing Perry. "I can see a slow deterioration though."

"Did you tell her about Dan?"

"No. It'd be too much of a shock. She was so fond of him. The only problem is, it's her birthday coming up and she'll expect him then. He always makes a point of visiting on her birthday, or *made* a point, I should say."

"Yeah, that's my brother for you. He put a lot of store in birthdays."

"Yes, he did," she said, remembering the personal presents she'd been the recipient of each year on her own birthday. But she mustn't think of that now. Dan was gone and the task ahead was moving on.

"Anyway, the reason why I was ringing was, I've been thinking while I was away, you're right, a memorial for

Dan might be a good thing. It'll give family and friends the chance to . . ." she purposely paused to convey difficulty, "a chance to say their goodbyes." Perry's advice had been to go ahead and he was never far wrong.

"I'm glad you've reconsidered," the relief was evident in Connor's voice, "it'll help us all, even you, I'm sure of it."

"You're right, but I wouldn't know where to start organising something like that."

"Leave it with me. I'll get an appointment with a funeral director. We could go together . . . if that's what you want?"

"Course it's what I want. I couldn't do it without you. You have to be involved."

"Thanks. It might actually help me, I'm barely getting through each day. I can only imagine how hard it is for you."

She inserted a convincing level of anguish into her voice, "It is so hard, but I've got you and Ruth, and I thank my lucky stars every day for that. Anyway, I'm sorry to have to cut you off, but I've got an appointment at work. They've asked me to come in."

"Are you thinking of going back?"

"No, the opposite actually, I'm going to tell them today I'm not coming back."

"Are you sure? You might find work could help. Not straight away, maybe after the memorial. It'd be nice to have something to focus on."

"Yeah, I hear what you're saying, but I really don't want to. I want to focus on my mother right now."

"Of course, you do what's best. I'll catch you later, then."

"Will do. Thanks, Connor."

She cut the call. No way was she returning to work. Once they'd had the wretched memorial service, she was moving to Leicester and would temporarily stay at her mother's house. Perry could then visit, or she could meet him in hotels. Anything was better than having minders Ruth and Connor scrutinising her every move. And even though she couldn't sell her own house, she would be able to rent it out. Dan had to be found soon – the length of time it was taking, was killing her.

After a short drive to the medical practice, she locked her car and approached her place of work for the past couple of years. Her stomach was in knots as she knew her work colleagues would be fawning over her when she went in. They'd all been generous with their cards and flowers, but right now she could barely face their condolences and well-meaning hugs. People of late seemed intent on hugging her, which she hated. She'd never been a hugging sort of person. But she'd have to put up and shut up as today was about terminating her employment and taking her one step closer to being with Perry. And despite him urging her once the memorial service was over, to return to work, there wasn't a cat in hell's chance she would. She wouldn't miss this place and certainly not Elspeth breathing down her neck at every opportunity. The only thing she would miss was working with Sarah. They always had a laugh together and were good friends.

She was bang on time, according to her watch. Good – she needed to be in and out of there quickly. Sarah was actually off work today and calling round her house once Lorna had done here. It was a lovely day, she'd dragged the garden furniture out of the garage so they could have a drink in the sunshine, and maybe lunch alfresco, too. Although she told Connor and Ruth she preferred solitude, in reality, it sucked. Looking forward to her friend visiting had lifted her spirits a little.

As she tapped on the admin office door and walked in, her work colleagues each jumped up from their desks and rushed towards her for the obligatory hug.

"It's so lovely to see you," newly married Amy said, "We've missed you so much."

"Aw, thank you. How are you doing, you look fab. Married life suits you."

Amy flushed, "Never mind about me, how are you doing?" she asked with a slight tilt of her head. Everyone was silent, waiting for her to speak. What they were expecting she wasn't sure but she was well versed in going through the motions.

"I'm okay. Some days are harder than others."

"I'm sure," Amy nodded sympathetically.

"Did you get our flowers?" Becky, her admin colleague asked.

"Yes, I did." As if anyone was remotely interested in flowers. She was sick to death of bloody flowers. "Thank you." She glanced at the wall clock, "I've got an appointment to see Elspeth, so I'd better not be late."

"Call in and see us before you go, yeah?" Amy said.

"Of course." She had no intention of doing so. Her days at the practice were done. As soon as she'd finished with Elspeth, she was out of there.

She made her way to Elspeth's office. It had a small glass window which enabled her to see directly into the admin office and the staff working. No doubt she was watching her right now.

Lorna knocked, and once summoned to go inside, she cracked her lips in a semi smile at the Rottweiler sat at her desk. Recently widowed, it wasn't expected she'd be a full ray of sunshine.

"Hello."

Elspeth stood up. "Hello, Lorna. Come in. How are you?"

Her expression seemed respectful and her voice was kind, but Lorna knew it was false. However, she had to play the game.

"As well as can be expected."

"Please, take a seat," Elspeth nodded at the seat opposite her. "We're all terribly sorry about what has happened. I can only imagine how hard it must be for you. You're getting plenty of support from your relatives, Sarah tells me?"

"Yes, they've been marvellous. We've made a decision to have a memorial service for Dan and then I may look at moving away."

"I see. Have you any idea yet where you might move to?"

Lorna painted on the wounded soldier expression. "My mother has a house in Leicester. She has dementia and is in a care home there. I'm going to stay there for a while until I get back on my feet and then decide what I'm going to do."

"I do understand. You must do what's right for you. I'm just going to buzz Dr Varma as he asked me to let him know when you came in. He wants a quick word."

"Oh, right."

Elspeth picked up the phone and keyed in the internal number. Seconds later, the door opened and Dr Varma came in. "Lorna," he extended his arms, so she felt it necessary to stand and be drawn into them. It felt most uncomfortable. She pulled away as quickly as was acceptable but remained standing. Sitting opposite Elspeth at her desk had made her feel almost subservient. No doubt that was the effect the witch was striving for.

"What a wretched business for you," Dr Varma said sympathetically, "I am so sorry about your husband, and the other lady that was killed. What an enormous shock it must have been."

"It was. Still is, actually."

"I'm sure. And both so young."

"They were, yes. I'm in the process of organising a memorial service for Dan and then I'm probably going away for a few months to be near my mother in Leicester. She's in a care home there."

"Ah, I see. We could maybe offer you a sabbatical if that would help?" He turned to Elspeth for affirmation it would be acceptable under the circumstances, but her face was rigid. Not that she'd dare argue though with the GP who paid her salary.

"We wouldn't be able to pay," Elspeth said through gritted teeth, "that's the thing, as we'd need to replace Lorna, but we could certainly look at extended leave without pay."

Dr Varma looked uncomfortable and much as Lorna would love to push it, she couldn't be bothered. It wasn't as if she was ever coming back. And she knew ultimately he'd agree with Elspeth. GP partners were a tight-fisted bunch in her experience.

She gave Elspeth an insolent glare. "You've no need to worry, I won't be coming back."

Elspeth made an exaggerated, not understanding frown, while Dr Varma shuffled uncomfortably on the spot. Lorna carried on, "I know you've never liked me, even though I'd worked hard for this practice long before you came to it. But you've always had it in for me . . . it's no good looking at me like that, you know what I'm talking about. It's sad really that as a grown woman you've seen fit to single me out for scrutiny while the other ones, much younger than me are pulling the wool over your eyes. But you've missed all that by focusing on me all the time, trying to trip me up and catch me out."

"I've done no such thing," Elspeth snapped. "My focus has always been to make necessary changes, as that's what I'm employed to do. And let's be straight, you haven't always been co-operative."

"That's enough," Dr Varma interrupted, before

turning to her with compassion in his eyes. "You've suffered a terrible loss, Lorna, and we fully understand your desire to move forward with your life. We'll ensure that you're given one month's termination of your contract from today and won't of course enforce that you have to come in and work, due to your current circumstances."

"Thank you," she nodded gratefully. She knew any second he would leave as there'd be patients waiting and she didn't want to be on her own with Elspeth a minute longer. "I think it's best I go now if you'll excuse me. I've said what I came to say."

"Yes, of course, I'll walk you out," he smiled kindly, no doubt wanting to minimise any further contact with Elspeth. He held the door open for her and she walked out of the office. Elspeth was no doubt smarting, but she didn't acknowledge her as she followed Dr Varma through the corridor, into reception and towards the exit. She was expecting him to say goodbye at the automatic door, but surprisingly he followed her through it to the outside of the building.

He touched her arm gently, "I want you to come to the surgery to see me . . . as a patient."

"Why? There's nothing wrong with me."

"I'd like you to come," he ignored the question, "how about Friday afternoon? I have some time set aside for paperwork. You could come at a time to suit you."

"That's kind but there's really no need."

"I think there is. A check-up might be helpful before you move on." He didn't give her a chance to respond further. "We can talk properly then. And please let us know when you have a date for Dan's memorial. I'd like to book some time out to attend and I'm sure some of your colleagues would too."

"I'll let you know. And despite what Elspeth thinks of me, I have enjoyed working here. I'll miss it."

"That is nice to hear. We've enjoyed you working for us and I'll be happy to provide you with a reference for any future employment, when you're ready, of course."

"Thank you," she said meekly. As if she was ever going to work again. She'd be too busy living with Perry and his inheritance.

"Well, I'd better crack on," he raised his eyebrows, "patients waiting and all that. Do take care of yourself. Grief can be terribly exhausting and complex. We'll discuss it more on Friday."

She nodded compliantly, doubting she would see him as a patient, even though she could definitely do with some medication for her shredded nerves and sleep deprivation. Rather than growing into the role of the grieving widow, the pretence was becoming increasingly more difficult as each day passed.

Chapter 33

Lorna got into her car in the health centre car park and messaged Sarah.

A chilled glass of wine at mine when you're ready X

As she drove the short distance home, she put the air conditioning on as it was getting warm. Her desire had always been to have a cabriolet car, something nippy and quick but Dan would never have one. Far too much money, he'd say, for a few months a year to drive around with the top off. Well, she'd be having one soon, that was for sure. Perry would buy her one. Despite her increasing anxiety about what they'd both done, she still got a lift when she thought of their future and the surplus money they'd have. Perry had said it was for spending and that's what she intended to do.

She pulled into the drive at the front of the house, applied the handbrake and switched off the engine. She'd always had an eye for class, and the impressive, detached town house smacked of quality. That's why she'd pestered Dan for it. Once she'd spotted it being built, she had to have it. And the way in which she'd co-ordinated the interior with the soft furnishing, was a great source of pride. She stared at the large bay window with her designer French vase dominating the sill and the beautiful swags and tail drapes that she'd had to have. They were made by a German designer and the cost of the material had been astronomical, but they'd been worth every penny. The window looked stunning. Her gaze was drawn to the top of the bay and the small open window on its latch. Her heart started pounding . . . she hadn't left the window open. She knew that categorically. Was someone inside the house?

As she exited the car, she purposely banged the door hoping the noise would disturb anyone if that was the case.

"Good morning, dear," Phyllis was hovering in her front garden clutching a watering can. "It's so hot for these poor pansies; I'm trying to keep them hydrated. How are you?"

Lorna didn't have time for busybody Phyllis, she wanted to go into the house.

"As well as can be expected," she said, swiftly walking past.

"That's good," Phyllis edged along, keeping up with her, "although I must say you look as if you've been losing a bit of weight."

Only Phyllis could be impolite to someone recently widowed. Lorna ignored her comment. "You're going to have to excuse me, I'm in a bit of a rush. I have a friend calling to see me so I need to tidy round before she gets here."

"Oh, I wouldn't worry about tidying up. Your friend isn't coming to see the state of your house, she'll be here to see you."

"You're right." She didn't give her chance to reply as she headed towards her front door and put her key in the lock, desperate to get to the lounge. The open window was really bothering her.

"Bye," Phyllis called as Lorna closed the door. She was being rude and knew it, but she didn't care. Why was the window open?

The house felt empty. She was pretty sure nobody was inside but still, her hand was shaking as she opened the lounge door. And even though the open window had spooked her, her stomach dropped as if she was in a lift plummeting downwards as she stared at Dan's reading chair in the bay window. Its position had changed. The chair was a source of argument between her and Dan. He always moved it the way he preferred it to get the maximum light, whereas she preferred it in the position that suited the room and was always quick to move it back. Never did she go to bed without the chair being in its correct place. She used to chastise him about the brass casters making indentations in the carpet, but he took no notice. His flippant reply invariably was to leave it where he put it, as he was the only person that used the seat in the window and it was fine the way he had it. But she never took any notice of him. What did he know about interior design and positioning of furniture?

Her eyes remained fixed on the burgundy velour armchair and the small open window above it. Someone had been in the house and put them like that. She wasn't imagining it. She knew categorically they had. There was no way she would even move that chair to that position and she certainly hadn't opened the window before she left that morning.

She swiftly checked around the rest of the house, half expecting drawers to be open and contents strewn all over the place. But everything was as she always left it. As far as she could see, nothing was untoward. Even her jewellery was where it should be, neatly organised in the bedroom drawer. Satisfied that nothing had been taken, she returned to the kitchen and reached in her handbag for her phone to call Connor. He was the only person with a spare key so it must have been him. But why move things around? It didn't make any sense. She pressed his number but a knock at the back door stopped her waiting for an answer. She hung up.

"What's going on?" Sarah asked as Lorna opened the door, "It's not like you to have your door locked."

"Sorry, I've only just got back from the surgery."

"Oh right." Lorna pulled a face, "How did it go?"

"Let's grab a glass of wine. I thought we could sit outside and I can tell you all about it. Is a glass of rosé okay?"

"Perfect."

They sat together in the garden underneath the parasol to keep the searing sun off themselves. Despite the shade, it was warm and sticky.

Sarah took a gulp of her wine. "Just what the doctor ordered. So come on, tell me, how did it go with Elspeth?"

"Exactly as you'd expect. She tried to fake concern but I could see straight through her. Dr Varma came in and wished me well. Such a contrast since the last time when he was berating me for the delay on that referral that somehow got in my drawer by mistake. Anyway, he was lovely, he even suggested I go see him as a patient."

"Really? And will you?"

"I'm not sure. I don't really know what he can do. It is what it is. I just have to work through it. Plenty of women lose their husbands."

"Yeah, but not as young as Dan, and in such tragic circumstances. Anyone would be struggling."

"Mmm, I'll have to see. It certainly wouldn't hurt having a chat with him."

"No, it wouldn't. Anyway, were they shocked about you leaving?"

"I think relieved more like. Dr Varma made noises about me taking a sabbatical, but I said no and that I wanted a clean break."

"Are you really going to your mum's? I don't get why you have to dash off from here when it has all your memories of Dan. And we're all here to support you, you'll have nobody in Leicester. Why the rush?"

Because I want to be with the man I love, she wanted to scream.

"I know it seems odd, but honestly Sarah, to me the house seems oppressive now. I'm not comfortable here anymore."

"You might feel differently when . . . you know . . . they find Dan?"

"Maybe, but how long is that going to be? The Greek authorities told me it could be months and I need to prepare myself that it might be never."

Sarah leant across and squeezed her hand, "It's so awful for you that your life's on hold, while that other chap, what's his name . . .?"

"Perry."

"Yeah, Perry, he gets to move on with his life. He's lucky . . . sorry, that's not the right word, but you know what I mean. By having a funeral for his wife, he gets closure." She took another sip of her wine, "Do you think he'll come to Dan's memorial?"

"I don't know to be honest," Lorna lied, "I'm not really in touch with him. At first when we got back from Greece we exchanged a few messages, but nothing since his wife's funeral. He understood I couldn't face going with . . . no news on Dan."

"It must be hard for you both," sadness was etched on Sarah's face, "you've got the accident in common, but neither of you want to relive it. It's probably best you don't keep in touch."

Lorna's mobile interrupted them. "Do you mind if I take this. It's Connor ringing me back."

"Of course, go ahead."

She pressed accept.

"Hi, Lorna, did I miss a call from you?"

"Hi, Connor, yes, but it wasn't urgent. I just wanted to know if you stopped by the house at all this morning while I was out?"

"No. Why, what's wrong?"

"Nothing's wrong. I've just got it in my head that someone had opened the bay window while I was out. I hadn't, but it was open when I came back." She didn't mention Dan's chair had moved.

"Not me. Does anyone else have a key . . . a friend or anything?"

"No, just you. And a friend wouldn't let herself in, I'm sure. I thought the likeliest explanation was you."

"Nah, I'm afraid not. I bet you didn't shut it yesterday and it's been open all night. You don't use the front lounge much anyway do you?"

"Not really." Certainly not now, anyway. They used to most evenings as it has the large wide screen TV, and invariably Dan would sit in his window seat until he lost the light.

"Are you okay? Do you want me to come round?"

"No, honestly, there's no need. I've got my friend here, which is nice."

"Good you've got some company. I'll ring you tonight, then."

"Yeah, okay."

"Bye for now." He cut the call and she put her mobile down on the table.

"What are you on about?" Sarah asked, her perfectly sculptured eyebrows frowning.

"When I got back from the surgery, the small window at the top of the bay was open. I didn't leave it like that, I know I didn't. That's why I was asking Connor if he'd been in the house and opened it."

"And it sounds like he hasn't?"

"No."

"Then you must have and you've forgotten. You're bound to be all over the place right now. I'm sure that's what's happened. You've just been thinking about something else and your mind hasn't registered you've done it. I do that all the time with my hair straighteners. I forget sometimes if I've switched them off. I always have done, but I don't seem to recollect doing so."

Sarah meant well, but Lorna knew categorically she hadn't opened the window and forgotten. She'd not even set foot in the lounge that morning.

"It's not just the window though," Lorna sighed wearily, "Dan's reading chair has moved. I have it a certain way, which Dan never liked. So he used to move it when he was reading. I'd always put it back though when we went to bed. It irritated me to death so I know I wouldn't leave it the way it was when I came in. Seeing his chair had moved, sort of unnerved me."

Sarah frowned, "Are you sure nobody else has a key?"

"No, only Connor."

"That is odd then. You don't think you might have been sleepwalking or something and moved it yourself? It would explain a lot."

"Don't be daft. I don't sleepwalk. At least I don't think I do."

"Well, I don't know then. You're not worried are you?"

"No, not really. Like you say, it's just really odd."

"Maybe it might help for you to see Dr Varma? Especially if you have opened the window and can't remember doing it. I'm no expert on grief, but you have been through an awful lot. You must be on tenterhooks every minute of the day, waiting for news."

"You're not wrong there. I'll have to see. I might take Dr Varma up on his offer and go and have a chat. Anyway," she reached for Sarah's glass, "I'll get us a top up and then I can tell you how I told Elspeth she could stuff her job."

"Oh, God, I can't wait for that. Someone finally standing up to her."

Lorna made her way into the kitchen and opened the fridge for the rosé wine. Unease still flowed through her veins about the window and chair . . . something wasn't right. But she pushed it to the back of her mind as she filled the two glasses, ready to embellish what happened with Elspeth. Although she had told Elspeth she wasn't coming back to work, the way she had done so wasn't half as exciting as telling her to stuff her job would have been.

She selected some olives from the fridge and, after placing them in a bowl, she reached in one of the cupboards for some cocktail sticks and a tray to carry it all outside.

"Here we go," she placed the tray on the table and took her seat. "Before I forget, thanks for coming to see me today. The days are really long, you know, waiting for news. I'm glad to have some company."

"Hey, don't be daft. That's what friends are for." Sarah reached for a cocktail stick, pierced an olive, and chewed on it. "You'll get through this, I know you will.

Get the memorial service over, and I'm sure you'll feel better after that."

"Let's hope so," Lorna gave a nod of agreement when in fact, nothing was further from the truth. Right now, it seemed like an enormous mountain she had to climb. She didn't see the memorial service making one bit of difference. As far as she was concerned, the only way she'd be able to move on was once Dan's body washed up.

Chapter 34

The funeral director had sympathetically taken her and Connor through the proposed memorial service.

"Is there anything else you would like that maybe we haven't considered?" the middle-aged man in his sombre black suit and fixed compassionate expression asked.

"No, I think that's everything." She turned to Connor, "Are you happy with it all?"

"Yes, it all seems fine to me . . . under the circumstances."

The funeral director nodded. "I'm not trying to say any funeral is easy, but it is harder to conduct something of this nature when your husband . . . is still missing, Mrs Lloyd. But I can assure you, the service will be fitting."

"Yes, I'm sure it will. Thank you."

"And you've met with the vicar, I understand?"

"Yes, it's all sorted," Connor answered. He'd helped her with the epitaph imparting anecdotes from Dan's youth.

"If you think of anything else before Friday, you know where we are. We'll collect you all from your house at ten fifteen."

Outside, Cnnor gave her a hug before she got into her car.

"You're coming to us on Friday after the service, no arguing," he said holding onto the car door as she got in. "Ruth wants you to come the night before, but I said you wouldn't."

No, she wouldn't. Her evening would be spent talking to Perry. Like every evening.

"You know me well. I'll be fine, I quite like the solitude of being on my own. But that's kind of Ruth so I will stay after the service. But only for one night though, then I want to go home." She hadn't yet told Connor that she was intending to move away. That could wait until after the service.

"Okay, I'll tell her. I'd better get back to work. I want to see Nigel before he goes on holiday."

"Thanks Connor for all you've done. You are doing an amazing job keeping the practice going. Dan would be so proud of you."

He'd really stepped up since the accident. Even she'd been surprised how supportive he'd become.

"And you," Connor smiled affectionately, "he'd be proud of how well you've done too. Let's do our best on Friday to make it all about Dan. "

"We will. We'll make sure he gets a good send off."

"Okay, speak later. I'll call you tonight."

Her heart was a little lighter as she parked her car on the drive and headed inside the house through the kitchen door. She put her bag down and glanced at the kitchen clock. Another hour and Perry would ring. He'd had an appointment himself that morning in London to meet with the solicitors about his father's estate. He'd been buoyant on the phone the previous evening, the twelve months searching for his father's daughter were almost at an end.

She made her way towards the kitchen unit and reached for the kettle, intending to fill it. As she touched it, she almost jumped back as if she'd got an electric shock. The kettle was hot. It had recently boiled. She stared at it. She didn't get it. She'd been away from the house that morning for over two hours and even then, her last coffee had been early before her shower and getting ready. What the hell was going on? The kettle had been most certainly recently boiled. The only person with a key was Connor and she'd only just left him, so he had no time to dash to her house and boil it. And why would he? There had to be another explanation. Someone had to have access to the house. And whoever it was, was letting her know they were watching. The hot kettle confirmed she wasn't going mad with the window that was left open and Dan's chair being moved. It was obvious someone was trying to frighten her.

But who, and more importantly, why?

Chapter 35

Perry was sitting in the prestigious London office of his late father's lawyers. David Blyth was the partner dealing with the estate and tasked with finding the elusive illegitimate daughter. Perry was confident they wouldn't locate her.

"Before we start, may I offer my condolences and those of the partners on your recent loss?"

"Thank you." Perry nodded. He didn't want to get into a conversation about Ingrid, least of all anyone with a legal background. "It's been a difficult time."

"Yes, I'm sure. Can I offer you any refreshments?"

"Not for me, I'm fine."

"Right, well I'll come straight to the point. Despite the enormous resources we've ploughed into trying to locate your father's daughter, I'm afraid we haven't been able to. Therefore, at the recent meeting with the partners to discuss the estate, the consensus was that we resolve the estate, and I'm in complete agreement with that. Your father's stipulation was that we searched for twelve months following his death, and at this moment in time, we're only weeks away for that period to end. My instinct is, that it's highly unlikely we'll unearth anything now after all this time."

"I see. Do you think the child could have died? You know, when it was born?"

"We considered that but still came up with nothing. So, the plan going forward," he peered over his gold-rimmed glasses, "with your approval, of course, is to begin the transferral of documents relating to Gayton Manor and the estate. Your father bequeathed monies to others which we need to make you aware of, and there are caveats that need to be honoured which we'll go over with you."

"Yes, I know about those."

Perry appeared calm and matter-of-fact, but deep inside a surge of elation gushed through him. It was all coming together exactly as he'd always planned. And now there was no longer Ingrid in the equation, the old man's considerable wealth would be his. He knew of the bequeathed monies which had been discussed at the original reading of the will. They were a pittance compared to what he would inherit.

After further discussion about the probate process and the distribution of his father's considerable assets, Perry left the offices and walked the short distance to his car and checked the meter. Only minutes left – timing was everything. It felt like a good day. He got into his car, started the ignition and headed home. All he ever wanted was now within his reach. Due to his endeavours, there was no longer a legal wife to make a claim on anything, and he'd been fortunate that Ingrid's father didn't live in the UK. He couldn't face seeing him regularly and have to keep up the pretence of mourning his daughter. Not that he owed him any respect. He'd never been parent of the year to Ingrid. It sounded like she hadn't had the best upbringing with him. Her mother had died from leukaemia when Ingrid was ten and apparently, during her teenage years, she became rebellious. When he'd initially met her, she was travelling around Europe with friends, but quickly they became a couple. She had always said, meeting him had transformed her life.

From the time of meeting, until her death, Ingrid had adored him, which he thrived on. His father had berated him furiously once he learned of their quickie wedding in Vegas, and even though Perry hated his self-righteousness, he'd been right. He'd put his inheritance at risk if they split up. He'd been hasty. It wasn't as if Ingrid was truly *the one* for him, either. That accolade was reserved for only one woman, Ingrid was always second best. And once he'd rekindled his relationship with Lorna, she became surplus to his requirements. However, getting rid of her without a divorce was a significant challenge.

But the answer came one dark November night. He'd had a vivid dream in which he murdered Ingrid. He'd woken up and remembered every single detail of the dream clearly, but dismissed it as a preposterous idea. However, over a period of time, it became more of a reality, particularly when he renewed his relationship with Lorna. Ingrid ultimately had to go, and divorce wasn't an option. During that time he was secretly meeting Lorna at her mother's house in Leicester, and he told her about the dream. Surprisingly, she wasn't as horrified as he'd expected. So, what began as a piece of fantasy, soon developed into a compelling strategy which gained momentum until eventually, it became a full-scale planning operation. And Dan quickly came into the equation with him and Lorna realising that if both their spouses died, they'd be free to be together. And they surmised no suspicion would be placed upon a rich heir, if two people had died in the boating accident opposed to just his wife.

It had been so easy to play Ingrid. She'd known the story about his father's illegitimate daughter and how he had teams striving to find her. On the few occasions his father met Ingrid, he discussed his desire to find his genetic daughter, so it hadn't been anything secret. But Perry did have an enormous secret. One he hadn't shared with anyone, not even Lorna.

The drive home was slow. There was obviously some sort of accident ahead as he'd been virtually static for fifteen minutes or so. He reached for a mint. The roundness of the mint with a hole reminded him of another time in his life when he was much younger. He would visit his father during the school holidays where he was left pretty much to his own devices. The old man was either busy with the staff and estate, or entertaining his latest floozy. So the young Perry had to make his own entertainment. He'd play in the woods with his bow and arrow, or his toy gun, shooting the enemy and galloping away on his pretend horse. He'd often bump into Ted, one of the older groundsmen on the estate. Ted was a great man for a young boy to chat to. He was full of exciting stories. They'd sit on a log and Ted would tell him tales of the woods, no doubt greatly embellished, but to Perry's young imagination, it was fascinating. Each holiday he'd look out for Ted, the old man that constantly seemed to suck mints, maybe to disguise his breath, stale from cigarettes. It was evident he was a heavy smoker from his nicotine-stained fingers and patches of yellow on his grey beard. But Perry only ever saw him sucking mints.

Each school holiday at Gayton Manor, Perry would escape into the woods and he'd always find Ted somewhere. Looking back, Ted was most likely looking out for him too as he always seemed to be there, waiting. Eventually, as the years progressed, Ted retired, but his father allowed him to continue to live in the grace and favour cottage on the outskirts of the estate.

A favourite topic of Perry's was conversing about the parties that used to take place at the great house. Perry remembered those and how the house was decorated luxuriously, the vast array of food laid out in the great dining room and the band playing beautiful melodies in the ballroom to entice the attendees to dance. They were always happy times. His morose mother had lived for those parties. She was always at her best socialising. The young Perry didn't understand how she'd lived for alcohol, but as he grew older, he barely saw her without a drink in her hand. She couldn't function before breakfast without vodka. It had been a terrible time watching her deterioration which ultimately led to her having to leave the house and live in an apartment his father bought for them.

One particular day, walking in the woods with Ted, it started to rain heavily so they'd sheltered in an old, dilapidated hut and Ted continued his tales about the staff employed at the great house. And for some bizarre reason that Perry never understood, Ted shared a huge secret with him and made him promise not to repeat it. Apparently, in his youth, Ted had been fond of a young girl, Mary, that worked in the kitchen. And although Mary appeared to be fond of Ted, seemingly whether through persuasion, or possibly force even, she had become involved with Perry's father. Eventually, she became pregnant and had to leave the house.

Ted seemed to be in a different world talking about Mary. He was saying the words out loud, but it seemed like he was cocooned in his memories as he continued to talk but stared into nothing, almost as if Perry wasn't sat alongside him. He explained how he'd always kept in touch with Mary, through letter writing, so he knew when and where the baby had been born.

Perry didn't keep his promise; he went straight home and told his mother. She'd been horrified. Her fear was that Perry, her only child they had adopted, was going to end up sharing his rightful inheritance if this genetic daughter of his father was ever found. So his mother had devised a plan, and Perry had executed it. It hadn't been easy. He was not even an adult when he did it. But it was a means to an end. As his mother said repeatedly, Ted seemed to be the only one that knew of Mary and her child. He had to go.

To lure Ted into the woods and push him off the muddy embankment towards the river, had taken guts. Perry's heart felt like it was on the outside of his chest, it was thumping so hard as they strolled thought the trees with twigs crunching under their feet. His head was pounding, with perspiration dripping down his back, even though the air felt chilling and numbing. As the rain began to fall, Ted suggested they picked up their pace to get to shelter. Perry chose his moment, waiting until Ted was at a high point of the huge embankment and close to the edge. He lunged forward to give him an almighty push, steadying himself as the embankment's edge crumbled and Ted toppled over. Perry remembered vividly the noise of a pair of jays screeching, but he didn't look down. He ran as fast as his wobbly young legs would take him back to the safety of the main house.

Ted's body had eventually been found and foul play hadn't been considered. He'd been an old man walking in the woods, lost his footing and slipped. And the secret about Mary had died with him. But there was one other secret, one that Ted had told Perry which he hadn't shared with his mother. The young Mary had indeed given birth to a child, but it hadn't been female. She'd given birth to a boy. But she didn't want his father to ever find them as she feared if he'd known he had a male heir, he'd somehow take him away from her. So she'd asked Ted to tell the few staff that knew, she'd given birth to a girl. And it was for that specific reason, Perry had always been confident that his father's *daughter* would never be found. All the time they were searching for a female instead of a male and he was the only person that knew. There was always a chance the son could be found, but it appeared the elusive Mary had covered her tracks well. She almost seemed to have disappeared. And now, according to solicitor David Blyth, they were giving up looking and were to begin distributing the estate.

The traffic started moving but Perry's mind was still in the past. He thought about Ingrid who he'd just buried and how compliant she'd been in his plan. She'd known the story of the illegitimate daughter and had soaked it all up. And one day, he dropped the bombshell the lawyer had found his father's daughter, and it was a woman living in Nottingham going by the name of Lorna Lloyd. It took time to persuade Ingrid that she had to go. But he played on her love for him and her emotions. And then the further subterfuge that she was going to end up with half their inheritance, which wouldn't be fair on any future children they might have together.

The whole plan took months of preparation. Pretend meetings with lawyers, telling lie after lie to Ingrid and eventually persuading her that they had to go to Nottingham and plan the demise of Lorna, always with the assurance that he'd be responsible for the killing, not her. And Ingrid bought it, because she loved him, unconditionally. After initially being sceptical that Lorna was the right woman, an evening at Lorna and Dan's house for dinner persuaded her finally. In the kitchen with Lorna chatting, Ingrid had questioned her about her parentage. Lorna had lied admirably about her mother working in the kitchens of a huge estate and at eighteen becoming pregnant by the son of the house. Her mother would never disclose to her where that had been. Lorna told Ingrid about her mother being in a care home with dementia, but on good days she could remember her past and she would say how she'd been chased away from the estate with a lump sum of money and had to make her own way in life. Her mother had quickly married and Lorna had explained she loved her stepfather as if he was her own. Ingrid bought it all, hook, line and sinker. Lorna had asked she kept her confidence as it wasn't a story she shared often. Even Dan only knew scant details. After returning to their home next door that night, Ingrid eagerly told him what Lorna had disclosed. Lorna had played her part convincingly.

Eventually, the traffic moving jolted him back. He put his foot down eager to get home to his town house in Chelsea to speak to Lorna and tell her about the solicitors and their proposal. It was all coming together perfectly.

As he opened the front door, the pay-as-you-go phone he used to communicate with Lorna was ringing. He rushed to the coffee table and picked it up. "Hi, darling, I've just got in."

"Someone's been in my house, playing tricks on me."

"Sorry? Who's been in your house?"

"I don't know," she snarled, "but someone has."

"Why . . . what's happened? I don't understand."

"The lounge window was wide open and I hadn't left it like that. Dan's chair had been moved to a different position than I have it in, and just now when I came in, the kettle had been boiled and I've been away from the house for almost two hours."

"But how could anyone get in? You've got an alarm."

"I don't use it."

"Why not?"

"I just don't," she snapped, "does it matter? Why would someone come into the house and try and scare me?"

"I don't know. But the first thing you have to do is put the alarm on. That'll ensure nobody does come in."

There was silence, as if she was hesitant about telling him something. "There's something else . . . you don't think . . ."

"Don't think what?"

"I know this is going to sound like I'm going mad, but . . . do you think that Dan . . . that Dan could be alive?"

"Don't be ridiculous . . ."

"No, hear me out. You know that neighbour of mine, Phyllis with the cat."

"Yeah."

"She came round and said that Dan wasn't dead. Reckons her late husband speaks to her and said Dan's not passed over."

Could she not hear how absurd she sounded?

"For God's sake, you aren't listening to crap like that,

surely? Come on . . . you know better than that. As if he survived. Think about it, seriously. He'd hardly be playing tricks on you now, would he? Dan's dead, sweetheart. I have no idea what's going on, but it isn't him doing these things. You're sure it's not that batty woman coming in your house? It sounds the sort of thing she might do."

"No, it wouldn't be her. She doesn't have a key. I'm scared, Perry," her voice cracked, "something's wrong."

"Nothing's wrong. Just keep calm. You need to concentrate on getting through this memorial. And first things first, put that alarm on every time you leave the house."

She started to sob. "Nothing's like we planned."

"It's exactly like we planned," he said firmly. "Look, why don't I come over the day before the memorial service and book a hotel room close by and you can visit. That way I can see you. And I'll spend the whole time reassuring you, there is nothing to worry about. I'll check out the following morning and come to the service, then go back to London."

"That would be nice," she sniffed, "I feel dreadful, Perry. I can't eat, I can't sleep. My nerves are in shreds. I don't even want this memorial. I feel it's somehow jinxed."

"Hey, nothing's jinxed. You've done brilliantly. We're close now to being together for the rest of our lives. Just hang on in there."

She was fragile and needed his reassurance. Dan's body not being washed up was a huge, unexpected hitch in the whole plan. But it would happen soon, he was sure of it.

"I'm trying but it's hard. I don't want to be here. I want to be with you."

"And you will be, soon, I promise you that. Just hold on tight. I need you to be strong. Let's get the memorial over and we'll make some plans, okay? Can you do that?"

"I'll try."

"Good girl."

"I love you so much."

"And I love you, too, sweetheart. Always. Never forget that."

Chapter 36

Lorna's name flashed on the screen at the GP surgery with instruction of which room she was to go to. Reluctantly, she'd made an appointment with Dr Varma on the Friday afternoon as he'd suggested, even though she was certain it was stress making her feel so tired. The lack of sleep was having a significant impact; it was making her question her state of mind. Things were definitely happening in the house, which were nothing to do with her. She was exhausted trying to think of an explanation.

She tapped on the consulting room door and waited for Dr Varma to invite her in.

He looked up as she entered, "Good afternoon, Lorna, come and take a seat."

"Thank you."

"I'm glad you came," he said as she sat down in the chair next to his desk. "I wasn't sure you would."

"No, I wasn't either, but here I am."

"Yes," he smiled encouragingly "and we've plenty of time to chat as I don't have patients waiting today. Therefore why don't we make a start by you telling me how you're really coping?" He looked over the top of his gold-framed glasses at her, "And I don't want the spiel reserved for family and friends, I'd like you to be frank with me. I can see you've lost a bit of weight so food clearly isn't at the forefront of your mind."

It wasn't. Alcohol yes, to numb things, but little food. It was probably why she had a permanent empty feeling in the pit of her stomach.

She took a deep breath in. "Food hasn't been a priority I must say. So I think I may have lost some weight. I can feel my clothes are slack."

"We'll get you weighed before you leave today, so we can monitor that."

Monitor? No way. Today was a one-off visit to get something to help with her shredded nerves, she had no intention of returning.

"What about sleeping?" Dr Varma asked, "That must be difficult for you."

"I can't sleep," she said wearily, "I'm awake until the early hours, but even when I do finally nod off, if feels like I'm dozing almost and not getting into a deep sleep. So in the morning I'm sluggish and feel sick most days."

"I see."

"That's why I came. I think I'm doing as well as I should be under the circumstances," but my family and Sarah," he'd know she meant Sarah from admin as most knew they were friends, "suggested I might get something from you to help." She shrugged, "Just as temporary measure more than anything really."

"Of course. Loss, grief and bereavement can manifest itself in many ways and you have certainly experienced a significant event that has impacted on your mental health and wellbeing. So, I can certainly give you something to help, such as a low dose anti-depressant, but I don't want you to be alarmed. Often the word anti-depressant can give all sorts of connotations; therefore, I think a better term is mood enhancer. Something that will give you a lift for a few weeks, and as you begin to get stronger, we can reduce the dose and ease you off them. They aren't addictive in any way."

"That sounds perfect."

"You say your family urged you to come and see me. Are there any other concerns?"

"Just what I've said really. I'm not eating and sleeping . . . and . . ."

"And?" He raised an eyebrow.

She let out a sigh, "It sounds silly saying it out loud. Some odd things have been happening in the house and there's no explanation."

"Such as?"

"I found a small window open and Dan's reading chair had moved when I returned to the house. Family think I did both of those things, but I didn't. And then, a day or so ago, I came home after being out for a few hours, and the kettle was hot, as if it had just boiled." She shook her head, "It's made me think I'm going mad."

"Well, let me reassure you that you aren't going mad. What you're telling me are classic symptoms of stress. And that combined with not eating and not sleeping, is clearly taking its toll."

"So, what are you saying? I'm imagining all this stuff?"

"I'm not saying that at all. Let me reassure you that

bereavement manifests itself in many ways, so you've made the right decision coming to see me. I'm sure once you start taking the medication, you'll begin to feel better."

"Will the tablets help me sleep at night?"

"Not specifically, no. But I can prescribe something that will. But before I do that, you mentioned earlier that you feel sick most days. I wonder whether there is a possibility you could be pregnant?"

Lorna huffed. "God, no. I'm on the pill."

He glanced at the computer screen. "Yes, I see that. Do you stop for seven days each month?"

"No, I take it continually. The practice nurse said I could."

"That's right, you can. But I'd like to rule out a pregnancy before I give you the prescriptions. Although I'm sure the symptoms you describe such as the tiredness and sickness are most likely due to the stress you're under, but equally, they could also be due to pregnancy. We can easily do a test to eliminate that while you're here."

"Oh, right. I know I'm not pregnant, though, I take the pill religiously at the same time each day." And she did. The last thing she ever wanted in her life would be a baby. She'd be sterilised if she could and had made enquiries once before, but they wouldn't consider it due to her age and fertility prospects should she change her mind.

"You've not had any breakthrough bleeding while taking the pill?"

"No," she answered truthfully, she hadn't. That's why she was confident the pill wouldn't let her down. It was one hundred percent effective as far as she was concerned, she never worried about pregnancy. A discussion that always stuck firmly in her mind was in the tearoom when one of the young admin girls was fearful she might be pregnant even though she was taking the pill. The discussion, led by one of the nurses, had been about the efficacy of the pill and, if there was breakthrough bleeding, the importance of using condoms as the pill might not be totally effective for that month. So she'd always known that, but she'd never had any breakthrough bleeding so it didn't apply to her.

"If you take a seat in the waiting room, I'll get the practice nurse to take a urine sample from you and test it. Once we get a negative, I'll call you back in and I'll prescribe the necessary medication I want you to take. I'll need to see you again in a couple of weeks to see if things are improving. If not, I can adjust your medication accordingly."

"I might not be here in a few weeks," she reminded him, "I think I mentioned when I was last here, I most probably will be going to stay at my mother's house in Leicester after Dan's memorial next week."

"Yes, you did say. It isn't a problem. As soon as you move, register with a GP and they can see you to monitor you on the medication."

She nodded compliantly, even though she wouldn't be seeing another doctor. All she wanted was something to help her get over the next week or so and the wretched memorial. After that, she'd be with Perry, so all of this nonsense with the house and someone playing tricks on her, would be a million miles away.

She reached for her bag and left Dr Varma's office to sit in the waiting room, silently smarting he hadn't just given her a prescription so she could get out of there. As if she possibly could be pregnant. The whole charade was a complete waste of time.

Dr Varma waited while she took her seat in his office again.

"Well, it's a good thing we did the test. It's going to come as a shock to you right now I know, but you are actually pregnant."

"What! I can't be," she shook her head in denial, "I take the pill religiously, I always have done. I never miss. And I've never had any breakthrough bleeding."

"I hear what you say, but you are most definitely pregnant. Although the pill is a reliable method of contraception, it isn't one hundred percent I'm afraid. Lots of things can render it ineffective. For example, if it's not taken at the same time every day, if just one tablet is missed in error, or if there is an episode of diarrhoea or vomiting. Any of these can stop the pill from being absorbed, which could result in ovulation. And of course if you are ovulating and having sex, the outcome can be a pregnancy. Sperm can live up to five days inside a female just waiting for that egg."

"But I can't have a baby," she stammered, as a memory flashed up in her mind about a tummy upset.

Vaguely, in the recesses of her mind, she recalled being off work for a day or so with a diarrhoea and sickness bug. But she'd still taken the pill, hadn't she?

"I think the best thing for you right now is to go away and have a little time to think about things and come to terms with it. It's an enormous shock, I can see that. Talk to your family, you'll need their support."

"I don't need to talk to anyone," her voice was warbling with emotion, "I don't want a baby. That's why I take contraception, to stop this sort of thing happening."

"Yes, quite. But sometimes nature has a way of circumventing the best of plans. And this could be a blessing in disguise with recently losing your husband. It could be that his legacy living on will be a source of comfort to you in the months ahead, and certainly the years ahead."

"How far on is the pregnancy?"

"I don't know. We'll need a scan to determine that, as we don't have a date of your last menstrual cycle with you taking the pill without a break. But if you want to pop up on the table, I'll feel your abdomen and I might be able to ascertain if the uterus is already growing. It won't be accurate of course, but it might give you some idea."

She laid down on the table and eased her trousers down so her tummy was exposed. His cold hands pressed on her abdomen. "I'd say, possibly, you're at least ten to twelve weeks already. Your uterus is certainly protruding. You could even be further on than that if you have a retroverted uterus."

She put her hands where Dr Varma had on her tummy. "I can't feel anything."

"No, you probably can't. A retroverted uterus means one that is tipped backwards, aimed towards the rectum instead of forward towards the belly. It's quite common and may explain why you haven't noticed a small protrusion. If that is the case, you could well be further on than the weeks I've suggested. It's hard to tell from examination alone."

He moved to the sink to wash his hands while she adjusted her clothes and made her way back to her seat. Tightness gripped her chest, like a steel band of tension. It couldn't be happening. It must be a dream. Surely, any minute, she'd wake up. She couldn't be pregnant. And whose baby could it be? Perry was mixed race, Dan was white.

"I'll get you booked in for a scan to ascertain how many weeks pregnant you are," Dr Varma said with his fingers swiftly moving along the keyboard.

"I don't want a scan. I need a termination as soon as possible."

"As I said," he paused from typing, "I think the best course of action right now would be for you to go away and talk things through with your family, rather than making a hasty decision. It's unlikely, once you've got over the shock and become used to things, that you'll feel like this."

"I won't. I don't want to talk to anyone. I don't want a baby."

"I can see this has come as an enormous shock to you, but my advice is to give yourself time to think. If you do wish to pursue a termination, which I personally wouldn't advise, you will need a scan to determine how far the pregnancy has advanced. It does make a difference to the type of termination offered if you decide to go down that route, as you know."

Of course she knew. A medical termination in the early stages of pregnancy, but any further on would require a general anaesthetic. She wasn't bothered which. All she wanted was to get rid of the baby.

"What about the medication and the sleeping pills?"

"I'm afraid neither are an option until we discover the age of the foetus. I'll call the hospital and get you in for an urgent scan."

Her heart was beating so hard she could hear it in her ears. She needed to get a termination as soon as possible. Perry definitely wasn't the sort to want children, and she certainly didn't. Their whole plan had been so they could be together and enjoy Perry's inheritance. And they were so close to achieving that. A baby wasn't in the equation. She simply couldn't have one.

Chapter 37

Lorna was visiting the care home out of duty to see her mother as it was her birthday. She wasn't intending to stay long. Since the pregnancy news, she could barely think straight let alone play happy families with her disagreeable mother.

"Did you enjoy the garden centre?" she asked taking a sip of tea from the tacky china cup reserved for visitors at the care home. She checked her watch. Perry was checking into a nearby hotel at two p.m.

"What garden centre?"

"The one you went to on Tuesday. Mrs Leeman told me when I came in today that the carers had taken a group of you to the garden centre for afternoon tea. She said you loved the cakes and the fruit scone you had."

"I haven't been anywhere for afternoon tea. Was she talking about those soggy offerings they serve up here? Because they're a poor excuse for scones, I can tell you."

There was no point in arguing with the aging Elizabeth Mann. Even before Alzheimer's disease cruelly affected her brain, her mother wasn't an endearing woman. Lorna had struggled most of her life to feel any warmth towards her. It was her late father that she'd adored. How he'd fallen in love with her mother in the first place was baffling. She most definitely wasn't a woman that was easy to love.

"They do that, you know," her mother continued, tightening her cardigan around herself as she did so often when she was about to embark on another long moan, "they tell lies. They lock you away in here for hours on end and then make up stuff like going out for afternoon tea. It's all rubbish. I tell you, the sooner I'm home from here, the better."

Lorna sighed. She hadn't visited her mother for a while and she could tell as soon as she'd arrived, her temperament hadn't improved. Thankfully, she'd have no idea how long it had been since she last visited, but the staff would know. But they'd understand. She was a grieving widow.

Her mother's eyes narrowed and focussed on Lorna's head, "What have you done to your hair? It really doesn't suit you like that, it makes you look old." She continued to stare and Lorna knew there were more disparaging remarks to come. Her mother had never been able to stop herself. She should be used to it after all these years, but her cutting remarks still had the ability to hurt. "You've got unkempt and unruly hair, just like your father. Funny," she shrugged, "that's what I liked about him, his thick curly hair," she gazed for a moment as if remembering, and then stiffened, "and look how that turned out."

Lorna stifled the urge to get up and leave. Half an hour more and she was out of there. She hated visiting. Her mother always had the ability to make her feel like a child. Lorna used to envy the girls at school that had mothers who were proud of them and giving compliments was the norm. Her best friend's mother always had a kind word when they were done up in their skimpy clothes going off clubbing. It was such a joy to get praise. Sadly, she never received any from her mother. It would always be a criticism. *That makeup doesn't suit you, you haven't got the right legs for short skirts, pull your tummy in, it's getting flabby.*

"Have you coloured it or something?" her mother continued to scowl through her half-rimmed glasses that could do with a good clean. "That's not your natural colour."

"Just highlights, which I've been having for years." She tried to change the subject to get her mother away from scrutinising her, "I wonder where Moira is, it's unusual for her not to pop in." She made the pretence of looking towards the corridor for her mother's one and only friend whose room was adjacent to hers. Friend was a loose term, as Moira had no idea really what time of the day it was.

"What does Daniel think about your hair like that?"

Her insides clenched at the mention of her husband's name. He was the last person she wanted to be discussing. "I'll ask on my way out where she is," Lorna said, trying to move the conversation on, "I hope she's alright. I guess she could be having a lie down."

"Daniel looks like he's lost weight to me. You're not feeding him convenience foods, are you? I hope he's not been over-doing it at the gym." Her mother gave her the familiar *I'm always right* look, "You need to keep an eye on him, gyms can become a bit of an obsession. I told him that when he was here. Are you listening to me?"

"Course I am." She wasn't though, her thoughts were on her late husband. "Dan hasn't been here, not recently anyway." Once it was out of her mouth, she inwardly chastised herself. She knew from reading Alzheimer's information when her mother's mind deteriorated initially, it was advisable not to tackle people with dementia by contradicting their thought processes or giving them new information – it was best to let them chat on regardless. Seemingly, they couldn't fathom out change. Their long-term memory was invariably intact and her mother certainly lived in the past, she could remember as far back as her school days, yet if asked what she'd eaten for breakfast she'd have no idea.

"He has been here," he mother repeated, "he came yesterday."

There was no point in arguing with her. She didn't know Dan was dead, and she wasn't about to tell her.

The door opened and Sandra, one of the domestics, came in for the cups. Lorna reached for her mother's cup and put it on the trolley alongside her own. Her mum lifted her head towards Sandra, "My son-in-law was here yesterday, wasn't he? Lorna doesn't believe he came."

"I'm not sure, Mrs Mann," Sandra smiled politely as she stacked the cups neatly and placed the spoons in a jug, "I see a lot of visitors coming and going, but I'm never certain who they're here to see." She nodded kindly as she made her way out of the room pushing the trolley.

"Well, I'm telling you he came," her mother said with her *I'm always right* look plastered on her wrinkled face, "and he brought flowers." She was looking around the room but there were no flowers other than the solitary vase with the flowers that Lorna had brought.

"See, there." Her mother pointed to the vase with the pink and red carnations and the single birthday card with *my dearest mother* in bold letters, taunting Lorna as she was far from her dearest mother. She didn't bother correcting her mother that she'd brought the flowers.

"Such a thoughtful man. When is he coming again to see me, do you know?"

"No, I don't. Anyway, I think it's about time I made a move. It's a long drive home and I'd rather do it before it gets dark." She reached for her handbag from the floor and leaned across to her mother, kissing her cheek dutifully, trying desperately not to inhale her fusty ageing smell. "I'll see you again soon."

"When?" her mother scowled.

"In a few weeks maybe, I'll let the care home know." Before another word was uttered she was out of the door. Seeing her mother always knocked her equilibrium out of kilter. She invariably reverted back to her younger self, trying so hard to please her, but never actually achieving it. If only she could have been a loving mother, maybe then she'd have visited more often. Dan always came with her on her mother's birthday. He made quite a fuss of her then, which always irritated Lorna. Her mother hadn't been the sort of woman that deserved a lot of attention. The only reason she'd been there today was out of duty. But it was the last time. She was finally going to embark on a new life. And it couldn't come soon enough.

The walk from the rooms to reception seemed endless despite the speed of her steps. The smell of stale urine permeated through her nostrils and the artificial lights were as oppressive as usual. Lorna couldn't get out of the place quick enough. She approached the main desk and picked up the pen to sign herself out of the visitors book. Despite not listening to her mother's innate ramblings, she found herself turning the page to the previous day, knowing full well there wouldn't be a visitor's signature from Dan. But she was wrong. At 2.10, there was a signature in, and at three o'clock, there was a signature out. In black ballpoint pen and in a scrawl, she stared at *D A Lloyd.* It couldn't be. She instinctively squeezed her eyes tight shut and then opened them, as if the scrawl would magically disappear. Someone had forged Dan's signature. As if they were trying to get into her mind. What she hadn't been able to fathom though was who would do such a thing. And why would they? None of it made sense.

The receptionist looked up from the keyboard she was working on as Lorna signed herself out. "Nice to see you, Mrs Lloyd," she reached across her desk to the electronic door release, "and once again, we're all terribly sorry for your loss."

"Thank you," Lorna said turning towards the main door. There was no time for pleasantries. Not when she knew someone was going out of their way to frighten her . . . and they were doing a pretty good job. Her heart was beating so ferociously, she felt almost short of oxygen.

The sun was blinding as she walked outside. She eagerly took a huge breath of air and continued deep breathing as she made her way towards her car. Her head began to throb as it always seemed to after visiting her mother. The relief she'd felt that today was the last day she'd be visiting for a while, had now been replaced by further anguish. The pregnancy was bad enough but she was taking care of that. However, seeing Dan's name had been like a knife plunged into her tummy and it slowly being twisted around.

Once inside her car she rummaged in her handbag for some aspirin, took the top off the bottle of water from the cup holder, and washed two tablets down. By the time she drove to the hotel to see Perry, her headache would be long gone. But her tummy muscles twisting with anxiety wouldn't. Dan's fake signature in the visitor's book had spooked her.

Who the hell would do that?

Chapter 38

Seeing the pleasure on her face as she writhed beneath him, moaning for him, made Perry all the more frantic. It didn't take long. Soon, he was slumping down beside her and pulling her naked body into his.

"That was well worth the wait," he said, stroking a hand over her hip.

"God yes," she said, "I needed that."

Their lovemaking was special. It always had been. Often it was quick the first time as they'd been apart, but he knew the next time, it would be much more leisurely. And soon they would have all the time in the world. Initially, he hadn't been keen on Lorna moving to her mother's, but that was because he was hoping Dan's body would be found. Now it still hadn't, they couldn't wait for ever to move on with their lives, and he so wanted to be with her without distance between them. They couldn't be open about their relationship just yet, but to be able to see each other was vital.

He kissed her head, "Don't forget, tomorrow after the service, I'll come and give my condolences to you and Connor, but then I'll make my excuses not to come to the wake."

"I wish you could come," she sighed, "I'd feel so much better if you were there, even if it is in the background."

"Yeah, I know, but I can't. It's easy enough to make my excuses. People will know I lost my wife too and the significance of the day would be hard."

"If only I didn't have to go through with this tomorrow. I'm really jittery about it all."

"What do you mean, jittery?"

"About the odd things that have been happening. They've really unnerved me."

"You've not had any more, though?"

"No. I use the alarm like you said."

"Good." He didn't want to spend their evening together analysing what he suspected had been her fragile state of mind. He didn't believe for one minute anyone had been in the house. The likeliest explanation was that Lorna had done the things herself. She'd played her part brilliantly in the whole thing, but understandably she'd wobbled since returning home. Neither of them had prepared for Dan's body not being recovered.

"There's something else now though."

His antenna raised and he eased himself up onto his elbow and saw her eyes filling up, which was unusual for Lorna. As far as he was concerned, she was equally as tough as him.

"What is it?" He stroked the side of her face, "Tell me?"

She swallowed. "My mother reckons that Dan's been to see her."

"What?" he scowled, "Doesn't she have Alzheimer's?"

"Yeah, she does. So I didn't take a great deal of notice. She always goes on about him. That's nothing new."

"What's bothering you, then?"

"When I went to sign myself out in the visitor's book in reception, Dan's signature was in the book for the day before. A time in and a time out."

"You're kidding."

"Course I'm not kidding. It was there. DA Lloyd."

"Well, it can't have been his signature. Someone's having a laugh."

"I hardly think impersonating someone dead is having a laugh."

"It's a figure of speech," he dismissed, "what I mean is, it's a prank. Someone's trying to scare you."

"But why would anyone do that? They barely know me at the home."

"Yeah, but they'll have seen the stuff in the media. They'll know your husband died and there isn't a body."

"What's to be gained by faking Dan's signature as if he visited Mum, though?"

"I don't know, sweetheart, but we both know categorically he hasn't been visiting. It's some sort of warped humour done by someone trying to scare you. Think about it, it can't be much fun working in a place like that. They'll have to make their own entertainment working with old people all day. Whoever has done it probably was watching for your reaction. They'll be having a laugh right now, I bet you."

"Do you think?"

"Yes. So stop worrying, it's nothing."

"I'm tired of it all," she drew her mouth into a

straight line and bit her lip, "I just want to move to Mum's. I have to get away. I'll go mad if I don't."

"Yeah, but we still have to wait an acceptable amount of time for us to publicly be an item."

"I know that, but at least I can see you when I'm at Mum's house, which will be much better."

"It will, yeah. And pretty soon, we'll have the rest of our lives together. And that can't come soon enough. I'm dying to show you Gayton Manor where I spent a lot of my childhood during the school holidays. You'll love it."

"I wish I'd have known you as a child. Were you a good endearing child, or a naughty one?"

"A naughty one, and a rebellious one. You wouldn't have liked me one bit." He laughed.

"I bet I would you know, because I was exactly the same." She was smiling again now, which was a relief. He hated seeing her upset. "So," she carried on, "we'd have been two rebellious kids, ripping up trees together. God knows what our kids would have turned out like."

"Our kids?" he pulled a face to show his displeasure, "don't be getting broody, whatever you do," he warned, "that's the last thing I'd ever want."

"I don't want them either. I was just joking about what they'd be like."

"Yeah, well don't joke, I can't imagine anything worse than screaming brats around us. The future is you and I, nobody else. I'm not sharing you with anyone."

"Good." She leaned forward and kissed him.

He pulled away. "Let's save that for after dinner." He

leant toward the bedside table and checked his watch, "We better get ready. I've booked us in the restaurant in an hour."

"Okay. Shall I get showered first?"

"You'd better. It'll only take me five minutes."

"Lucky you. Wish I was a bloke."

"Well, I'm glad you're not," he winked.

She laughed as she threw the bedclothes back and made her way towards the bathroom. He watched her go. Her figure was perfect to him, but he could see she'd lost weight, which was understandable. They'd been through an awful lot together and were on the brink of everything they wanted. Soon, they'd be living the dream on his hefty inheritance. But she'd unnerved him mentioning children. There was certainly no place for them in their new life together. The future was about the two of them. And as soon as Dan's body was found, things would be easier as she'd be able to settle his estate and cut her ties with his family. Right now, all she had to do was get through the memorial service. Although he'd initially been reluctant to attend, he'd come round to the idea. It was the right thing to do. He wanted to be there in the background, with his strength willing her on.

They were almost there.

***

Staring at her nakedness in the mirrored bathroom, Lorna examined her tummy. It was protruding a little but not that you'd think there was a baby in there, it was more like she'd eaten a five-course dinner. Being with

Perry at the hotel was marred by the pregnancy shock. Earlier that morning, she'd received a phone call from the hospital inviting her for a scan the following day, but she'd had to decline as it was Dan's memorial service. She'd been offered an alternative the day after. As soon as she'd had the scan, she'd push for the termination. However far on she was, she knew they'd do it quickly. And after that, she was moving to her mother's house. So even though the pregnancy weighed heavily on her mind, it was all in hand. And Perry was right, someone was messing about at the care home. As if Dan would be visiting her mother. It was too ridiculous for words. He was dead. Tonight she needed to try and put it all out of her mind. The plan was in place. She had to get through the memorial service, have the termination and move to her mother's house. And, any day now, she most probably would get the call that Dan's body had been found.

As she came back into the bedroom and Perry headed for the shower, she put on her cropped white trousers and turquoise blouse and stood back to look at herself in the huge, mirrored wardrobes. It felt nice to dress up for a change. A tinge of excitement surged through her that she'd be having dinner with the man she loved. He was right. Now was their time and the last thing she needed was a baby getting in the way. It wasn't as if she knew whose baby it was anyway. That would only be apparent when it was born by the colour of its skin. But it wasn't going to get to that. They had a bright future together with enough money to live an elegant lifestyle. That's why they'd done what they had. Children didn't feature at all in their future life. The termination was an absolute necessity.

She picked up her phone to call Connor. He'd said he would ring that evening but he thought she'd be at home. The last thing she wanted was her time with Perry interrupting. She wasn't staying the whole night at the hotel, she would return to her own home that evening, but it would be late. She needed to be at home first thing as Connor and Ruth would arrive early for the service.

He picked up, "Hi, Lorna."

"Hi. I'm just calling to say I've got a headache so I'm going to have a bit of something to eat, a soak in the bath and then going to get an early night."

"Yeah, I must admit, I feel ropey too. It's the stress. We'll feel better when we get tomorrow over with. Hang on a sec . . ."

She could hear Ruth saying something in the background.

"Ruth's just asking if you want her to come over for a while tonight?"

"No, I'm fine, honestly. I'm just tired and want an early night. I'll pack an overnight bag to stay at yours tomorrow. We'll all be exhausted after the service, I'm sure."

"We will, but it's the right thing to do. People want to pay their respects, Dan was a popular man."

"Yeah, I know he was. We'll make sure tomorrow is special for him. Right, I'll see you here in the morning then?"

"Yep, we'll be there early. Try and get some rest, it'll be a long day tomorrow."

"Will do. Thanks Connor, you're such a support helping me."

"Hey, we support each other. We'll always do that."

"I know we will. See you in the morning. Night night."

She cut the call. Roll on tomorrow and the tricks would be over finally. Whoever was doing them would realise it was pointless. Especially once she'd moved away to begin her new life and cut all ties with the old one.

Chapter 39

Tuesday morning, Dan's memorial day was as gloomy as Lorna felt. She'd barely slept and the nausea was worse than ever. The rain deluge was unrelenting and battering the kitchen window as she sat sipping tea and nibbling an arrowroot biscuit to try and settle her tummy. She'd showered and dressed early, ready for Connor and Ruth's arrival. Despite the twins protesting they wanted to attend the service, their parents had said no and were dropping them off at school first before coming to her.

A tap on the front door interrupted her melancholy thoughts. As she made her way down the hall, she silently said a prayer that it wasn't Phyllis at the door with some prophecy that Dan was going to appear at the memorial in person. Most days, she managed to give the old bat a wide berth, but whenever she did see her, it was obvious she was bursting to engage her in conversation.

As she opened the front door, she gave a sigh of relief to see a neighbour from further round the cul-de-sac. Due to the weather, she was wearing a waterproof coat with a hood, and clutching a bunch of pink and white chrysanthemums.

"Oh, God, Sheila, come in. What a morning."

"I won't come inside, but I'll just get a bit of shelter for a minute," her neighbour said, stepping inside the door and standing on the doormat, at the same time closing the front door shut behind her.

"I've just come to apologise," she eased her hood down, "and to let you know that Alan and I won't be at the memorial today. We were meant to be flying out to Tenerife this evening at eleven, but we had a call last night to say the flight was rescheduled for five o'clock. So we'll have to leave for the airport shortly."

"That's alright," Lorna said with a forced smile, "it can't be helped."

"No, I know, but we do feel bad. We'd have liked to have been there."

"That is kind, but please don't worry. To be perfectly honest, I'm not terribly keen on this memorial service, I somehow got cajoled into it. Are you sure you won't come in?"

"No, honestly, I won't. I told Alan I'd literally be two minutes. Here, just some flowers to let you know we're thinking about you."

"Thank you. They're lovely."

"I'm sure the service will be fine, and you never know, once it's over," she smiled sympathetically, "it might help you."

"Yes, I'm sure you're right."

"You're getting lots of support I hope?"

"Oh, yes, definitely. My brother-in-law and his wife have been amazing. He's taking it really badly, as he and Dan were close, but he's been an absolute brick. I couldn't have got through it without him."

"That's good. And I see Phyllis has been helping."

"Phyllis," Lorna frowned, "helping? I'm not sure

about that. Hindering more like."

"Oh," Sheila pulled a playful face, "it's like that, is it? I thought maybe she'd been doing a bit of cleaning for you or something. I've seen her popping in while you've been out."

Lorna's chest tightened. Phyllis, in her house. How? She didn't have a key . . . or did she?

"Anyway," Sheila continued, "I'd better get off." She gave Lorna a hug, "I'm sure it'll all go well today. We'll be thinking of you."

"Thank you both," Lorna said watching her neighbour as she pulled the hood over her head and opened the front door. "I appreciate you coming. Do have a lovely holiday."

Her eyes followed Sheila as she walked down her drive and towards her own property. Lorna's melancholy mood from five minutes earlier had turned thunderous. How dare Phyllis set foot in her house?

She grabbed a pair of boots and hastily put them on. Her intention was to sort the interfering old bat out once and for all, but just as she closed the front door behind her, Connor's car pulled into the drive.

"Go in, both of you," Lorna urged as Connor got out of the car, "the kettle's boiled. I'll only be a minute."

"Where you off to?" Ruth frowned from her side of the car, "and where's your coat?"

"I'll be back in five, honestly." Lorna hurried past their car, down the drive towards the gate.

She banged loudly on Phyllis's door with her fist.

"I'm coming, I'm coming," the old bat called from inside. Lorna's heart was thumping and her blood pressure had to be sky high as fury raged through her.

Phyllis eventually opened the front door. "Hello, dear."

"Have you been in my house?" Lorna snapped.

"What . . . er . . . what do you mean?"

"Have you got a key to my house and been in while I've been out?"

The colour from Phyllis's face faded.

"I know you have. You've been seen on CCTV," she lied.

"It . . . it isn't what you think."

"And what do I think, eh? I'll tell you what I think. That you've been in and moved Dan's chair, opened a window and boiled my kettle. It was you, wasn't it?" She could tell by her pallor that it was. "What a wicked old woman you are. How could you?"

Connor rushing up the drive towards them stopped Lorna in her flow.

"What the hell's going on?"

"It's her. She's been in my house." Lorna glared at Phyllis, "She's been the one playing tricks."

"What tricks?"

"The window open, Dan's chair moving position and the kettle being boiled."

Connor only knew about the window, she hadn't mentioned the other two incidents. But he clearly got the drift judging by the disparaging scowl on his face.

"What?" he glared at Phyllis as she stood in her doorway, "And it's you that's been doing this?"

"I'm sorry," Phyllis flinched, "I was trying to get close to Dan, that's all. But I couldn't. There were no vibes. He's not passed over to the other side, you see, I would have known, sitting in his chair."

"You're mad," Lorna spat. "Have you any idea the impact it's had on me, you moving things around my house? I've even visited the doctor because of you. My nerves are frazzled, you stupid woman."

"That's why I've been trying to help in my own way," she shook her head, "I don't believe Dan is dead, but you won't listen."

"That's enough," Connor said firmly, "today is difficult enough for us. We're having a service to celebrate my brother's life, and this is only adding to the stress we're under." He reached for Lorna's arm, "Come on, we're finished here."

Lorna shrugged his arm away, "I want my key, now," she glared at an ashen Phyllis.

Phyllis eased the front door to and went inside the house. They waited seconds for her to return clutching the key. With a sheepish expression she handed it over.

Lorna snatched it from her. "Where did you get it?"

"Dan gave me it once. Said it was for extra security. He told me you didn't always use the alarm."

"Well I do now. So you keep away from my house. And do not attend the memorial today. The last person I want to see is you. Have I made myself clear?"

"I . . . I wasn't coming to the memorial," Phyllis

stuttered, "I don't believe Dan is . . ."

"Shut up. Just shut up," Lorna shouted, "no more. Keep away from me. And keep your warped views to yourself otherwise I'll be going to the police. Do you understand?"

"The police," Phyllis's voice juddered nervously, "I meant no harm. I am truly sorry to see you this upset."

"So you should be. Remember what I said," she snapped, "anymore nonsense or interfering from you and I'm going straight to see the police. This is bordering on harassment."

"Please don't do that. I've said I'm sorry."

Lorna jabbed a finger. "If I get so much as a peep out of you, I will. So don't you forget that."

Connor almost had to drag her away and lead her towards her own house. She could have punched her. All the anxiety about someone being in the house she'd put her through. She'd even considered that Dan was alive and doing it all, even though Perry had reassured that he'd hardly be sneaking into his own house and frightening her. His first stop would have been the police.

Once inside her house, Connor made her sit down at the kitchen table. He placed a small glass of brandy in front of her. "Here, drink this."

"I can't, honestly, I feel sick."

"Maybe have it in a minute then. You need something to calm you down."

Her heart was racing madly, she could feel it. Ruth was making coffee but the smell was nauseating. "Could

I have tea Ruth, please?"

"Course you can. Coming up." While Ruth was busy making the drinks, Connor sat down and explained what had gone on next door.

"Drink this, it'll warm you up," Ruth said placing a tea in front of her and taking her seat. She scowled, "So, what you're saying is, that woman has a key and she's been coming into your house while you've been out?"

"Yes," Lorna sighed, "and I've been frantic about it all. I thought I was going mad seeing things happening which I hadn't done. I've even been to the doctors."

Ruth squeezed her arm, "You should have told us, I had no idea. How dare she?"

"It's okay. To be honest, it's almost come as a relief. I thought I was seriously losing it."

"I bet. What did the doctor say?"

"He just mumbled on about stress playing tricks on my mind."

"And did he give you anything?"

"Er . . . no, nothing yet. He's done some blood tests," Lorna lied, "we're just waiting for the results."

"At least you've got your key back now," Connor chipped in, "so the old bat can't come in anymore."

"Yes, thank God. What a terrible woman she is."

Ruth took a sip of her coffee, "I hope you told her how much she'd upset you?"

Connor widened his eyes. "She certainly did that."

"What?" Lorna screwed her face up, "Do you think I was too harsh?"

"You were a bit. She looked quite shaken when you

threatened her with the police. I hope she doesn't have a stroke or anything."

"She won't. She's as tough as old boots that one."

The tea was having the desired effect as Lorna's heart rate felt like it was slowing down. Ruth put a hand on Lorna's knee. "You're damp now, have you got something else you can put on?"

"It's fine. I'm not changing now." She looked up at the wall clock, "They'll be here shortly."

"Yeah, they will. What a day for this to happen. I can see it's really upset you."

It had, but not as much as they would imagine. She was furious yes, but it confirmed she was being stupid imagining Dan was alive and doing those things. As if.

"I'm okay, honestly. I'll just use the bathroom and then I'm ready."

"You're not having this?" Connor nodded towards the brandy.

"No, you have it. It might help you."

He picked up the glass and stared at it, "I'm not sure a glass of brandy is going to help that much, but I'll have it anyway."

He was right. The next few hours were going to be an ordeal for them all, more so for her than Connor and Ruth. They'd get closure, whereas she never would. Dan was gone, but she was going to have to live the rest of her life haunted by what she'd done. And there was nothing that could ever erase that wretchedness.

Chapter 40

Lorna sat in the front pew of the church with Connor and Ruth. Connor had asked for a special photograph she liked of Dan and had it enlarged and framed so the congregation could focus on it during the service. It was a particularly nice one of him, taken about a year ago in Cornwall where they'd spent a lovely few days. The water was so blue in the background, it could almost be the Caribbean. Dan was glaring at the congregation from the altar accompanied by a posy of red roses and freesias, with a simple message of *With love always* from her, Connor, Ruth and the twins. They'd suggested a more personal message just from her, but she'd dismissed it. That would be far too hypocritical.

Although still smarting from her confrontation with Phyllis, some of the tension had been replaced by a sense of relief. At least now she knew. She'd tormented herself since the incidents on whether or not she was going mad. And stupidly considered Dan might turn up at the memorial. Now she knew that was completely absurd. There was still the pregnancy, but she'd be having the scan tomorrow and then moving on with the termination. So, gradually, things were getting sorted, which was good as she was desperately weary.

Perry was sat on the adjacent row to her, close to the aisle, purposely she was sure so she'd feel his presence.

And she was acutely aware of him. Evidence of their previous night's lovemaking at the hotel, she could still feel. As she'd pulled into her drive in the early hours, she'd wondered at the time if beady-eyed Phyllis had clocked her coming in. But she no longer cared. Phyllis wouldn't bother her anymore, and very soon, she'd be out of that house. All she had to do now was get through the service, play the grieving widow at the wake, then she was home and dry, resigned to the fact that for the time being, the sea wasn't going to give Dan up. But as Perry said, it would do eventually. They just had to be patient.

Out of her peripheral vision, sitting alongside Perry, she spotted Dan's previous wife, Victoria. All elegant and suitably dressed in full mourning attire which looked classy and elegant. She'd met her earlier on in her and Dan's relationship, when she'd joined one of their yearly meet-ups to celebrate their deceased son's birthday. Dan had insisted she went. No doubt terrified someone might suggest he was having an affair meeting a random woman in a restaurant. It was evident straight away that Victoria was Dan's ideal type of woman with her pretty face, her upper-class southern accent and her engaging, eager-to-please manner. She'd been Dan's first love and Connor and Ruth were always gushing about her.

Lorna kept her focus straight ahead rather than acknowledging anyone. The service was, above all, a celebration of Dan's life and accomplishments, but there were no smiles. Although the church was packed with classmates, colleagues, distant cousins and friends, the mood was sombre. The vicar droned on in his monotone voice, "So, as we thank God for Dan's life, short as it turned out to be, we are reminded about the huge void he has left in his wife's life and that of his brother, his sister-in-law and his nieces, whom he adored. We must pledge to support them all in the days and months ahead."

There were prayers and a poem, before the vicar concluded and invited those attending to the golf club for refreshments and to share their memories of Dan with the family. Connor had asked him specifically to invite everyone. Getting through it was going to be a significant challenge, but it would be the last challenge, she told herself. Throughout the service, she'd kept her eyes averted from Dan's photo. It was too much of a vivid reminder of what she'd done.

The vicar asked them all to remain seated while the family were taken to the church entrance to greet them all as they left. In turn, each aisle filtered out and formed a queue, waiting patiently to speak to them. Lorna found their condolences difficult to deal with. Connor and Ruth were doing a sterling job stood at the side of her and thanking each one for attending. She had to accept the hugs from everyone, telling her how sorry they were and she responded accordingly. The only light was Perry further down the queue. She was still hopeful he might come to the golf club if only for one drink, even though he'd been pretty clear he wouldn't. And a further frustration was that she wouldn't be able to call him that evening as she was going to be staying with Connor and Ruth, so they'd have to make do with texts.

"Lorna," Victoria said in her upper-class accent as she leant in for the obligatory hug. "I'm devastated for you," she reached and hugged Connor and Ruth, "and you both, too."

"Thanks for coming, Vic," Connor said, "we know how much Dan meant to you."

"To us all," Victoria corrected, "we all loved him."

Lorna shuffled uncomfortably on the spot. Although she had nothing against the woman, she didn't feel it appropriate for her to be so gushing about Dan. After all, following the death of their son, she'd quickly ditched him and married someone else.

"You're coming to the golf club, I hope?" Ruth asked.

"No, I won't. But please," she looked at Lorna, "accept my sincere condolences. Dan was one in a million and I can only imagine how terrible it's been for you." She squeezed Connor's hand, "And he loved you so much."

Connor's eyes filled up and he grabbed her for another hug. "I know he did. Thanks Vic. Keep in touch now won't you."

"Yes, of course I will." She grabbed Lorna's hand. "You only had Dan for such a short time, I know, but he loved you dearly." Victoria paused, swallowing back tears, "Take comfort in that in the coming days ahead."

"I will." Lorna faked an appreciative voice, "Thank you so much for coming." It was good riddance as far as she was concerned. Connor and Ruth had been far too gushing. She was an ex after all.

After what felt like an eternity, Perry was in front of

her in his navy suit and white shirt showing off his amazing hazel-coloured skin. He gave her a courtesy hug, and for literally seconds, she inhaled his familiarity.

"I'm so sorry, Lorna," he included Connor and Ruth, "for you all. This is such a terrible time."

"Thank you," Lorna said in her soft, mourning voice. "It's kind of you to come, it can't have been easy." She turned to Ruth, "This is Perry, Ruth. It was his wife, Ingrid that was in the accident with Dan."

Ruth clasped his hand. "I am sorry for your loss, too. And Lorna's right, it's kind of you to come today."

He shook Connor's hand. "I wanted to pay my respects. Although I'd not known Dan long, I liked him. I could see he was a good man and how much he loved Lorna."

"He did," Connor nodded, "he had a lot of love to give. Will you join us for a drink at the golf club, it's only down the road?"

"No, I won't. I'll head back to London. But thank you anyway." Before he walked away, he smiled kindly at Lorna, "Look after yourself, and do keep in touch. I'd love to know how you're getting on. In a month or so, you know, when things settle a little."

"Yes, I will. Thank you again for coming. It really does mean a lot."

"You take care," he nodded and walked away.

As staff from the Health Centre and Doctor Varma walked away, Connor breathed a sigh of relief. "Right, that's the lot. We'd better go do the last bit. You okay?" he squeezed her arm.

"I'm fine."

The undertaker hovered waiting to drive them to the golf club. He was clutching the photograph of Dan, no doubt he'd hand it over when they got there. Ruth linked her arm with hers and they made her way down the uneven church path towards the gate and the waiting Daimler, with Connor and the undertaker a couple of paces behind.

"I thought the service was nice, didn't you?" Ruth said making conversation.

"It was," Lorna agreed, barely able to remember a word.

"I don't know about you, but I'm ready for a drink."

"Yeah, me . . . "

Two men approached the church and stood at the bottom of the path they were descending. Both were wearing jackets and ties, one youngish, maybe about her age, the other much older, but she didn't somehow feel they were mourners. Unless they represented an organisation of some sort, she hadn't recognised everyone that had attended. With purpose etched on both their faces, they stopped directly in front of her.

"Mrs Lloyd?" the older of the two men asked.

"Yes."

"Lorna Lloyd?"

"Yes," she said, unease surging through her veins. "What is it?"

"I'm Detective Inspector Graham Morton and this is Detective Michael Kelly."

Lorna glanced at their warrant cards. *Had they found*

Dan's body?

"You're under arrest for the murder of Ingrid Hunter . . ."

"What?" Connor barked, "Is this some sort of joke?"

"It's no joke, sir, if I could ask you to step out of the way."

The younger Detective carried on speaking, "You have the right to remain silent. Anything you say can and will be used . . ." Her arms were placed behind her back and she felt the metal of the handcuffs as they were applied, and although he continued with his spiel, she was barely listening. It couldn't possibly be real.

"No, I won't step out of the bloody way," Connor snapped, "I have no idea what is going on here, but now isn't the time."

Ruth began to protest, "We have a wake to attend. We can come down to the station and sort out whatever this is after that."

"I'm afraid not, madam. Excuse us."

Lorna was almost frogmarched by the officer towards the waiting BMW. He opened the back door and eased her inside, putting a hand on her head to prevent her banging it. He fastened up her seatbelt, closed the car door and took his seat in front behind the steering wheel.

"What's happening?" she protested as the senior officer took his seat beside the driver, "There must be a mistake . . . this is my husband's memorial service."

Connor put his face to the passenger window and raised his voice, "I'll sort this, Lorna, don't worry. I'm coming to the station, I'll be right behind you."

Her heart was pounding so loudly, she could hear it in her head. Sweat began to trickle down her back. She wanted to protest further, but the words wouldn't come. Her mouth was dry. She stared in disbelief out of the window to an equally disbelieving Ruth standing watching. Incredulous was her expression and she'd started to cry. It couldn't be happening. What had the Detective said – she'd killed Ingrid? She hadn't. Perry had. But how did they know?

The heat in the car was oppressive. As the car slowly pulled away, Lorna looked beyond Connor and Ruth, to the church entrance they'd just come out of.

And there at the entrance he stood.

Watching.

Dan Lloyd, her husband of seven years . . . was alive.

Chapter 41

The wait for Lorna to face justice had been endless for Dan. It had taken incredible resilience to be where he was now, purposely stood at the elevated doorway of the church, making sure she couldn't miss him as the police car was driven past with her handcuffed in the back seat. Connor hadn't yet seen him, nor had Ruth, as they were further down the church path at the gate, focussing upon the scene in front of them as their sister-in-law was hoisted unceremoniously into the car and driven away. He watched the funeral director speaking to them both, no doubt waiting to take them to the wake but unsure now whether Connor and Ruth were going straight there, or the police station?

The drizzle had lifted and the sun was trying to break through, almost like an omen as Dan walked down the pathway towards his brother with a heart that felt almost as if it was bursting out of his chest. As if sensing someone was coming up behind him, Connor turned around first, followed by Ruth. Acute shock was evident by the slow, disbelieving shake of his head . . . next, the widened eyes of realisation . . . and finally, a cry of astonishment. Dan, eager to close the gap between them, quickened his pace into a run. Uncontrollable tears streamed down his cheeks, his gut aching with love at the sight of his stunned brother.

"What the fuck," Connor cried incredulously. Dan prevented him saying any more by grabbing him and wrapping his arms around him tightly.

"Tell me I'm not dreaming," Connor said with his head buried in Dan's shoulder.

"You're not dreaming," Dan sobbed, "it's me, I'm here."

"Where the hell have you been?" Connor eased himself away, "I can't believe it!" He rubbed his wet eyes, "You're supposed to be dead."

"I know." Dan pulled his brother towards him again, and Ruth joined in with the hug. "This is surreal," she squealed, sniffing back the tears. Dan savoured the love emanating from them both. His suffering had been appalling, and the trauma of Greece was going to take time to heal, but right now, he was back in the only place he wanted to be.

"I can't believe you're here," Connor extracted himself again, "Jesus Christ, we've just had a service for you. We've spent weeks grieving."

Dan swallowed back the tears.

"The police have arrested Lorna," Connor indicated with his head in the direction she'd been driven off. "Do you know what's going on?"

"Yeah, and I'll explain everything properly. But right now, you need to know that Lorna and Perry killed Ingrid and tried to kill me. They set the whole thing up."

"No," Ruth's mouth dropped open, "that can't be true. Lorna's taken things really badly," she shook her head disbelievingly; "she's no murderer." She wiped her cheeks, "And we've just seen Perry, he came to the service."

"The police know that too. They've been waiting to see if Lorna went ahead with it. They know they're in a relationship. They did it, definitely, the police have evidence. I've given my statement, so they'll both be charged."

"I can't take all this in," Connor reached in his pocket and pulled out a handkerchief. "First of all, you return from supposedly being dead," he paused to blow his nose, "and now it seems your wife, who we've been supporting, is a murderer. It's too much."

"It's a massive shock, I know," Dan squeezed Connor's arm, "but I'm here now to sort everything out."

"Has Perry been arrested?" Ruth asked.

"He will be."

"But he's on his way back to London. He just told us," she indicated with her head to the church.

Connor scowled, "It feels like my body's going to explode or something."

"I'm sorry," Dan reached out and squeezed his shoulder, "it's a massive shock, I know."

In the midst of the reunion, they'd all forgotten the undertaker, waiting at a respectful distance, until he cleared his throat to remind them he was still there.

"Oh, God," Ruth put her hand to her mouth, "the wake. What are we going to do? People are expecting us."

"Maybe it's best you go and make an announcement.

You don't have to go into details. Just say you've been informed I'm alive but you don't know any more than that."

Connor blew out a breath, "Christ almighty, this is like a bloody dream. What happens now . . . where are you going?"

"Home. And now Lorna's gone, I can."

"You don't want to come to the wake yourself?"

"I thought about it, but it'll be too much for everyone. Best you go and tell them. Then come to mine and I can explain everything."

"I'm not sure I want to let you out of my sight," Connor gave a weary little smile, "I'm scared you're going to disappear again."

"I'm going nowhere. My days of being away are well and truly behind me."

"I can't see Lorna being involved in this. Are you absolutely sure? She's pretty cut up about it all."

"I bet she is," Dan snarled, "guilty conscience, that's what that'll be. She's done it, bro, honestly. The police have enough to throw the book at them both."

"And to think we've been there for her, supporting and trying to ease the pain."

Doubt was etched all over Ruth's face, "I can't believe it either. Lorna's been through hell, waiting for news."

"All fake. She's played you . . . she played us all. It seems that none of us really know her."

"You're telling me," Ruth said, disbelief still evident on her face.

"Anyway, enough about her. What about the girls,

where are they?" Dan couldn't wait to see them but knew they'd need to be prepared.

"They're staying at a friend's house tonight." Ruth looked at Connor, "I think when we've spoken to Dan and understand it all, we'll have to go and bring them home."

"Yeah, good idea," Connor said, "it'll hit the media soon, I'm sure. We'd better go to the wake first of all." He turned to Dan, "I've just thought, you can't get in your house, you haven't got a key."

"Phyllis has next door."

"Not anymore she hasn't. Lorna took it from her. And I hardly think turning up at her house is the right thing to do, even though she's the only one that thought you were still alive."

Dan widened his eyes, "Really? Good old Phyllis. Shall I head to yours then? You've got a key to my house."

"Yeah, maybe that's best. I tell you what. Let's get in the Daimler to take me to the wake and I'll go in and explain things. They'll understand I can't stay once I make an announcement. You get the driver to carry on with Ruth to our house and I'll get a taxi back."

"Sounds like a plan. You've become quite pragmatic since I've been away, I see."

"Yeah, I've had to," Connor grinned, "since you died and left me." He reached in for another hug. "This is going to be the best news I've ever delivered."

Dan savoured his embrace. After his hellish experience, it was a joy to finally be back. His focus moving forward was to concentrate on his family that loved him . . . it was plainly evident now that Lorna never had.

Chapter 42

"Here you go," Ruth placed three glasses of brandy on the kitchen table and smiled lovingly at Dan. "First of all, let's drink to the fact you're safely back with us."

"Cheers Ruth," Dan said and turned to Connor who'd just got back and sat down. "How did they take the news?"

"Pretty stunned at first, but it soon turned to celebration. I didn't elaborate, I couldn't. I just said we'd had news you were alive. I've left those that wanted to stay drinking to your good health and stuffing themselves with the buffet."

"It'll go down as one of the best wakes they'll ever attend," Dan said with a grin.

"Tell me about it. I still can't believe you're here, it feels like some sort of television drama."

"It does a bit, but it's definitely real and I can't tell you how good it feels to be back."

"How the hell you're going to have an explanation for all this, I've no idea," Connor said, running his fingers through his hair, "where the fuck have you been all this time?"

"Connor!" Ruth scolded.

Dan took a huge gulp of his brandy. The heat felt comforting. "It's hard to know where to begin. I know it's an enormous shock."

"Shock doesn't come close to covering it. I'm trying to figure out why my brother has allowed us all to grieve for him, when all the time, he's been alive and well. And to let us have a memorial service for you, for Christ's sake, why?"

"I know it's bad, and I'm truly sorry for what I've put you through."

"I don't get it. Lorna is capable of a lot of things, but murder?"

"You'd better believe it. The pair of them hit Ingrid and I with a boat hook and shoved us overboard. I was lucky and somehow woke up and was able to swim for my life, literally."

"But why the hell didn't you let us know you were alive?"

"I couldn't, not at first anyway."

"Allowing us to think you were dead is unforgivable." Connor was fighting back the tears, "It's been terrible."

"I know it has. But let me explain and maybe you'll not judge me so harshly." Dan gave a huge sigh, "I hardly know where to start." He knocked back the last of the brandy and began by discussing how they'd first met Perry and Ingrid Hunter and had become friends. Of course, he didn't realise then that Lorna had already known Perry, nobody did. They'd played him well, each of them. It was all simple enough for Dan to discuss how Lorna, Perry and Ingrid, had pestered him about the holiday. He relayed it all well until it came to being in Greece. Then he faltered, recalling their evil act.

"I find this is the hardest part of it all," he blew out a

breath.

"Do you want more brandy?" Ruth asked.

"In a minute, let me get this out first. It isn't that I've a problem remembering, it's more that it's easier to try and forget."

"Yes, I'm sure. Just try though, so we can make an effort to understand."

"About four days into the holiday, we were supposed to go out for the boat trip. I now realise the whole purpose of the day was to get us as pissed as they could. It was a great day, roaming around and seeing the sights, and we had a fabulous lunch that went on for about two hours. I'd had more than enough wine, so when we returned to the villa, I wanted to go to bed and sleep it off. I now realise with hindsight, I was actually being plied with more alcohol than any of them.

"Anyway, despite trying to go to bed, they insisted we went out on the boat. I wasn't keen. Even in my plastered state, I didn't want to. I'm still not entirely sure even now if they slipped something into my drink. I remember a euphoric feeling, a sense of not caring about anything, which is unusual for me. I'm quite measured normally, as you know," he raised his eyebrows.

"Perry took the boat out for miles, but I don't remember particularly sensing any danger. Eventually, after yet more drinks and a ridiculous shot of God knows what, Ingrid called us over to the edge of the boat on some pretence of seeing an unusual fish. The last thing I remember was an enormous blow to my head."

"Do you know who hit you?"

"It was Perry. He'd just approached, carrying a heavy-duty boat hook. He looked over my shoulder to the water, looking for the fish. I remember Ingrid pointing that she'd spotted the fish again. I turned my attention back to the water, and then came the blow to the head."

Ruth and Connor listened patiently. He knew they must have questions, but they didn't interrupt.

"Anyway . . . I came to in the water but in a daze. I think instinct kicked in and despite struggling to move, I somehow pushed myself upwards, knowing my survival depended on it. I honestly reckon if I hadn't been as fit as I was, I'd have been a goner. Eventually, somehow, I managed to get to the surface. That first breath," he shook his head, remembering how it felt to gasp some air into his lungs, "I can tell you, was something else. But I was terribly disorientated. I wasn't entirely sure then what had happened. I don't think at that moment in time, I even knew my own name. I had no idea where I was or how I'd got into the water. Intuition told me I needed to swim to keep out of danger and stay alive. I think half of the time I swam under the water, so great was my fear that danger wasn't far behind me. I felt I'd escaped from something, but didn't have any idea what. I heard an explosion, maybe even two, I'm not sure, I just kept on going. I was disorientated and on the edge of losing consciousness. I remember vividly, bright lights flashing in front of me. I thought maybe I'd had a stroke or something. But I kept on swimming. I knew my life depended on it."

Ruth interrupted, "I don't get how they didn't see you

if you were in the water and swimming."

"No, I don't either. I can't fathom that out. But as I say, instinctively, I stayed beneath the surface, well I say instinctively, to be honest, I'm not entirely sure if it was pure fatigue. I can only assume they were too busy covering their tracks to look for me. The Greek authorities will now know Perry rigged the explosion on the boat.

"The next part was filled in for me by Vasilis, a Greek fisherman who found me washed up on the beach, unconscious. Seemingly, he was returning from a fishing trip to his home to the west of the island where he lives with his wife. After checking to see if I was breathing, his wife came to his assistance and they got me to the house in a wheelbarrow and put me to bed. He told me that I slept for almost twenty hours. When I woke up, I had no idea where I was or even who I was. Vasilis could only speak in broken English, but he was able to say I needed a doctor. I rejected that and asked if I could stay and rest. I hoped my memory would return once I'd got over whatever trauma I'd suffered.

"How long before your memory returned?" Connor asked.

"Weeks, but I was actually with them for over a month. My memory was there somewhere in the back of my mind. It was like when you wake up and have dreamt something nice, and it's in there," he tapped his temple, "only you can't recall it. But it's dormant in the deep recesses of your brain.

"Anyway, after about three weeks, the fog started to

clear and piece by piece, I remembered exactly what had happened. Vasilis then shared as best he could, the information about the boating accident which he'd thought involved me, and then I realised I was presumed dead."

Dan was full of remorse as he looked at the two people he loved most in the world. "I'm sorry. I should have contacted you then, it was unforgivable not doing so. But once I learned that Ingrid's body had been found, it crushed me. I still find it difficult coming to terms with what Lorna and her lover had done. What an evil pair. I thought about the law and how easily Lorna might get a slick lawyer to somehow get her off with it. You know, coerced by her lover, and I didn't want that. I wanted to get justice for Ingrid, a young woman they chose to snuff out."

"So, what happened next? How did you get out of Greece?" Ruth asked sipping her brandy.

"Vasilis helped me to get back into the UK. He had a friend that travelled regularly and was prepared to smuggle me in the back of his lorry. I am a British Citizen so it wasn't like I was an illegal immigrant, and by that stage, I was past caring anyway."

"Bloody hell," Connor said, "it would have been much easier to go to the police."

"I know it would. But like I said, Lorna might have walked and I wasn't having that."

"So, once you were back in the UK, what happened then?"

"I hitched my way to the Cairngorms. I remembered

where you'd hidden away when you got into debt that time. I went to Arthur's, that neighbour, intending to tell him I was going to stay at the same cottage. I knew where that key was we put back when we left, under the pet headstone. But the old boy offered me a bed at his. He's unwell and I think he wanted the company. He's not got long for this world."

"I can't bloody believe all this time we were grieving, you were there."

"Yep," he smiled, trying to add a bit of humour into an intense discussion, "you can't get rid of me that easily. Anyway, I stayed there and continued to recover. I wanted some time to elapse for Lorna to continue the façade of the grieving widow. I thought the longer it went on, the less chance of her pleading some sort of coercive control from Perry and getting away with it."

Ruth raised her eyebrows, "She still might do that."

"Yeah, I'm sure she'll try. But she's been complicit by organising the memorial service. I hope that when she comes before a jury, they can see how cunning she is."

"But how did you know what was going on with Lorna? Who knew you were alive?" Connor paused, "Phyllis?"

Dan scowled, "No, what's made you think she'd know anything?"

"Because like I said, she never believed you were dead. Kept going on about you hadn't passed over to the other side. She really spooked Lorna. Now I can see why."

"Yeah, I bet. But no, nobody knew at that stage until

I eventually went to the police and told them everything. They put a tail on Lorna. Their intention was to wait until today to see if she went ahead with the memorial service. That's pretty calculated and I don't think it'll do her any good when the case comes to court. It's mercenary."

Ruth shook her head, "I'm still struggling to get my head around it all. I can't believe Lorna's capable of this. Perry must have had some sort of control over her. She's not a murderer."

"That's exactly what she is Ruth. Imagine how I'm struggling to come to terms with it. I was married to the woman. I nearly lost my life because of her and him. They deserve everything that's coming their way."

"So what now?" Connor asked.

"I resume my life."

"What about Lorna?"

"What about her?"

"Will you go and see her?"

He shrugged, "What is there to say? Why did you want me dead? I know why. There's no doubt that the legal process is not going to be easy, but nothing can be as terrible as waking up in the middle of the ocean knowing that you were meant to die. Nothing's worse than that."

Ruth squeezed his hand reassuringly. "I can't believe what you've been through. Thank God you made it. You know we'll be there for you. As difficult as this is to get our heads around, you're alive and that's all we care about. We've had such a terrible time, Dan. Poor

Connor has been beside himself with grief."

Dan's eyes welled up as he looked at his dear brother. "I know. Me too. But I'm back now and going nowhere. I promise." He reached in and pulled Connor towards him. For a few seconds, time paused as the normally capable, strong and stoic older brother, became vulnerable as he allowed the relieved tears to flow freely.

Chapter 43

Dan's life had changed for ever. He'd spent weeks dreaming of returning and getting back to a degree of normality, but it was going to take time. The realisation he'd been married to a woman that was prepared to kill him was taking some getting used to. While he'd been away, it had somehow felt as if he wasn't directly involved, as if it had happened to someone else, but now he'd returned home, the realisation of what had occurred was even more heinous. He'd been the focus of media attention which he hated, but he found being back at the office therapeutic. And there was one bit of light on the horizon. Victoria. She'd got his new number from Connor and telephoned him straight away when she heard the news. As with them all, she'd been stunned having spent weeks mourning him. They'd made arrangements to meet up that afternoon, which he was looking forward to.

The telephone ringing in his office interrupted his thoughts.

"Hello."

"Mr Blowers is on the line."

"Thank you, put him through." His solicitor calling was becoming a daily occurrence. More recently he'd had to meet with the prosecuting barrister to go through his statement and his forthcoming appearance in court.

"Good morning, Dan."

"Morning. What can I do for you?"

"Well, it's a bit of a difficult one . . ."

"Don't tell me," Dan interrupted, "she's changed her plea to guilty."

"No, it isn't that, I'm afraid. That would be easy to deal with. It's much more complicated. I've just received a call from a social worker involved with your wife, it now appears that Lorna is pregnant."

"Christ," Dan cursed, "the poor little bugger, having those two criminals for parents. I don't get why this information is being shared with you, though?"

"Because it's not as clear cut as you suggest, I'm afraid."

Dan shook his head, "I'm not with you?"

"Lorna doesn't know who the father is. She claims it could be either yourself or Perry Hunter."

"You're kidding me."

"I'm afraid not. That's why they're involving me. Arrangements are going to have to be made for when the baby's born as to what'll happen to it."

"Do you mean adoption?"

"Yes . . . or, if it happens to be your baby . . . if you would want to bring it up."

Dan squeezed the bridge of his nose in disbelief. Could things get any worse? "I can't believe I'm hearing this. God alive, can this woman cause any more bloody havoc?"

"Seemingly, the next step is to meet with the social worker for a discussion. I think it's best if I accompany you to any meetings. Although this is personal, we don't want anything to compromise the prosecution's case."

"I'm not meeting anyone. I've enough on with the barrister and all the legal stuff. I want to move on with my life. I'm certainly not discussing any baby that won't even be mine. It'll be Perry's."

"I do understand. But as I said, at the moment, they can't be certain who the father of the baby is. And I guess, you can't be certain either, unless," his solicitor paused . . . "unless of course you weren't having sex with your wife?"

Fuck, fuck, fuck. They were having more sex than ever before Greece and during their time there. But that was ages ago.

"How many weeks pregnant is she?"

"They're not sure. Seemingly, the prison are organising some scans and antenatal care. She's actually been moved to HMP Peterborough as there's a unit for expectant mothers."

"I can't get my head around this. We didn't want kids. That's why we took precautions. How the hell has she got pregnant?"

The line was silent.

"Look, I'm going to have to think this through. Can I call you back?"

"Of course. You certainly don't have to meet with anyone if you don't want to. They'll do a DNA test on the baby once it's born and we'll be informed of the result. You don't have to make any decisions right now. My job is to inform you that a meeting has been offered."

"I get that. Thanks. Leave it with me, would you. I'll be in touch."

"Yes, whenever you're ready."

Dan cut the call. Bile burned in his throat. A child would tie him to Lorna for ever. His thoughts drifted to his precious little boy with so many health needs, he barely survived past his first birthday. But he loved him desperately and if willing a child to live would have worked, then his son would be alive today.

He stood up and walked towards the office window. People outside were going about their business, walking to and from work, nipping in and out the shops, while he'd been hit with a sledgehammer. One thing he was certain about was, he wasn't seeing a social worker to discuss anything to do with Lorna. As far as he was concerned, he wanted them to lock up her and Perry and throw away the key. And he was going to testify to make sure that happened. He had to, for Ingrid, a lovely young woman that Lorna and Perry had discarded like a piece of meat.

He sighed deeply. There was a fifty per cent chance the child Lorna was carrying was his, and no way was he in a position to bring the baby up on his own. Even if he was, the baby had Lorna, a murderer as its mother. Eventually, she was going to get out of prison, and however old the child might be, she'd want to see it. And another thought occurred to him, like a light bulb moment – being pregnant might just help her defence when the case came to court.

The thought of a child coming into the world that might be his caused his heart to skip slightly, but he had to suppress it. His head told him not to get involved. No way could he bring up Lorna the murderer's baby. It'd be Perry's, he willed silently.

He winced. But what if it wasn't?

Chapter 44

Dan's first instinct had been to cancel his coffee date with Victoria, but he hadn't. After his solicitor had dropped the bombshell about the baby, any joy he'd felt about meeting up with his ex, had disappeared. Now all he felt was an overwhelming sense of despair with one thing dominating his thoughts. Could he turn his back on his own child?

Victoria was already seated in the corner with a mug in front of her as he opened the coffee shop door. As soon as she saw him coming towards her, she rushed forward and wrapped her arms around him.

"God, Dan, I can't believe you're here." Despite it being a bitterly cold day, warmth flooded through his veins. It was comforting, locked in her embrace; instinctively, he tightened his arms around her. He'd felt vulnerable since returning to his normal life, almost as if he was still a victim, not a survivor. Victoria's radiant smile lit up her face as she pulled away, "It's a miracle, it truly is." Tears glistened in her striking eyes, one blue and the other brown, "I was devastated when I thought we'd lost you."

"Thanks, Vic," he smiled tenderly, "with hindsight, lying low wasn't one of my smartest moves. I should have come forward sooner."

"Well, you're here now, and that's the best thing in

the world as far as I'm concerned." Her beautiful face was full of genuine warmth as she took her seat. They'd talked on the phone a few times so she knew the details of what had actually happened to him in Greece.

He pulled out a chair opposite her. "I can't tell you how good it is to see you. You look great, by the way, and today isn't going to be all about me. I want to know how you've been keeping."

"I'm absolutely fine," she wiggled the ring-free third finger of her left hand, "divorce going through now, sadly."

"I'm sorry it didn't work out for you. You deserve to be happy. I wanted that for you more than anything."

"I know you did. You're a good man. How are you? You look like you've lost weight."

"Yeah, I have a bit, but it's going back on now. Ruth insists on cooking me meals which consist of roast potatoes, Yorkshire puddings and calorific puddings smothered in custard."

"Oh, right," she pulled a playful face, "that's no hardship for you, is it? You love that sort of food."

"Yeah, it's still a struggle, though," he winked, "but I'm doing my best."

The waitress appeared, "Can I get you anything?" she asked Victoria.

"Yes please, same again for me."

"And a large black coffee for me please," Dan said.

Victoria waited until the waitress walked away. "So, tell me, how are things really?"

"Okay," he shrugged, "it's not easy with the court

case pending. My solicitor must have me on speed dial or something as he seems to contact me on a daily basis. Being back at work though is helping."

"I bet. Hey, it's a good thing you had Connor to hold the fort."

"Yeah, he really did come up trumps in my absence. I've seen a real maturity about him since I've been back. Thankfully the wobble he went through with the gambling, seems to be well and truly behind him now, which is a relief."

"You're lucky to have each other. I always wished I'd had siblings."

"You're right, I am lucky. I've actually suggested to Connor that he goes to university on a part-time basis to train as a chartered accountant."

"That sounds brilliant. Does he want to?"

"Let's just say, he's coming round to the idea. I want him to get the qualification and invite him to become a partner at some stage. He deserves that if nothing else. There'd have been no business left without him. It's hard to find a way to thank him for what he did."

"Well, I can't think of a better way than supporting him to train as an accountant. What an opportunity."

They paused while the waitress appeared and put their coffees down.

"Thank you," Dan said.

Victoria nodded her thanks and waited until they were alone. "Have there been any long-term effects of the blow to your head? Have you been checked out?"

"I've not seen anyone, no, but I'm fine now. Fine that

is apart from the pending court case." He released a heavy sigh. "It's not every day that you have to give evidence that's going to put your wife behind bars."

"No," she said, adding sugar to her coffee and stirring it, "I can only imagine how difficult that's going to be for you. You're not a vindictive man, far from it."

"I like to think I'm not, but if I'm absolutely honest, all the time I was in Greece recovering, I wanted the pair of them to suffer for what they'd done. But they weren't suffering one bit. It seems they were carrying on with their lives just waiting for my body to be washed up."

Sympathy flooded her eyes, "It's terrible, it really is. You said nobody knew you were alive. Didn't Connor have any inkling?"

"No, nobody knew."

"How terrible for him, Dan, I can't imagine what he went through. And Ruth and the girls, they all love you so much."

"Yeah, it wasn't nice for any of them, but Connor of course suffered the most. I regret that now more than anything."

"Well, you have to move forward. You're here now and that's what counts."

"You're right," he smiled and took a sip of his coffee. "Anyway, that's enough about me for now. How are you . . . since splitting with Mike?"

"I'm okay," she scrunched up her pert little nose which he'd always found attractive, "I realise now, he was a rebound thing. You and I had lost Tommy and our precious world imploded. After the split, Mike was simply there. And I enjoyed him being there. I wanted everything to happen between us that did. It was the light against the darkness. And for a little while, it worked, but then momentum petered out. We found ourselves living in the same house but not together. Eventually, he met someone which I am genuinely pleased about and the good news is, she's having a baby."

He was probably the only person who could read that, despite the cheery exterior, her heart would be breaking about her ex having a baby with his new partner . . . something she couldn't give him. He placed his hand on hers on the table, they shared a huge bond together. "I'm so sorry, Vic."

The hysterectomy she'd had which he'd given consent for as she couldn't at the time, was always there in the back of Dan's mind. His chest ached with sadness. She'd been the most beautiful mother to their son, and since his death, she covered her heartache well. It was especially sad that she couldn't have more children.

Her lovely face smiled back at him. She knew he recognised her pain. Momentarily, he hesitated telling her about the bombshell he'd received that day. But he had an overwhelming urge to speak to someone and relieve the tension of the tight knot in his stomach, and nobody was better than Victoria to share it with. She was pragmatic and a sorter. His best interests would be hers and he was confident that she'd put him on the right path. So, despite his misgivings, he cleared his throat and plunged in. "Speaking of children, I had a call from my solicitor today, seemingly Lorna's actually pregnant."

"Oh no," her mouth dropped open.

"Yeah, and can you believe, she doesn't know who the father is. The baby either belongs to her accomplice, or it's mine."

She squeezed his hand. "Oh God, Dan, that's awful. What happens in cases like this? Can she have the baby in prison?"

"It sounds like that's what's going to happen. The trial is set for next year now, anyway. So she'll have the baby in jail." He shook his head, "What a start eh, for any child."

"And then what happens?"

"It'll be taken away into care initially pending the outcome of the trial. That's if it's Perry's baby, unless of course he has family to take care of it, I guess."

"What if it's your baby?" she asked cautiously.

He blew out a breath. "That's the million-dollar question right now. She's likely to get a hefty sentence for being an accomplice in the murder of Perry's wife, and then a sentence for the attempted murder of me. I don't think she's going to be out much before fifteen to eighteen years, unless of course she gets away with it by pleading she was coerced by Perry."

"Do you think that's likely to happen?"

"Not if I can help it. But she's resourceful, and it will have crossed her mind that this baby might help her cause in terms of the jurors."

"Yes, I can see she might get a sympathetic response."

"Precisely. But if she gets what she deserves, the child will be an adult when she gets out. I want to build my future away from her. I've already started the process of divorce."

"It's truly awful, Dan." He found it comforting she'd kept hold of his hand. "So you're now going to have to wait until the baby's born for DNA tests?"

"Yep, that's about it. Perry's mixed race though so it might be evident as soon as it's born, although I did read on the internet that it's not always noticeable at first when babies are born as the pigmentation could take days before it changes. So yes, it most probably will be a DNA test."

"Gosh, how terrible having to wait. How far on is the pregnancy, do you know?"

He felt almost bereft as she released his hand to sip her coffee.

"No, I don't. To be honest, I know very little. I don't think she does actually. Seemingly, they are in the process of doing tests."

"So . . . I hardly dare ask. If it's your baby, will you bring it up?"

"I honestly don't know, Vic. Rebuilding my life will be even harder bringing up a child as a single parent."

"Yes, I can see that. But if you do decide to bring up the baby, you'll just have to allow people to help. You'll do it, Dan, that's the sort of honourable man you are. If anyone can step up, you can."

"Thank you, that means a lot. I can't tell you how nice it is to be able to talk to someone about it. Connor and

Ruth have been brilliant through all of this, but I haven't told them yet about the baby. I know Connor will want me to walk away and I'm not sure I can do that."

"Of course you can't. Without being over-dramatic, there's a child's future at stake here."

"You're right," he nodded, "you always are. I really don't know how it went so wrong for us. We were happy, weren't we?"

"Yeah, we were. And I still think of Tommy all the time, do you?"

"All the time."

"But," she said brightly, "soon you might have a new child to focus on. You were a fabulous dad and I know if it is your baby, it'll have the most fantastic childhood with you."

Whether it was because he'd felt lonely and vulnerable since the accident, he wasn't sure, but his chest seemed to almost flutter hearing the enthusiasm in her voice and her confidence in him. It made him feel as if he could conquer anything that was thrown at him. He smiled lovingly at her, because he did love her . . . he always had done. "That truly does mean the world. I wish things had been different. You too should have gone on and had more children."

"Yeah, but that's life, we don't always get everything we want. And the hysterectomy was necessary to save my life."

"I know it was, but I hated making that decision."

"It was the right one," she reassured, "I had wonderful years with you, and one with our beautiful boy."

"You're an amazing woman, you know that. Not an ounce of bitterness in you. Mike was a fool to let you go. And I was too."

"What's done is done, Dan. It was a terribly difficult time for us when we lost Tommy. Instead of pulling together, we lost ourselves somewhere along the way."

"You're right. But I hope now we can see each other from time to time. Not full-on or anything, but maybe dinner occasionally. If I end up as a full-time father, I'm going to need all the friends I can get."

"I'd like that. And I don't know whether I should be rooting for you, or hoping it doesn't happen."

"No, me neither." He looked around the cafe and realised that him and Victoria were the only customers left, with their empty cups in front of them. And by the looks of one of the waitresses sweeping up, they were waiting to close.

"Crikey," he looked at his watch, "how long have we been here?"

"Too long by the look of things," she grinned, reaching for her bag.

"Have you got to dash off?" he asked, "or do you fancy a bite to eat now? Don't feel you have to if you've somewhere to go."

She smiled, lighting up her familiar face he knew so well. "I haven't got anywhere to go to, so supper would be lovely."

"Great. Give me a sec and I'll pay for the coffees."

He walked towards the cashier. "Sorry. We were so

engrossed in conversation, we hadn't realised the time."

"No worries," she said, "It's refreshing to see a couple concentrating on each other and spending their time chatting rather than on their mobile phones."

"I know what you mean, but we're not a couple," his eyes drifted towards Victoria putting her jacket on, "we were once, but that was a long time ago. We're just friends now."

"Yeah," the woman winked, "sure you are."

Chapter 45

The immaculate office Dan was sitting in felt oppressive. He'd come straight from his own place of work, across town to his solicitor's pristine, upmarket office. He'd taken a seat next to his solicitor, George Blowers around a huge glossy twelve-seat table having been introduced to the woman opposite. Yvonne Barr, the social worker who had been assigned to oversee the future for Lorna's baby when it was born.

"Mr Blowers tells me you've been appraised of the situation regarding your wife's pregnancy," she said.

"I have."

"Then you'll understand that, as yet, Mrs Lloyd does not know who the father of the baby is."

"Yes, I'm aware of that."

"Good. The reason for today's meeting is to ascertain exactly what happens when the baby is born. Mrs Lloyd has been moved to a secure mother and baby unit until she gives birth. Once she has, the baby will be taken into foster care until the outcome of the court case is known. If she is found guilty, she'll remain in custody for the duration of the sentence imposed by the courts. If this is the case, she'll then decide if she wants the baby to be adopted."

"Yes, I understand."

"I've met with Mrs Lloyd and her wishes are, if you

are the genetic father of the baby and are willing, that you have custody of the child. But if Mr Hunter is the genetic father, then the baby will be put up for adoption."

"How far on is the pregnancy?" Dan asked.

"She's currently almost thirty weeks pregnant. The due date is," she looked at the paperwork in front of her, "November the 8th."

Dan did a quick calculation in his head. Lorna must have been pregnant before Greece.

"Have the screening tests been completed?"

"Yes, they have. Mrs Lloyd has had all the relevant blood tests, scans, and her physical health is being monitored."

"And everything's normal?"

"Yes. Even though she was much later than normal in receiving antenatal care, all the relevant tests appear to be satisfactory."

He prayed that was the case. His own son with all his health concerns was never far from his mind. Tommy's little life had been snuffed out because of them. The paediatrician had reassured him and Victoria that none were hereditary, but he'd never wanted to test that theory. Now he might have no choice if the child Lorna is carrying was his.

George Blowers cleared his throat, "I've advised my client about all of these issues and offered him more time to think about things. You'll appreciate, he's had a traumatic time of late."

"Yes, of course. And you're right, no final decisions

will be made until the baby is born. Then we'll carry out a DNA test to establish parenthood. Today's meeting is more about intention."

Dan had already made his decision. It had been made for him really. He couldn't abandon his own child.

"If the baby is mine, then I will have custody."

"Thank you. That's helpful to know at this stage."

"I do need to ask, though, if I am the father, and Lorna goes to prison for what she's done, does she have any visitation rights? Can she demand to see the baby?"

"No, she doesn't. But, if she is found guilty, and you are the father, you'll need to consider the child's welfare. It might be . . . erm . . . prudent for the mother to see it from time to time. Whatever happens, if for example Mrs Lloyd does spend a period of time incarcerated, it won't be for ever. She will come out and resume a life where she may want to be part of her child's upbringing."

That was exactly what he was afraid of. He wasn't stupid; this baby could sway the court into a more lenient sentence for Lorna. The prosecuting barrister had informed him that Lorna was prepared to take the stand and give evidence. Seemingly, her defence was coercion by Perry as her lover, and if she was lucky and the jury believed her, it could mean a much lesser sentence, if indeed one at all in relation to her part in Ingrid's murder and his attempted murder.

Dan deliberately didn't respond to the social worker's suggestion. "So, now it's a waiting game, I take it?" he asked.

"Yes, I'm afraid so. I have some scan pictures if you'd like them?"

"No . . . thank you. I'd rather not until I know if it's my child."

"Yes, I do understand." She smiled kindly. "I'll speak to Mrs Lloyd and tell her your decision. So for now, I think that's about it unless you have any further questions?"

"Can I ask if you know the sex of the baby?"

"Yes. Would you like to know?"

Did he? What difference would it make? If it was his child, he was going to bring it up regardless of anything else.

"Yes, I'd like to know."

"It's a girl."

"Thank you." He looked at George Blowers. "Have we covered everything?"

"For now, yes." His solicitor turned to the social worker. "Thank you for coming and explaining things to my client. It's been helpful."

She nodded and reached for her briefcase. Dan watched as she placed the documents relating to Lorna inside. His gut contracted as he wondered how many lies his wife was spinning them all.

The social worker stood up. "I'll be in touch, Mr Lloyd."

Dan shook her outstretched hand. "Thank you."

She turned to George Blowers and shook his hand also. "I appreciate you facilitating the meeting, Mr Blowers."

"You're welcome."

After George Blowers buzzed his secretary to show the social worker out, he indicated for Dan to sit down again.

"You okay? Can I get you anything, a coffee, tea?" he asked, pulling his chair away from Dan's so it was easier to talk.

"I'm fine, thanks. Glad it's over really. It's just the waiting now to see whose baby it is."

"Yes, I can see that's going to be a strain. And then the court case, it's a lot."

"It is. But none of it is choice, is it? It's got to be done."

He dreaded the court case coming but in equal measure he wanted it all to be over and done with. He'd met with the prosecution barrister, Alastair Millington several times to go through his evidence and how he was likely to be cross-examined. Rage surged through him every time he thought that Lorna might walk after all she'd done. He'd been extremely lucky to be alive to tell the tale, Ingrid less so. He needed to fight for her. She'd been a lovely woman and in the short time he'd known her, he sincerely liked her. Perry was at least pleading guilty, but Lorna wasn't. As if Lorna would ever lie down and take anything. Her nature was rebellious. And his biggest dread was the thought she might get off lightly. He couldn't resist asking George's opinion. He was after all an experienced legal professional.

"You were there with Alastair the last time he went

over me giving my evidence in court. Do you share his view that there's a strong possibility that Lorna might be acquitted?"

"It's a difficult one to call. She's admitting she was complicit, but using coercion by her lover as her defence is a clever move. The jury might go for it. It's topical right now. Lorna was a respectable woman, worked in a GP practice and doesn't have a previous criminal record. She was a regular visitor to her mother in a care home and subsidised the care home fees. And the fact that she will have recently given birth might just add the sympathy card."

"Yeah, that's what scares me. If she walks free after what she's done then there isn't any justice."

"No, I quite agree. But . . . you'll be an exceptional witness for the prosecution in terms of being a survivor of their heinous crime. That's why Perry Hunter has had to plead guilty. There is no defence for him. You're living proof of what the pair of them did, and if they had succeeded, nobody would be any the wiser.

"I hope and pray you're right. There is one thing that I'm still puzzled about, though. I get that Perry and Lorna wanted to be together, hence Perry renting next door so they could carry out their plan. What I don't get is, how he convinced Ingrid to move there. Yes, it seems he dabbled in buying and selling property, but of course bought nothing while he was there. The police told me that. So, I wonder how he persuaded Ingrid to rent next door?"

"Maybe he took her round some properties to be

convincing?"

"Yeah, maybe, but she told us she did admin for the company he worked for. But there was no company. I just don't get why she would go along with that lie?"

His solicitor shook his head, "I don't suppose you'll ever know."

"No, I don't suppose I will," Dan said wearily, pushing his chair back and standing up. He reached out his hand. "Thanks for facilitating the meeting with the social worker."

"My pleasure. There'll be a bit of a lull now until the baby's born. As soon as I hear anything, I'll be in touch."

"Cheers, George." He raised his hand, "It's okay, I can see myself out."

As he made his way towards his car, Dan suppressed the gloominess of the court case and the mystery of Ingrid and allowed his mind to consider that soon there would be a baby. A girl, the social worker had said. He reached in his pocket for his phone, intending to call Victoria. But he stopped himself. What was the point in sharing the news?

Especially as it most probably was Perry's.

Chapter 46

Eight months later . . .

Dan was standing with Connor in the garden of his house. They were both clutching a glass of red wine from a bottle of Dan's best reserves he saved for special occasions. And today was certainly one of those. It was his daughter, Rosie's christening. He'd hired caterers and a small marquee in case of inclement weather, but he needn't have worried. The sun was shining on all the guests in their finery, and after the past year, it was a joyous occasion. There weren't hordes of guests, but the intimate gathering was of people that meant the most to him.

They'd had the church service and the guests were back at the house enjoying the fare on offer. He spotted his neighbour Phyllis out of the corner of his eye, bending a poor victim's ear. Dear old Phyllis, she'd been fussing round him for months now, like a mother hen.

Dan's gaze was on Victoria, sitting on a bench amongst the trellis of coloured clematis, holding his daughter in her beautiful christening gown that she'd gifted Rosie. When he'd asked her to be Rosie's godmother, the tears had flowed down her beautiful face. But they were joyous tears and he was honoured to think she was going to be part of his daughter's life.

Connor reached in his shirt pocket for his sunglasses and put them on. "Well, you certainly didn't need that DNA test to prove Rosie is yours, she gets more like you every day."

"You think so?"

"I know so."

Dan smiled proudly as he looked across at Rosie who seemed to be enjoying all the attention from the women. Instead of being fractious as she was passed around, she appeared to be loving all the fuss judging by the smile on her chubby little cheeks.

"She's really placid, isn't she?" Connor said, "she didn't cry once when the vicar doused her in water."

"No, she didn't. But she's good most of the time. And Caroline is worth her weight in gold as a nanny. It was my lucky day finding her."

"Yeah, she is. Why's she not here today, anyway?"

"It's her sister's fortieth."

"Ah, right. Good job you've got Victoria then, as a stand in. Motherhood suits her. It was nice of you to ask her to be godmother alongside Ruth."

"I couldn't think of anyone better. Vic loves Rosie . . . like we all do."

"Yeah, and that little bundle has certainly captured the girls' hearts. They asked Ruth if we were going to have another."

"Bloody hell. Is that likely?"

"No," Connor said emphatically, "much as we love Rosie, neither Ruth nor I want to start again with all that."

"I don't blame you. It's hard work, there's no doubt about that. I'm lucky with the support I get from you all."

"We love helping." Connor's gaze was pensive as he looked around the guests. "When you think of the past year, it's amazing how things have turned out, isn't it?"

"It is. Family means everything. That's why I chose Rosie's name, after Mum."

"I love you gave her that. It suits her."

"Yeah, it does somehow, doesn't it?"

Connor took a sip of his wine. "There's something I want to ask you," he screwed up his nose, "but maybe now's not the time."

"What? Don't tell me you can't cope with the academic work of your course?"

"Don't be daft. It is bloody hard though, but I will stick it out until I'm qualified."

"What's bugging you then?"

"Ruth doesn't want me to say anything. She said to leave it."

"Well, if it's something that's bothering you that much, ask away."

Connor took a deep breath in. "You know at the trial when the prosecuting barrister asked if you knew for certain who hit you over the head with the boat hook . . ."

"Yeah?" Dan had been expecting this.

"You said you weren't sure which of them it was, Lorna or Perry."

"That's right, I wasn't."

"But you told Ruth and I that day in our kitchen when you explained it all, that you knew it was Perry that hit you from behind on the boat as the women were sitting next to you."

"Did I?"

"Come on, Dan. You know you did."

Dan didn't answer straight away. Of course he knew. The day was etched on his mind and haunted his dreams. That and the memory of waking up underneath the water and thinking he was going to die.

He knocked back the last of his wine. "I also said at the time, Perry may have slipped something into my drink. I think, whatever it was, clouded my memory, if I'm totally honest. Either that or the blow to my head."

"So, in court, you didn't lie by omission?"

"What?" Dan scowled playfully, "You sound like a bloody barrister. I'm beginning to wonder if you're on my side."

"Just answer the question, sir," Connor joked.

"Like I said, I can't be certain who hit me. And who cares anyway."

"I don't care. I'm just curious, that's all. Lorna got what she deserved, and Perry did too as far as I'm concerned. But I reckon she only got her sentence because you cast doubt on the extent of her complicity. Without that, she might have walked."

"Yeah, but I think Ruth's right, it's best left now, anyway."

Victoria approached interrupting their conversation. She looked stunning in a white fitted dress that tapered in, showing off her trim waist, but what made her even more beautiful and feminine to Dan, was his baby daughter in her arms wrapped in a shawl.

"She's getting a bit tired, Dan. Shall I give her a bottle and put her down for a nap?"

"Yeah, good idea. Do you want me to come?"

"No, you stay with the guests. I'll come out again when she falls asleep."

"Okay, thanks Vic. You know where the monitor is, just bring it out with you when you come, would you?"

"Will do."

His eyes followed her graceful walk as she made her way into the house.

Connor eyed him suspiciously. "Victoria's looking rather splendid today. How are things going with the two of you?"

"Okay," Dan nodded nonchalantly.

"Okay?" Connor raised his eyebrows, "That doesn't really say much. It looks to me as if something might have shifted between you both. Are you okay as in you're still just friends, or okay as in you're now in a relationship?"

Dan tapped the side of his nose playfully, "I'll let you know when there's something to tell. I don't want to rush into anything."

"Rush into anything? Christ, you'll be collecting your pension before you sort yourself out. The woman clearly cares about you. I should make my move if I was you before she gets fed up of waiting."

"Since when have you been an expert relationship

adviser?"

"Since you've been dragging your heels. You two are meant to be together. After everything you've been through, you deserve to be happy."

"I am happy. I have a beautiful daughter, you, Ruth and the girls. Why do I need to complicate things? Remember, I'm no dead cert on the relationship front."

"I disagree. You're a dead cert in everything you do."

"You would say that, you're my brother."

"I know. And you haven't answered my question."

"What question?"

"Are you and Victoria okay as in still just friends, or okay as in you've moved on to a relationship?"

"The third one."

"What third one?"

"We might have moved things up a notch."

"Really?"

"Really."

"And . . ."

Dan handed Connor his empty glass and winked, "And another for me when you're ready."

EPILOGUE

Lorna was sitting in the recreational mother and baby unit of the prison waiting nervously. It was the day she was going to meet her daughter for the first time since she'd given birth to her. The labour had been a difficult one, she'd had to endure almost fifteen hours of pain and suffering. Consideration had at one stage been given for a caesarean section, but she'd managed to give birth naturally. Initially, she'd held the baby, but not for that long. By the time she'd counted her fingers and toes and seen her eyes open and close, the tiny little bundle had been whisked away by the authorities. It would have been different had she chosen to breast feed, but she couldn't face anything like that. The pregnancy had taken its toll on her body and that was more than enough. The last thing she wanted was a baby on her breast every few hours so it had been her choice she'd been taken away.

Yvonne Barr, the social worker, was sitting with her in one of the chairs that were supposed to be comfy and recreational for public visits, but were actually made of leather and stiff and cold. She was dressed in typical social worker attire – black leggings and a floral top flowing like and enormous tablecloth over her midriff. A few chairs away, sitting at a discreet distance, was the prison officer, Pamela Hurley, a bulky and tall woman who the inmates didn't mess with due to her size.

Whether she knew the inmates called her Burly, Lorna wasn't sure, but it certainly was apt.

Yvonne had set the meeting up with Dan and laid down the parameters of the visit. Seemingly, when Dan arrived at the prison with the baby, Yvonne was going to meet with him away from the recreational room and bring Rosie to her. Dan would remain outside in the waiting area for the duration of the visit which was supposed to be one hour. He'd specified to Yvonne that he didn't want to see her. Lorna understood perfectly. And, after what he did in court, she didn't particularly want to see the vindictive bastard of a husband who had scuppered any chance of her getting out of prison.

Images of the trial were never far from her mind. The injustice of it all was still terribly raw. The defence case appeared to be going well until he took the stand. Dan was a personable man with an abundance of charm. Not in an obvious way where he put himself about as if he was something special. He just had one of those engaging faces that instilled trust. And he certainly used every scrap of his appeal when he took that stand.

When her defence barrister had challenged his version of events, she'd allowed herself a tiny smidgeon of hope, especially as Perry had already pleaded guilty to the charges. That more or less got her off the hook. Or so she thought. Even thinking about that day in court, made her sick to the pit of her stomach. The smell of the courtroom still lingered and she could still visualise the faces of each individual jury member. There had been an equal number of men and women, and despite being warned repeatedly by her legal team not to stare at any of them, she surreptitiously eyed them, trying to ascertain if their thoughts were favourable to her.

The barrister defending her had inspired a degree of confidence. He was a self-assured man, in his sixties and clearly had a wealth of experience. And while he didn't give her false hope by any means, he appeared confident that if he couldn't secure an acquittal, he'd manage to achieve a relatively short sentence. And due to the time spent on remand, she could walk free after the case.

She watched eagerly from her position in the dock reserved for the prisoner on trial with a slight acceleration of her heart as the barrister representing her, challenged Dan on the stand.

"In your evidence, Mr Lloyd, you state that you are unsure whether it was Mr Hunter or Mrs Lloyd who hit you from behind on the boat."

"That's correct."

"You already know that Mr Perry Hunter has pleaded guilty to the murder of his wife and attempted murder of you. Therefore, I put it to you, Mr Lloyd, you do know that your wife didn't deliver that blow to your head, as she has already testified. She couldn't have done as she was sitting beside you when it happened."

"I'm sorry," Dan put on a puzzled face, "Is that a question or an observation?"

"An observation. The question I do have is, can you categorically deny that it wasn't Mr Hunter that hit you. And please remember that you are under oath."

Dan paused, as if gathering his thoughts. But Lorna

knew him better than anyone. He was acting. She watched her husband take a theatrical deep breath in. "I'm afraid, no matter how hard I try, I can't be certain who hit me. I came to in the middle of the sea, not knowing if I was dead or alive. I forced myself to swim, literally for my life, to get to the surface. And I thank God every day that I did, and I'm here today to give evidence. I have no idea whatsoever which one of them hit me from behind. But I was hit, with a significant blow to my head, as was Mrs Hunter. I was the lucky one . . . sadly, she wasn't. I'm afraid I can add no more than that. I only wish I could."

Lorna wanted to scream out at the injustice of him being so vague. Even she could see, with her non-legal brain, Dan's testimony had the ability to cause significant damage . . . all by saying so little. As if she'd hit him with the boat hook – he knew she hadn't. But his act had been convincing and the vagueness of his evidence had sewn seeds of doubt in the jurors' minds.

The social worker sneezed loudly. Lorna glanced at the wall clock while Yvonne, searched around her bag for a tissue.

"I would have thought they'd be here by now," Lorna said.

"Yes, me too." Yvonne blew her nose. "Maybe there's a bit of a traffic hold up."

"He knows it's today?"

"Yes, of course. I confirmed it with him myself."

The door opened and one of the junior prison

officers came in. "There's been a telephone call to the prison. Mr Lloyd says he won't be bringing the baby today as she's developed a bit of a cold."

"Oh, dear, that's a shame," Yvonne said, "thank you for letting us know."

"You're welcome." The prison officer closed the door behind her leaving the three of them alone. Lorna was seething. She didn't think for one minute the baby was unwell.

"This isn't on," she spat, "there'll be nothing wrong with the baby. It'll be Dan. He won't want me to see her."

"I'm sure that isn't the case. He certainly didn't give me that impression. We can reschedule another visit. I'll speak to him and sort out another date."

"What, so he can do this again? Don't bother."

"Look, you're upset, it's understandable."

"Yes, I am upset because I know what's going on here. He's done this on purpose. Just like when he gave his evidence. He lied when he was asked if he knew who'd hit him over the head. That's why the jury found me guilty."

"But he didn't lie. He said he wasn't sure."

"And that put doubt in the jurors' minds. He knew exactly who hit him and that it couldn't possibly be me. How could I when I was sat alongside him?"

"There isn't anything to be gained by going over all this now, especially with me. I'm here as a facilitator for the baby's well-being. I can't help with anything to do with your sentence, you'll need to speak to your legal team for that. I'll make contact again with Mr Lloyd through his solicitor and fix up another time for him to bring Rosie in."

"Yeah, you do that," Lorna snarled, "but I'm telling you now, he'll not come. Or if he does, it'll just be the once and then we'll get a million excuses for the next time. He'll see to it that I'm using the baby as part of my appeal to get the sentenced reduced."

"And are you?" Yvonne asked.

Lorna didn't answer. How could she when she was doing exactly that. Eight years was a ridiculous amount of time she'd been given. All the evidence pointed to coercion by Perry. And it was all going so well until Dan's evidence and his vagueness about who hit him. It cast enough doubt in the jury's mind and ultimately, they found her guilty. All she could do now was use the baby as leverage for her appeal.

Burly Pamela stood up. "We'll get you back to your cell."

Lorna followed the prison officer out and back towards her cell. Her sentence was long enough, but poor Perry had got fifteen years for killing Ingrid and eight for the attempted murder of Dan. It was far too harsh. Her one true love still dominated her thoughts every moment of the day. She'd prayed that he'd have been the father of the baby, anything to tie her to him, even though distance and years separated him. Images of his handsome face constantly flashed through her mind, particularly at night. She hated using the defence that he'd coerced her into taking part in the crimes, but it had been a means to an end. Her expectations had been raised by the legal team conducting her defence who'd argued that pleading coercion was her best chance of being acquitted. But they hadn't bargained on Dan's evidence.

But now, her focus was on winning her appeal which the legal team had launched straight after sentencing. Eight years in the disgusting prison was the stuff of nightmares. And Dan, who'd deceived them all and pretended to be dead, had ended up the hero with a baby that he'd always secretly wanted, even though he'd sworn to her, he didn't. It had all worked out well for him. As she trailed alongside the prison officer, a thought struck her, like a light bulb going on. If that stuck up Victoria wasn't married, Dan could get back with her and they might bring up the baby together. That didn't bear thinking about. The image was too painful, like a knife being plunged deep within her.

They reached the cell door, wedged open, which was the norm during the day. Her cell mate Sandra, a middle-aged woman from Liverpool who'd embezzled money from her employers, looked down from the top bunk bed with an expectant expression.

"How did it go, hon?"

"It didn't."

"Why?"

"The baby has a cold so my husband didn't want to bring her."

Sandra jumped down from the bunk and wrapped her arms around her. "Aw, I'm sorry, love. That's a bummer."

Lorna pulled away. "Yeah, it is." She hated people hugging her.

"What now?" Sandra asked with genuine concern on her face.

"I have to wait for another visit. God knows when that'll be." Lorna climbed on to the lower bunk bed, hoping Sandra would see that she didn't want to talk. She must have got the message as she headed towards the door. "I'll give you a bit of time on your own."

Lorna gazed around the oppressive cell with the dark grey suffocating walls, barely eight feet by six, with only one way in and no windows. When the door was shut, the only light was creeping under the door. The isolation was a slow torture and the stimulation zero. The only piece of furniture apart from the bunk beds was a small square table with only the one chair despite there being two inmates sharing the cell. Sandra's family pictures of children and grandchildren were on the wall above the table. A space had been left for her precious photos, but she had none. Who could she put up? Hardly Dan, and she didn't want to see her mother's condescending face staring at her on a daily basis. She didn't even have one of her daughter. They'd offered her one at the birth, but she'd said no. What was the point?

A solitary tear ran down her cheek. Not so long ago, she had everything. A husband that loved her, family, a job, friends, and a comfortable lifestyle. But now, all that had gone. Even her dear friend Sarah had returned the letters she sent unopened to the prison. And she had no idea if Dan was still supporting her mother in the care home. Knowing him, he would be – she'd have to remember to ask the social worker next time she saw her if she could find out.

An image of Dan playing happy families in her home with their daughter, gnawed away at her. More tears streamed down her face as she rolled onto her side and curled herself into a ball. The pain of not seeing Perry crucified her. What was he doing? Was he laid on his bunk pining for her? They loved each other and should have been together right now, living the dream with his substantial inheritance. Sobs wracked her body at the injustice of it all.

How on earth could a man – rendered unconscious by a significant blow to the back of his head, his lifeless body tossed overboard in the sea to drown, actually survive to tell the tale? They couldn't. Yet Dan Lloyd had. None of it was fair. And if someone had said to her that Dan would try and influence a jury, she wouldn't have believed them. But he'd done exactly that. And in all the years she'd known him, she never heard him tell a lie, or fudge the truth. He was an honest man with integrity. Yet, he'd put the final nail in her coffin.

She pushed her face into the pillow, stifling the urge to scream out loud. She'd underestimated Dan's resolve and might have known that he would do *whatever it takes* to get justice.

THE END

Acknowledgements

The journey to completing a novel can take quite some time and involves much more than just the author, therefore, I'd like to take this opportunity to thank other contributors to this book. Top of my list is my brilliant and insightful editor, John Hudspith who I couldn't write without! Thank you Johnny!

To draw a reader towards a book, you need a gifted and talented cover designer and I have one with Jane Dixon-Smith (JD Smith Design). I'm thrilled with all of the book covers Jane has done for me, each one is special.

I have wonderful and supportive beta readers, Nico Maeckelberghe, Lyn Wilkinson and Denise Goodhand. They play an important part, and an extra bonus has been their enthusiasm for the story which has meant so much to me. Thank you, ladies.

Friends and family are equally as important and I am extremely fortunate to be surrounded by the best. Their desire for me to do well strengthens my resolve to produce a book worthy of their belief in me. I'm truly blessed to have their constant support.

As always, heartfelt and most important thanks and love go to my wonderful husband John, who never complains when he's on deaf and dumb dinners as I try to fix plots in my head! John, you are a star!

Special thanks must go to all the bloggers who willingly share my books when they are released. These supportive folks are out there industriously helping and directing readers towards my books and for that I want to say a huge thank you. With their help, more people read my stories and that's all I want.

Finally, to all my readers – I need every single one of you! Each email, review or message I receive saying you've enjoyed reading one of my books makes all the blood, sweat and edits worth it.

Thank you most sincerely – I am fortunate to have you.

~

If you have enjoyed *Whatever It Takes* and are able to write a review on Amazon or Goodreads, it would mean so much. Each review gives the book greater exposure which I hope will attract new readers. Any author will tell you, that is primarily why we write. We all want readers to enjoy our stories, and I'm no exception.

So, thank you in advance if you are able to write a few words about the book. And please do get in touch directly if you so wish, I love hearing from readers.

My email is **joymarywood@yahoo.co.uk.**

Other books written by Joy Wood

Dead Pretty
Secrets and Lies
Getting Away with Murder
Who's Smiling Now?
April Fool
Chanjori House
Knight & Dey
For the Love of Emily

Printed in Great Britain
by Amazon

45085629R00212